Re-incarnation a
MYTH OR SCIENCE

Re-incarnation a
MYTH OR SCIENCE

Ashok Kumar Chattopadhyay

PARTRIDGE
A Penguin Random House Company

ISBN: Hardcover   978-1-4828-5644-6
               Softcover   978-1-4828-5643-9
               eBook   978-1-4828-5642-2

Print information available on the last page.

To order additional copies of this book, contact
Partridge India
000 800 10062 62
orders.india@partridgepublishing.com

www.partridgepublishing.com/india

This book is dedicated to the grandmothers, grandfathers, and the true preachers of the world who influence their grandchildren and their followers through simple stories and gospels of the universal truths for enriching their moral values.

May our legacy continue so that future generations can be proud of their ancestors.

Acknowledgement

I discussed my perception about transmigration many times with my family members and in my friend circles even though I neither had the competency nor the license to do so. If not for the insistence of Ranita Chatterjee, my sister-in-law, I would not have ventured into writing this book. My wife, Sutapa, and my sons, Romit and Rohit, remained main architects while crafting this book. My close friends and brothers Dipten, Josef, Alok, Amar, Pradip, Chayanika, Chaitali, Franco, Pohar guided me while writing and compiling this book.

I shall remain grateful to all of them, including the ones who helped me with their valued suggestions at prepublication stage. I specially thank Partridge India Author Solutions, who have given me a platform to publish this book.

Finally, I recognise the fact that without *her* wishes, nothing can happen.

Contents

Chapter 1:   An Ideal Family 1

Chapter 2:   Concept of Birth 9

Chapter 3:   Social Environment 15

Chapter 4:   Mind, Body, and Intellect 28

Chapter 5:   Philosophy and Maturity 49

Chapter 6:   Death in the Family 68

Chapter 7:   Science and Spirituality 74

Chapter 8:   A Solemn Mission 78

Chapter 9:   Transmigration 82

Chapter 10: Present Proof of Reincarnation 91

Chapter 11: Humble Appeal to the Valued Reader 104

Chapter 12: Beginning of the Search 106

Chapter 13: Physiological Body 110

Chapter 14: Spiritual Gross Body 117

Chapter 15: The Subtle Body 121

Chapter 16: Science of the Subtle Body 126

Chapter 17: Birth of a Human 132

Chapter 18: Death of a Human 137

Chapter 19: Soul/Spirit/Atman/Ruh 141

Chapter 20: Cosmic Energy, Ionosphere, and Other
             Layers of Earth's Atmosphere 147

Chapter 21: God Time and Man Hour 160

Chapter 22: As We Sow, So We Reap 163

Chapter 23: Purification Process of the Soul 165

Chapter 24: Physiological Responses during
Meditation 179

Chapter 25: Migration of Energy and Its
Accumulation 186

Chapter 26: Radio/Telecommunications 203

Chapter 27: Humble Submission 240

1

An Ideal Family

Don't limit a child to your own learning, for he was born in another time.

Rabindranath Tagore

On 2 September 1983, in the early morning of hot and humid Calcutta, a child is born in a hospital. For some time, the child does not cry. Everybody in the maternity ward becomes anxious and starts wondering why the newborn is not crying. The doctor holds the boy upside down and gently slaps his hip. The boy suddenly starts crying. There is a momentary sigh inside the hospital room, which later turns into a stream of joy.

It is a boy child. The baby is perplexed with the new environment and continues to cry loudly. The nurse cleans him with hot water, wraps him in a piece of white cloth and gives him to the safe arms of his mother, with whom he is accustomed from the embryo stage. For so long, he has been quite happy to get all his biological needs easily through the umbilical cord, which has just been disconnected. Now he starts gasping for oxygen, trying to adjust to the hostile surroundings.

The baby stops crying, sensing the touch of his known shelter, and perhaps is confused with the paradoxical behaviour of the people around, who are laughing with joy. He learns his first lesson after birth: 'When I cry, others laugh.' It is true indeed; both births and deaths are paradoxical and full of mysteries. What we cannot explain scientifically, call it an act of God.

The elder brother of the newborn child asks his mother, 'From where and how did the baby come?'

Her answer is 'From heaven, my son.'

God indeed has created a robust and balanced evolutionary system of birth and death so that this planet can survive, but He keeps the magic wand in His own hands. There is a very common saying in our society: 'Births and deaths are fully in the command and control of God.' Even the doctors of this modern world believe it.

Three days later, the baby is taken to his home. A ceremonial welcome is waiting for him. The baby is first given to the hands of the most experienced person in the family, the grandma (grandmother), who after a very careful examination gives the opinion that her new grandson looked like his father. She predicted that this boy will be loved by all his friends and family members. Her final finding is that the grandfather of the family has been reincarnated as this boy. All elderly persons of the family ask her why she thought so.

Her answer is 'The birthmark of this boy is similar to that of his grandfather and that too on the same place.'

The brother asks his grandma, 'From where and how did this baby come?'

She gives the same answer: 'From the heaven and by the act of God.'

Therefore, the mystery of birth remains as misty in the inquisitive mind of the young boy. For him, heaven remains a place of supreme happiness—adorned in flowers all around and had the spiritual state of everlasting communion with God everywhere.

The mother of the newborn baby, although weak after the recent delivery, remains very alert and active with the child. The baby remains in hibernation during the days. His playing sessions start at night, and he registers his existence with his cry.

Back when the mother was pregnant, the grandmother used to tell her, 'During pregnancy, always think of good, holy things, and be positive. This will help the child to become pious and wise.' She used to narrate good gospels and stories containing high morals.

The brother remembers all such stories, and he reminds his grandma to repeat those directly to his newborn younger brother for a better result. He observes the activities of the baby very keenly.

One day he asks his mother, 'Why does the baby, without any reason, smiles for a while and then cries, raising his fists towards the sky?'

She explains that the baby can still recollect the sweet and sour memories of his previous life.

The boy wonders, *How can a baby express fear and annoyance when exposed to sudden light and certain sounds for the first time! How does a newborn child get his first experience of fear or joy when he has not experienced those before? Newly born chicks hide under the wings of their mother when they see an eagle flying close to them. Who taught them the sense of fear immediately after birth?*

He is convinced by his grandma that such experiences are inherited by the baby from his previous life. The immediate question from the boy is 'What was I in my previous life?'

Grandma thinks for a while and replies, 'You were a good, wise, and honest person and did many good works for others and never committed any crime.'

The boy wants to know how his grandma can be so sure. She calls the boy closer, then gently says, 'God was pleased with your good deeds of your previous life, so He sent you to us. You are living so happily here, and people love you so much. See outside in the slum. There are little children like you who are not so lucky and are facing so much hardship in their lives because they did not do as much good works as you did in your previous life.'

The boy stares at his grandma and asks, 'Is that a universal law of God?'

The prompt answer is 'Yes, there cannot be any exception to that.'

The boy is curious and questions, 'Now tell me how God sent a baby who slowly grew inside the stomach of my mother.'

The grandma replies, 'It is very easy, my son! When your mother was asleep, God quietly appeared and sowed a seed in her stomach as our gardener sows seeds in our garden. The seed then germinates and slowly grows branches, leaves, flowers, and fruits, and ultimately it grows into a big tree. In fact, the seed has all the latent qualities of a grown-up person. Your younger brother will also become a boy like you in the near future and then a man like your father.'

'Where is your mama?' asks the boy.

Grandma paused a bit and then replies, 'She has gone to heaven. At night, you can see countless stars twinkling in the sky. My mama is one of those. One day God will convert her into a small seed and sow it in the stomach of a very good lady.'

The boy enquires, 'Why does God not appear publicly?'

Grandma replies, 'If God appears publicly, then the bad people will directly ask for many good blessings from Him, which He does not like to bestow in order to ensure good governance of our planet and justice to the good people. Therefore, He carefully remains unseen to the general people. Those who obey His laws and commandments truthfully and pray regularly for His sight, He appears only to them, like the idols you see in temples, and fulfils their wishes. To see him, you will have to work very hard and may have to wait for a long time. But whoever sincerely prays for His sight, He appears before him at an appropriate time.'

'Then why should I not stop going to school, reading books, and start performing prayers only to invoke him?'

Before Grandma can reply, the baby starts crying loudly. The boy becomes concerned and runs away to see the baby, whom he has started loving from the very first day he was brought into the house.

He excitedly asks his mother, 'Why is the baby crying so loud?'

His mother replies, 'He is hungry, my son.'

His instant question is 'Can he sense hunger?'

'Yes!' his mother replies. 'Just like you.'

'Why can't my brother do everything that I can do now?' he asks.

His mother gently taps the head of the boy and says, 'I heard when your grandma explained to you the mystery of birth. Did she not tell you that this baby was like a seed in my stomach? In a few months, he has grown so much that he can now cry, move, and sense with his little organs.'

'Did you not feel hurt when the baby was inside your stomach?' the boy asks his mother.

'No, my son, I felt very good to bear this child. He used to float on some fluid inside my stomach. He used to swim, move, kick, and play.'

The boy asks again, 'Why, Mama, only mothers bear a child? Why not fathers?'

Mother thinks for a while and replies, 'God is very considerate. See, your father works so hard. He has to go to his office every day and also does physical work to earn money. But your mother does relatively less hard work. If your father would have bore the child, it would have been very difficult for him to do such hard work. God therefore has given this privilege to mothers only. He has also bestowed mothers with more kindness and love towards children, for which they are respected more in societies.'

The baby continues to cry. Mother then feeds the baby. Immediately he stops crying. After a little while, he starts sleeping.

The boy becomes inquisitive again and asks, 'What did you feed him?'

Mother softly replies, 'It was milk from my breast.'

'Was it just like how a cow feeds its calf?'

'Yes, of course!'

'Who has given you milk?'

'It was given by God for feeding the child. Milk formed with the birth of the baby and will remain until he starts eating other foods.'

The boy salutes God for His kindness, turns around, and hurriedly disappears. He goes to the terrace and looks at the glittering star-studded sky and tries to gauge the strength and kindness of God. He also tries to locate his grandfather's star. He cannot spot the one among the countless stars, but he enjoys the bright full-moon night. The moon is up in the sky.

He starts singing softly, 'Twinkle twinkle little star, how I wonder what you are, up above the world so high. Like a diamond in the sky.'

He looks around and discovers more stars. The more he concentrates, the more stars he discovers. He begins to enjoy the distant stars twinkling in the moonlit sky. The moon appears to him as the possible castle of God, encased by a bright translucent sphere. He looks around again and again to guess the size of the universe and becomes disappointed at one point when he realises that it is huge and beyond his perception. Suddenly, he hears the loud voice of his father calling him for dinner.

The little one remains intoxicated by the sight of the night sky. He asks his father excitedly about a star which he saw dislocating from the sky and falling down somewhere. His father explained that it was a shooting star.

He is not satisfied and asks, 'Was it an evil one? So God did not like it and therefore exiled it from His kingdom?'

Father becomes serious and enquires whether he had completed his homework. He is smart enough to realise that his father may not have a good time in his office and therefore may not have liked his question, so he remains silent.

The boy is loved very much by his sister. She tells him very interesting short stories, sometimes rhymes before going to bed. He shares his experience of the beauty of the night sky with his sister and then questions, 'How big is the sky? Is it bigger than our Earth?' Her answer is yes! He shares the information given by their grandma that their grandfather shares a space in the sky along with the stars.

His sister remembers a beautiful quote:

He is born in vain, having attained the human birth, so difficult to get, does not attempt to realize God in this very life. (Sri Ramakrishna Paramahamsa)

The boy tries to recollect all the information he has gathered and also his own findings, then summarises those to his sister.

- God gifts babies to mothers only, so mothers are more respected in families and societies.
- Babies grow inside the stomach of mothers, like the seeds in the garden soil.
- God arranges everything for our planet.
- Whoever does good works and remains honest, God sends them to good families.
- Everybody, after completing their tasks, goes back to heaven, a beautiful place of God in the sky.
- The sky is very big; there is no end to it. It has to be very big because in the end, all people from earth go there. It is a two-way process.
- People who are pious and pray every day can see God Himself, like we see the idols in temples.
- Sometimes people go back to their own family as a baby in their next birth.

2

Concept of Birth

Long ago you were a dream in your mother's sleep, and then she awoke to give you birth.

Khalil Gibran

The boy starts snoring softly and plunges into the darkness of the night. The dawn will again bring new challenges, new ideas, new questions, new information, and so on. Slowly this boy will become a youth. But his innocence, inquisitiveness, simplicity, tranquillity of mind, honesty, naughtiness, and over and above all, the purity of his mind shall not remain the same. The complexity and maya, the *hallucination* (nescience), of this samsara (earth) will slowly pollute him.

The sister is fifteen years older than her younger brother. He is only six years old now, and the youngest brother is just a few days old. She goes to college and is a student of physiology in the University of Calcutta. Immediately after her little brother is asleep, she smiles to herself and goes to prepare for her studies. She compares her perception with that of her brother and recognises that her understanding of life had been the same until she grew up to a girl, leaving behind her childhood.

Now she is attending physiology classes, and after being exposed to the complexity of the system of birth and the associated process of growing up, she now knows the truth. She is now very proud of her knowledge on embryos, mutation, cell division, hormones, DNA, and so on. She remembers her recent memory on this subject.

As a student of physiology, she recalls that her professor, on the first lecture on birth, had narrated the dictionary meaning of physiological birth, 'Birth is such a state that processes of life are manifested after the emergence of the whole body.'

It is an emergence and separation of the offspring from the body of its mother, which was seen in all mammals except monotremes. To produce a child, the parents have to be fertile. Fertility is the ability to conceive and bear a child, the ability to become pregnant through normal and synergic sexual activity. Hormones and the concerned neurological pathways should be in synchronism for sexual desire to be present. The sperm reaches the urethra through a physiological passageway.

There are many other legal definitions of birth. The most common of those is from the World Health Organization (1950):

> A live birth is the complete expulsion or extraction from its mother of a product of conception, irrespective of the duration of pregnancy, which, after such separation, breathes or shows evidence of life, such as beating of the heart, pulsation of the umbilical cord, or any definite movement of voluntary muscles, whether or not the umbilical cord has been cut or the placenta is attached.

The students in class realise progressively how a simple definition taught by their grandmas have become much more complex.

We habitually make things complex, but God has made it very simple and routine for His children. A woman is not aware how and at what precise time a baby is conceived. Out of 20 million to 500 million sperms ejaculated, 1 or 2 lucky sperms eventually fertilises her egg. In the prostate gland of man, a mixture of spermatozoa and other fluids is stored, which is called semen. The spermatozoa holds human DNA, which contains the complete set of chromosomes; normal cells have two. These appear to be living organisms under microscope. They seem to be moving energetically with the sole mission of fusing with an ovum. The sperms may take only an hour to complete the journey of about 20 centimetres to the egg in one of the fallopian tubes, but then their lifespan is only one day. Lashing their long tails like whips, they execute an intricate dance, wriggling, pushing, competing, and prodding the membrane of the egg cell for some hours. Thereafter, only one lucky sperm penetrates the outer membrane of the egg. The egg then hardens its skin to prevent other sperms from entering.

Then the fusion of the nuclei of the sperm and egg cell takes place. Within a very short time, two volumes of genetic information are bound together in harmony. The combined male and female cell starts to grow and multiply. After about thirty-six hours, the egg splits into two new cells. Each of these grows and divides again to form a total of four cells. Meanwhile, a six-day-long journey begins; the embryonic baby goes down the fallopian tube to the womb, multiplying its cells as it goes. By the time the jelly-like cluster of cells reaches the womb, it has a firm core and is known as a blastocyst.

The rapidly growing baby formation has to sustain itself during its journey down one of the two fallopian tubes as nourishment gets exhausted. By attaching itself to the wall of the womb, which is thick and supplied with rich blood vessels, the baby obtains nourishment. During this stage, rootlets called villi, which are put out by the baby, grow into the lining tissues of the womb, drawing food for its growing cells. This process is natural but complex indeed.

About a month after implantation, the blastocyst begins to take a human form with a rudimentary head, brain, and trunk. The heart begins to throb. About two weeks later, arms and legs germinate from the tiny buds. Then the cranial nerves of the brain and the baby's circulation system are formed.

Within two weeks of the egg implanting itself on the wall of the womb, it prepares for the formation of the placenta, the temporary organ which carries the function of the lungs, digestive system, kidney, liver, and blood supply. This system supports the baby till its own organs function. The placenta is attached to the baby through a tube which carries blood and nourishment, known as the umbilical cord.

Small blood vessels from both the placenta and the tissues lining the womb run close together, thereby a free absorption of nourishment by the baby takes place. This includes oxygen, salts, carbohydrates, and amino acids, which are the building blocks of human body. The spent and waste products from the baby are eliminated by the placenta, like a kidney, before the return stream goes back to the mother's bloodstream.

In two months, fingers, toes, muscles, some of the bones, etc. are formed. One month later, a mature baby of about 8 centimetres in size takes shape. In the next six months, it is of about 25 centimetres, and just before birth, it reaches the size of nearly 50 centimetres.

The human brain begins to form at a very early stage. It happens in just three weeks after conception. But in many ways, its developmental activities continue throughout life. It is because the same events that shape the brain during initial development are also responsible for storing information, new skills, and memories throughout life; however, the degree differs. The newborn baby is not blank. The primary visual areas, the somatosensory cortex, and the auditory cortex remain active. It can process visual impressions.

Clear behavioural responses to smell can be recorded in pre-term infancy from approximately the twenty-ninth week. Responses to low-frequency noise can be recorded from about the sixteenth week in the foetus's brain. If a twenty-two-to-twenty-three-week-old foetus is exposed to vibration, it reacts by moving. Newborn infants remember sounds, melodies they have been exposed to in their foetus period because of their short-term memory. 'It reminds us the story of Abhimanyu, the son of Arjuna, in the Mahabharata, learned how to enter in the circle of a most difficult formation of solders, from the discussion of his father, when he was in the womb of his mother.

The brain is far more impressionable in early life than in maturity. This impressionability has both positive and negative sides. On the positive side, the brain of a young child is more open and favourable for learning; on the negative side, the brain is more vulnerable to developmental problems if the environment in which the child lives is not favourable.

The wall clock pronounces it is eleven already. She suddenly returns to her normal state of mind and remembers about her homework to be completed. She envies her little brother for his age, time, and mind.

The sister has enjoyed her self-talks, which includes the following points:

• Birth is a state of being in which the processes of life are manifested after the emergence of the whole body.

- Out of the 20 million to 500 million spermatozoa, generally one sperm cell becomes successful in fertilising the egg, and then cell division takes place.
- It forms a blastocyst and attaches itself on the wall of the womb.
- Within a month of conception, the brain starts developing.
- Placenta provides the basic needs of the baby through the umbilical cord.
- In about ten and a half months, the baby goes out of its mother's womb, then the umbilical cord is cut, and the baby starts surviving on its own.

3

Social Environment

Human beings are not born, once and for all
on the day of their Mothers give birth to them,
but life . . . obliges them over and over again to
give birth to themselves.

Gabriel Garcia Marquez

There is a small temple behind the house of the boy, where a priest (pujari) lives alone as the caretaker of the temple. He manages the temple from morning till night, 7 days a week, and 365 days a year. The local community contributes some money to pay for the day-to-day expenses of the temple. The priest is very soft-spoken and is always seen in a saffron dress.

During festival days, the temple is nicely decorated with flowers and colourful lights, while the priest becomes the most focal person of the community. The priest performs pujas (prayers) every day. In the evenings, some of the ladies and old people living nearby visit the temple during regular prayers. On festival days, special pujas are performed, and most of the neighbourhood people come together and join the prayer. Sweets are offered to God, and after that, the prasad is distributed among the participants. The temple during those days transforms into a sacred place where people for a while forget their differences and enmities. They convert it into a social meeting place and celebrate the festivals together.

The priest likes the boy very much. They spend a lot of times together, discussing simple subjects of mutual interest and various stories of moral science. Both of them have no time constraint unlike others in that colony.

The boy waits eagerly till the afternoon to give the good news to his priest uncle of the arrival of the new infant in their home. He is very excited, and he narrates everything that has happened since yesterday and very proudly reports that his mother has brought a small baby into their home.

He continues further. 'The infant is very cute but always sleeps and cries loudly for milk when he feels hungry. He is not as active as me.' Then he shares to the priest with simplicity and verbatim all the stories which he has heard from his grandma and mother.

The priest asks what the baby looks like. The boy replies, 'He is cute. Grandma says he looks like my father, but I cannot find much similarity. I also do not understand the logic of her claim that our grandfather has returned back as this baby. By the way, since that morning, whatever I enquired about birth, Mom and Grandma said it was an act of God. Don't you think it is funny? Do you believe so? Where do we come from?' He goes on asking such questions and becomes excited.

The priest asks him to take some deep breaths, and he assures the boy that he will answer all his questions. He goes inside the temple, drinks some water, and then offers some sweets to the boy for the good news. He prays to God,

'Let this newborn live long, become wise, and bring more happiness to the society.'

The priest sits beside the boy and thought of how he should start answering the difficult questions raised by the little one. The absolute truth is not known to him either. Perhaps the same is not very clear even in this advanced scientific world. But he has promised the boy to respond. He decides to satisfy the boy with the old classical stories.

The priest starts, 'Yes, my son, all of us come from heaven at birth. The heaven is in the universe, which is infinite. There is no end to it. In it, the most beautiful part is paradise, where gods and goddesses live in their palaces. After death, people go to heaven or hell as per their performances in their past lives, which is known as karma. The results of karma are similar to the marks and grades you get in your school. The best students sit in front benches, and the bad ones in last benches. At the end of the year, only those students who pass the examination advance to the next class. Similarly, after death, our subtle bodies go to the various subtle regions of the universe according to our level of performances.

'The subtle body is called atman [spirit]. There it stays for some time and returns to earth, when it gets the chance, as a human baby just like your brother. The persons who are bad, are cruel to others, and commit crimes will go to hell, where they suffer. Such subtle bodies may not return back as human beings. Depending upon their bad works, they may be sent back to earth as other animals or even as non-living substances. From such a state, to become human beings, it may take several million years.

'Human life is very precious. You are very fortunate indeed to be born as a human being and that too with the most favourable conditions and in a good family. Notice those poor boys playing around the muddy field, they do not have proper clothes and proper food and may not get the opportunity to go to a good school.

'You had been a good person in your past life. God treated you well in heaven and again sent you to a good family. Therefore, you must continue to do well, study hard, respect your parents and elders, love your friends, and pray to God for giving you strength and knowledge so that you grow well. Remember that human existence is invaluable if it is used wisely.

'Your grandma is right. There are possibilities that a person may return to his previous home through rebirth. There are many case histories of such people in the world, where some young children had recollections of their previous birth—places they had visited, homes, and even important incidents. In some cases, identical birthmarks in the same places were found. Dr Ian Stevenson, a renowned scientist from the University of Virginia in USA, established about three thousand such cases to prove the reality of reincarnation. Many people still believe that reincarnation is not possible because the process of reincarnation has not been adequately proved by science.

'However, in India and, for that matter, in the Eastern world, most people do believe in rebirth. In our country, our wise ancient rishis, scholars, and saints strongly advocated and documented the facts or truth of reincarnation in all our holy books. They simply preached, 'As you sow, so you reap.' They described it as a karmic cycle.'

'What is a karmic cycle? Please explain it to me,' asks the boy, brimming with curiosity.

The priest then reminds him his earlier message of doing well in the present life to ensure a better and happier next life. The boy immediately nods in acknowledgement.

'My son, have you ever seen the sun rising from the west, fire cooling your finger, ice warming your body, birds sleeping late in the morning and dancing at midnight?.'

The boy replies, 'No!'

The priest then explains, 'All these cannot happen because they cannot defy the laws of the Almighty God. The universe, including nature, follows the dictum of laws and commandments of God without any exception. He has delegated a special power to human beings, the ability to think with consciousness. He has bestowed it on us for the good governance of our planet.

'Human beings have the capability of comprehensive discrimination and free choice over their actions. We can consciously shape and change our lives. That is why the cosmic law of karma is valid for us. The karmic law states that every action we take will at some point come back to us in the same way as it went out from us. Therefore, the most important precept that should be observed is to harm no one by our words, thoughts, and deeds.

'But alas, this special power is very often misused by human beings, and they defy His laws, exploit nature for their materialistic and selfish advantages, and disregard the inevitable consequences!

'People can become better by following His laws or can become worse by defying the same. Because of this special power of consciousness and reprogramming ability, we are unique, and are the best creation of God on earth. If we desire, we can improve ourselves. Those who defy His wishes, suffer sooner or later.'

'Uncle, does everybody have to grow old?'

'Yes, my son! This law of God cannot be exploited by us.'

The little boy then reveals his trump card and asks the priest, 'How does God transport a baby to earth? We cannot see the baby or even the seeds while being transported from the heaven.'

The priest remains quiet for some time, then eventually explains to the boy, 'You listen to music on the radio and see television every day, and you see your favourite heroes Mickey, Donald, Spiderman, and so on playing inside the TV. How do you see them? You cannot see them outside your TV set and arriving from the sky. Similarly, God through His transponder, transports the baby as waves from the sky, and it enters the body of its mother without being seen from outside. Life is like a movie. If it starts, the end is inevitable. Other people are like viewers. If you perform well, people will like you. If your performance is excellent, you get rewards from your admirers. If the performance is bad, you are considered a burden to the society.'

'Can we change the channel for a better program?'

'Yes, you can do so through better karma as I explained you before. Another example is rain and how it happens! The water in that pond behind this temple gets evaporated because of the heat of the sun and goes up to the sky. When it is evaporating as vapour, you cannot see it. It accumulates in the sky, forms clouds, and returns back to the earth as rainwater. When it comes back to earth, you can see it as water again.'

After a little pause, the boy asks, 'Have you seen God?'

The priest is a little taken aback, but then he appreciates this question profusely! 'Many years back, Swami Vivekananda, a great philosopher of India, asked this question to his guru, Paramahamsa Ramakrishna, who was a demigod. He answered yes, that he had seen God, and he promised to show Swami Vivekananda also. But, my son, I am an ordinary priest doing my karma in search of God, but I can see the embodiment of God standing before me.'

'Where is he?' asks the boy.

'I see Him in you.'

The boy feels embarrassed and starts laughing. The priest tells him it is not a joke.

> As body, mind, or soul, you are a dream; you really are being, consciousness, Bliss. You are the God of this Universe. (Swami Vivekananda)

The priest explains, 'God is omnipresent and omnipotent. He resides within human beings, in all animal kingdoms, in all matters or non-matters, in the sky, and in the universe. He shines more in the hearts of children. He Himself has become all. Nothing moves or happens without His wishes.'

The young boy now seriously becomes confused, and he questions again how one God can dwell in so many places and in so many shapes, colours, and looks.

The priest reminds the boy about his visit to Puri, a beach in the eastern part of India, last year along with his father. 'You must have seen the Bay of Bengal from the beach. Could you trace the end of the sea?'

His answer is no.

'What did you see?'

The boy replies, 'It was water and endless water without any shape and colour.'

'Is it not the same water that you see in the pond behind this temple?'

The boy nods in agreement.

'You see the same water in your home in a jar or in a glass or in a cup. The water takes the shape and colour of the container in which you keep it, but at the same time, it remains intact without losing its property.'

The young one sharply responds, 'If some dye is put in it, the colour of the water changes.'

The priest responds, 'Yes, that is true, but if you boil the contaminated water and then cool down the water vapour, it becomes colourless again.'

'That is true,' says the little one.

'If the container is broken, the water will escape and shall become shapeless and colourless. Similarly, God is shapeless, colourless, infinite, and He dwells in everything, in different colours and shapes and yet remains unseen. As fishes playing in the pond covered with reeds cannot be seen from outside, similarly God, screened by veil, plays invisibly in the hearts of human beings. The veil must be removed to see Him. The veil is like magic [maya], you may have seen being performed by some magician on stage.

'How to remove the veil? If you want to see the fishes in the pond, you will have to remove the dirt and weeds from the surface of the water. Similarly, if we can remove all dirt and impurities from our minds, then we can see God.'

The boy intervenes and informs the priest that, the other day, a friend of his father came to their home for dinner. He overheard the conversation with his father. His father's friend vehemently argued in favour of the non-existence of God. They are both mature and elderly persons. Then why are there differences of opinions in this matter if it is a universal truth?

The priest takes a deep breath, and with a smile, he replies, 'There are many types of people in this world with different colours, natures, and beliefs. It is not necessary that everybody has to be same. Whatever they see with the limited power of their sense organs or knowledge or experiences, they form their personal opinions. But the absolute truth remains the same and universal. The sun exists in the sky. At times, in a cloudy day, it gets covered by some passing clouds. The sun cannot be seen at that time. Does it mean that the sun does not exist in the sky?

There are blind people on earth. Maybe God was not so kind to them. They cannot see the sun or the moon at all. Does it mean the sun and the moon do not exist? God has given them the sense of feeling. If they want, they can feel the presence of the sun and the moon. Even if they cannot see the same, God has given them the virtue of belief. This simple belief will activate their senses to enjoy the creations of God. Do you know that Ludwig van Beethoven, a world-renowned German music composer and pianist was deaf? Hearing is the most important sense organ for a music composer. Still he overcame his shortcomings by his belief. There had been many physically challenged persons—like John Milton, Galileo Galilei, Franklin D. Roosevelt, Horatio Nelson, Helen Keller, and Stephen Hawking—who, with their beliefs and strong determination, became famous in this world with their creations. The mind of your papa's friend is veiled by maya. So he does not have belief in God.'

'Please tell me, Uncle, does God exist in so many deities of this temple? If yes, then why are there so many deities? Why not one? Is it not contradictory to your explanation that one god exists everywhere?'

The priest starts thinking that he has not met many grown-up people asking such valid questions. He asks, 'What is your name in your school?'

The boy says, 'Romit.'

'Now, Romit, if I call you by some other name—say, John—are you going to become someone else?'

'No,' replies the boy.

'Similarly, God has many given names. Different people call Him by different names, which do not affect the entity of God. Similarly, as I have explained to you, water pots may be of different shapes, but they do not affect the water in any way. No, the question is, why are the deities of different shapes? In some cases, it looks like a simple piece of stone.

'You may recall I have told you that to see God, there is a need for cleaning the surface of our minds and then going slowly deep inside. The mind and intellect are the tools with which the cleaning process is performed. At the first stage, the mind needs to be made calm. For doing so, we need to increase our concentration. A concentrated mind has enormous power. It is just like a magnifying glass. The sunlight cannot burn a paper ordinarily. But with a magnifying glass, if you concentrate the sunrays in a particular spot on the paper, the area becomes heated, and this can initiate a big fire. Similarly, you with the help of your concentration can activate your mind for the removal of the dirt lying beneath your heart and mind. As such, you require a concentrated mind to do well in your studies. To begin with, you may have to impose your faith on something which you believe most. One has to practise this exercise continuously.

'I have told you that people have different faiths and beliefs. They as per their faith can choose out of these idols in the temple the one that suits them best. Simple prayer regularly can be initiated to make their minds more disciplined. This is the cleaning process of the mind, and the idols are facilitators. Once the mind and intellect are purified, you can see God. Then you do not need these idols as you can see God directly. This is known as realisation of God and is the purpose of our lives. Such realisation liberates us from the bondage of sorrows and miseries. You will understand it later when you grow up, but you will have to start preparing yourself from now on.'

The readers may wonder how a boy of only six years can be so inquisitive and raise so many intricate philosophical questions of life? I alert their parents to please not underestimate or ignore such children. They were born with larger inbuilt computers than what we have been given so far. Don't you see how easily they play with their play stations, remotes of electronic appliances, and even with the computers? We grown-ups are not comfortable with modern gadgets. They are certainly more intelligent and matured than us at their ages. This is a good and healthy sign, but at the same time, it is a great challenge for the new society—channelling this young energy in the right direction. Otherwise, there will be phenomenal and uncontrolled increase in initiatives of subversive catastrophe in our beautiful planet. The indications are already very much alarming as seen in daily newspapers, TV news, and in other types of media in this regard.

The housemaid of the boy arrives and insists that the boy must go back home now for his lunch. He quietly gets up, thanks the priest for the good preaching, and assures him that he will come back again.

While going back home, he starts sharing with the housemaid the wise advice which he has learned from the priest a while ago.

Even though the boy is satisfied fully with the answers given by the priest, he still wants to verify the substances of the teachings with his father, whom he considers as the final authority. His father is an honest officer in a national company. He carries back home all his problems from the office. At times, after returning home, he starts complaining about the systems and procedures of the company to their mother, who does not understand the matter but still remains as an emphatic listener. He wants to change the whole world. It is therefore important for the children to gauge correctly the swing of their father's mood before proposing something.

That evening, at an opportune moment, he tells his father proactively that he has completed all his homework for school well beforehand. Then he says that the priest of the temple had told him that God had created everything, including all human beings, the nature, the sky, and the stars.

His father replies, 'Yes, my son! There is no doubt about it. Otherwise, who else can create the beautiful world that we see around us? Have you ever noticed the beautiful butterflies, the colourful flowers full of fragrance? See the colour combination, the pigmentation of their colours. Can any artist of this world do it? You have seen the mountains, the sea, the stars, the moon, and the sun in the sky. Can you even dream that humans could do those? Do you know that our Earth is no bigger than the head of a pin compared to our galaxy?

'We human beings may be infinitely small in size, but my son, God has favoured us with a unique power of thinking ability. With the help of our practically limitless, powerful mind and intellect, we can achieve any reasonable goals that we set in our lives.'

'But, Papa, I understand we can also defy some laws of God, as told by the priest, which no other species can do.'

Father becomes very pleased and asks him to go to his sister to sleep.

He disappears immediately from there and reappears in the room of his sister and excitedly relays everything that he has learned.

- God is the creator of the universe, including heaven and all creatures. He is infinite.
- A good person, after death, goes to good places in heaven and returns to good families for further improvement.

- Human life is very precious. We can see God by purifying our minds and intellects instead of waiting for a very long and uncertain evaluation process.

- God is present everywhere, but ordinary people cannot see Him because He has placed a veil before them, which can be removed by cleaning the mind and intellect.

- We must respect our parents and elders and love our friends. We should also remain disciplined in the society.

- God transports or sends babies to earth like how Mickey Mouse and Donald Duck appears in TV during a TV show.

4

Mind, Body, and Intellect

The mind commands the body and it obeys.
The mind orders itself and meets resistance.

Saint Augustine

The mind of a child is just like clay; it can be moulded easily. The subconscious mind of adults can also be reprogrammed if properly addressed and nourished. Nobody is born a criminal. God sends everybody to earth without much of basic defects so that they can rectify themselves and start good karma for the purification of their souls. He ensures, with some exceptions, that the basic memories are erased so that our conscious minds are not very much influenced by our previous lives and karmas. The bad elements are rewritten by human beings due to their ignorance of the truth. The urge of practising bad habits by people having evil DNA is very intense. The minds of such people draw happiness from evil acts.

In India such inherent inferior quality is called tamas guna. To become a noble person with high ideology in the society, one has to go against the natural tendency of such a mind; this quality is known as sattva guna. In between the two, there is another category, which is known as *rajas* guna. The sattva guna is the ideal quality in a human being as classified by Wises, whose results shall always be good for an individual or for collectives.

Rajas guna is the quality which is liked by most people as it gives kinglike pleasures to people, but its results can be good or bad in the long run. The results of tamas guna will always be bad. There cannot be any exception to the result of these basic rules for mankind as determined by Him. No matter how rich a person is or how powerful he may be...

The names of these basic qualities may be different in different countries. Whoever follows and practises sattva guna will be happy eventually and can remain in peace and harmony. It may sound very simple or may look very easy to practise and implement. But alas, in reality it is the biggest challenge to every individual, every society, and every nation.

We cannot yet wipe out the scars from the two world wars of the last century, but again we have started plunging into conflicts and warlike situations in different parts of the globe in the name of caste, colour, and religion to satisfy our egoistic nature and to demonstrate our power and supremacy. This egoistic nature is the veil which prevents us from realising that God is present. Under the influence of maya, we run after a mirage to find an oasis in the desert and eventually die without achieving any meaningful gain in our present lives.

While discussing such various subjects over the days and months, the priest one day realises that the small boy has become eleven years old and that his younger brother has also sneaked into their team at the age of five.

They have been regularly coming to the temple to see their priest uncle. Over time, the priest has become an inseparable member of their family. They have grown up under the moral protection of their grandmother, the love and compassion of their parents, the immaculate support of their sister, the company of good neighbours, and finally, the teachings of their wise priest uncle. These two boys have been lucky to get very good support from the priest in their very formative years since religious studies have now taken a back seat in the curriculum of schools.

The boy quietly goes to his sister and shares the treasure he has acquired. His sister attentively and with full interest starts listening. He tells her about the two new components he learned, the mind and intellect of human beings, which remain invisible but do back-seat driving of the body for its all actions and inactions.

His sister asks him, 'Do you know what components of the body are seen from the outside? Without even knowing the basics, you have started expressing interest which are subtle in nature.'

'Yes, my sister, please explain to me the basics.'

His sister with great pride, starts narrating, standing before an anatomical chart of the human body, 'The human body comprises of a head, neck, trunk (including thorax and abdomen), arms and hands, legs and feet, hair, skin, nails, eyes, nose, tongue, ears. These are visible from outside.

'There are organs which cannot be seen from outside as those are covered by flesh and skin, and those are brain, spinal cord, bones with cartilage, joints and marrow, muscles, nerves, stomach, liver, gall bladder, large intestines, small intestines, kidneys, urinal bladder, nasal passage, trachea, lungs, heart, blood vessels, veins, arteries, glands, pancreas, blood, other fluids, etc.

'These organs can be grouped in the following systems: nervous system, musculoskeletal system, circulatory system, respiratory system, digestive system, integumentary system, urinary system, reproductive system, immune system, lymphatic system, endocrine system.'

The boy responds, 'Oh, sister! We are much more complex inside than outside.'

His sister goes on saying, 'All these complex systems, both outside and inside, are made of various types of cells which you cannot see with your naked eyes. You will require a microscope to see those. Do we have many cells? Yes, at a full-grown stage, the estimated number of cells will be about 37.2 trillion. Within those cells, smaller particles are moving and generating an electric field around our bodies.

'The amazing part of it is that the cells, which I explained, keep on disintegrating and getting replaced simultaneously up to our old age. Therefore, our bodies right from our birth are not permanent. Within that lie your mind and intellect somewhere in complete subtle form. Those are not considered as physical body. Those are known as subtle body.'

By the time she finishes her 'class' on human anatomy, the little boy is snoring on the bed. She gently passes her fingers with compassion on the forehead of her sleeping brother.

The next day, the boy returns from his school in the afternoon, hurriedly finishes his lunch, and heads towards the temple. But the priest is not present in the temple. He sits down quietly at a corner of the prayer hall and starts thinking about the anatomy class he attended last night. By this time, he realises that the priest and his grandma are the only persons on earth who can explain things in a simple manner which he can understand and remember.

In the meantime, the priest arrives at the temple. The boy's first question is 'Why do you always wear a saffron dress?'

The priest replies, 'As you always wear your school uniform in the school, for me the temple is my school, and this is my uniform.'

'But you always wear this uniform,' says the boy.

'You are right, my naughty boy. You always come here with a bag full of questions.'

The boy quickly responds, 'Uncle, you are the only one who gives simple answers which I can understand easily.'

'Look, someone in the society has to serve the temples. You see, your father and other people living around here remain busy throughout the day with their office work. Your mother and the ladies of the society also remain busy for preparing food and doing other household work. Can you tell me who will prepare food, change dresses, and feed God? Therefore, I have volunteered to do these works for our society. People out of generosity donate in the temple. With that small sum, I buy all the necessary articles for the temple and also for my livelihood. I necessarily had to sacrifice other colourful and costly dresses to exercise some restrictions on my mind so that I can remain focused on doing selfless services to God and to the society. I have the privilege of having people around know me as the priest of this temple and give me special respect and honour.'

At once, the innocent boy replies, 'I shall also be a priest when I grow up.'

His good priest uncle does not encourage his idea of becoming a priest. He remains quiet for some time. On the contrary, he starts asking questions regarding his performance in school and advises him to do excellently in his studies, which is the foremost requirement even to become a good priest.

'By the way, why have you come to this temple at this hour?'

The boy responds, 'I have something to learn from you. Why are there such complications in human body? With so many parts, it becomes very difficult to remember. Can you make it simple and easy to understand and remember?'

'Wait, my son, let me drink some water, I am feeling thrust.' He actually needed some time to prepare his answer. Then the priest starts, 'Initially, human beings remain as a seed similar to that of a tree. Slowly it grows inside the womb of its mother. Even as a seed, it has the complete potential of a grown-up person. After birth, it gets nourishment from food and grows with all its organs. Those which are visible from outside constitute the gross body.

'The gross body consists of bone marrow, bones, blood, flesh, and skin. The container is made up with these and filled up with such matters. All these together constitute our fascinating body. This body comes into existence at the birth of an individual. After death, it will decay. From seed to the fully grown body, the growth takes place because of food consumed and assimilated day after day. It is therefore known as the food sheath [annamaya kosa]. This sheath does not react on its own. It cannot see, taste, listen, feel, or smell with the sense organs.'

The boy argues, 'It is not true, Uncle. I can do everything with my gross body.'

The priest continues, 'My son, when you sleep, this gross body remains in your possession. Can you do all that you are claiming?'

The boy thinks for a while and replies, 'Yes, Uncle, you are perhaps right. With the gross body alone, we cannot do our day-to-day activities.'

'Yes, we need something else to drive our bodies. Therefore, God has given us a vital air sheath, which is a physiological layer of human personality known as *pranamaya kosa*. This *kosa* (layer) is a subtle one. It is the subtle sheath of cosmic energy and nourishment that is necessary for life. With breath, we not only absorb oxygen but also prana, which influences our thoughts, emotions, and other sheaths. The manifestation of life in the physical body, which expresses itself in the gross body as five action organs, is called the vital air sheath. The five organs of action are hands, feet, vocal cords, organs of reproduction, and organs of excretion.

'The pranamaya kosa is therefore the driver of this body. It works as a glue between the gross body and other subtle bodies, which I will explain to you soon. This kosa is a modification of air. As long as it is attached to our body, all our body functions will continue. But if it leaves the body, all activities of the body will stop. Prana is inert by itself, which means it does not know anything about joys and sorrows by itself or those of others. Therefore, in our daily lives, we are not conscious about the pranamaya kosa.

'We need something beyond it to enjoy our lives. God is kind enough. He, for this purpose, has given us another kosa known as *manomaya kosa*, which is the mental energy sheath. It is subtler than pranmaya kosa. The mind along with our sense centres constitutes the manomaya kosa. The sense organs of our body can become active only when the mind is attached to them. For example, now you are attentively listening to me. Hence, your mind is fully attached to your ear. You are not able to see the beautiful butterflies flying around or smell the roses or even feel the biting of mosquitoes. This is because our sense centre is in our mind. If the mind is not attached to the sense organs, no perception is possible.

'This manomaya kosa is responsible for all our pleasures, sufferings, and miseries in life. It is the master of both pranamaya kosa and annamaya kosa. The mind can only conceive things known to it. Therefore, it is very important that this kosa has to learn many lessons so that you will have more happiness than miseries. The whole world exists in our mind. Every thought, every idea, and every feeling forms a separate world for itself. You go to school every day to enrich your mind with new knowledge, and this learning process continues throughout life. The more you learn, the more your mind can pervade a bigger boundary. It is important to not only expand knowledge but also to teach discipline to the mind so that it always provokes you to do good works for yourself and for the society as a whole. Only through proper controlling of the mind can we control our destiny? The best method is to foster good thoughts and follow the rules of the nature. Your sister is a student of physiology, so she studies the annamaya kosa. She must have explained the same to you in detail. There are two other kosas over and above the three that I have already explained to you, which you may not understand at your age.'

The boy starts insisting for the priest to continue as it is important for him to know; otherwise, he will not be able to outsmart his sister.

The priest continues, 'Do you love chocolate?'

The boy replies, 'Yes.'

'You see with your eyes an object, and then your mind takes note of the object and recognises it as chocolate. You start liking and wanting to possess it. If you do not get the same, you feel sad. If your friend takes it away, you may get angry. Up to this state of your mind, the desire of yours for the chocolate is controlled by the manomaya kosa. Now, say, your sister has cautioned you that if you eat too many chocolates, you will lose your teeth. So what will you do if someone offers you ten chocolates? You will take only one by putting some restriction on your mind. Even though your mind by its habit wants to take all of those, at the same time, it remembers the advice of your sister. This consciousness of human beings, which can discriminate between good and bad and accordingly pervades over the mind, is known as the intellectual sheath or *vignanamaya kosa*, the intellectual body, which is still subtler than the other two kosas. It is formed by the experiences, upbringing, and education in the present lifetime and also by the impression we bring from our previous lives.

'It is just like the electricity working in the bulbs as light, in the heater as heat, and in the refrigerator as cold. This mighty power of eternal consciousness—God, which is the spark of life in every one of us and is not only confined within—is present everywhere at all times. This consciousness playing in the pools of thought is the individual within whom the pride of doership is generated. The intellect by itself has no intelligence. It is just like a mirror in the darkness. It is this kosa we shall have to work on if we want to purify ourselves to make us free from the bondage of life.'

The boy responds, 'I fully understand this kosa, but I cannot understand the word *bondage.*'

'I will tell you a story to make you understand this,' says the priest. 'Long back, there was a prince in a kingdom. One day the prince wanted to see whether the subjects of the kingdom were happy or not. So he went out in disguise.

On the way, he met a person unable to walk properly. He was limping. The prince went to him and enquired whether he was happy or not. The man replied, "I have become old, so I'm unable to walk." "Does everybody become old?" the prince enquired. "Yes" was the reply. The old man also confirmed that he was very unhappy. The prince became sad and went on walking.

'After crossing a mile or so, the prince met a young person vomiting blood. He asked what happened to him. The poor person replied, "I am suffering from a bad disease." The prince asked again, "Does it happen to everybody?" The reply was "Yes, if there is a body, there shall be some disease or the other." He also expressed unhappiness. The prince started thinking about the miseries of people in his kingdom.

'No sooner had he reached near the bank of a river than he found one person lying in a cot which was being carried by four persons, and others around them were crying. He enquired about the incident. One of them informed that the man in the cot died, and they had come for the funeral of the body. The prince asked, "Is it compulsory that everybody has to die?" They informed him that whoever was born in this world had to die one day or the other.

'The prince, with a very heavy heart, returned to his palace. Some days later, in the middle of one night, he left the palace in disguise in search of freedom from such misery. He became a monk. After many years, he returned to his kingdom as a holy man with full realisation of God. He returned to teach others how to go beyond the clutches of such miseries of life. That wise person was none other than Gautama Buddha. There had been, and there may exist even now many such saints in this world.'

'Yes, Uncle, I also know him. I have seen his photos and statues.'

The priest again continues, 'The Buddha preached to mankind how to make themselves free from the clutches of birth, death, and miseries of life. This continuous cycle of birth, death, and suffering is known as bondage of human beings. It is just like the parrot you have kept in a beautiful cage. It gets food and care, but by its nature, it wants to fly in the blue sky, sit on trees, and sing in freedom. Similarly, we are caged in this body and chained by the kosas as I have told you.'

'Uncle! Then why people do not become free by following the lessons taught by the Buddha?'

'It is a good question. I have already told you that Almighty God is the greatest magician in the universe. With the hallucination (maya), He has created ignorance and egoism (*ahamkara*) in the minds of people, which has prevented them from following the noble paths of God. This is perhaps to maintain balance on the planet Earth. If everybody becomes saints, then who will do the day-to-day functioning of this beautiful planet? Very few people practise the preaching of the saints for liberation. They eventually become free and get attached to God Himself eventhough all have potential to become free. But everybody, without any exception, even after remaining in the active society (samsara), can remain happy by following His commandments and simple laws.

'God has given another sheath (kosa) to human beings as an incentive as well as a final hurdle for those people who want to become free. It is known as *anandamaya kosa* or the sheath of eternal bliss. It is full of eternal love and happiness. These small thought waves are said to be bliss thoughts, which generates joy and ecstasy. A normal person also enjoys this bliss during deep sleep. It is the most difficult sheath to overcome for uniting with God. Only through wisdom and knowledge can we free ourselves from this kosa?

'So far, we have understood about all five sheaths (kosas), which are the food, the vital air, the mental, the intellectual, and the bliss sheaths. People have three states of consciousness—the waking, the dreaming, and the deep sleep. But what is behind them all—not as an object yonder but as one's own self—is called spirit or *jivatman*, the individual atman that is a part of the universal atman or *paramatman* (Brahman, the creative power that manifests the universe).'

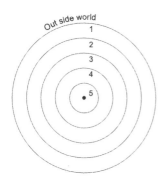

1. annamaya kosa
2. pranamaya kosa
3. manomaya kosa
4. vignanamaya kosa
5. anandamaya kosa

The boy becomes very happy and starts memorising only the five components rather than the several explained by his sister.

At half past two in the afternoon, the priest asks him, 'Don't you feel sleepy?'

The boy replies no. On the contrary, he expresses his willingness to hear some more from the priest regarding the relation between God and human beings. He also expresses his willingness to know why gods and goddesses have different postures, body parts and why some have multiple hands, multiple heads, and heads resembling other animals, like Ganesha, who had the head of an elephant.

The priest takes a little rest and starts again, 'Look, in a country like ours, the population is very big, and a large number of people do not get the opportunities for higher education. There is a need for mass education, particularly moral education, in the society for maintaining the discipline, law, and order. It is also important for them to learn the methods of living healthy and peaceful lives so that the population—even with a mixture of different castes, creeds, and religions—can blend and coexist happily in the society.

'The wise people of different countries have derived various methods to suit their people, depending on their nature, level of education, environment, weather, etc. In India, as what I have told you earlier, a large number of people do not get equal opportunities for higher education. They have different vocabularies, different habits, different lifestyles, different natural resources, etc. The wide variations in India pose great challenges to our, preachers, priests, saints to make common golden rules, guidelines, and practices for defining the way of a healthy life.

'They had chosen the simplest way for mass education—through simple stories having very high moral values. Such stories are quite exciting to hear, but at the same time, they advocate the universal truths. Those are actually moral science. If followed, the results shall be inevitably good. They generate hope in the minds of the deprived classes of people in the society that a better time will come in this life itself or maybe in the next life. Such stories prescribe the ideal ways of leading a life, earning money, performing work, developing healthy eating habits, behaving with different classes of people of different ages, forming relationships with others, sharing duties and ways of learning, etc.

'Stories and pictures are the easiest mediums for mass education. In the past, majority of the Indian population religiously followed those teachings. In general, the people of India, in spite of so many variations, used to live more happily and harmoniously with simplicity, more values, shared joys and sorrows, and close familial bonds. Over and above, they had stronger feelings of love and affection. Even now, rural India has not yet lost her old culture and traditions. Adopting the cultures of the rich and prosperous nations, which do not suit the environment of India, may have reduced the peace of mind of some people living in urban India, but the core values still persist. The people of India, even with so much diversity, still coexist without any major catastrophe.

'The laws and golden rules of happiness are similar and valid all over the world because those are universal and were valid million years ago and shall remain the same for millions of years to come.

'The question may arise on why, before any disaster, natural or caused by human beings, God does not forewarn people well in time so that innocent people can escape. Probably the reply is that He has created all human beings as the best in the universe, with complete consciousness, wise command and control system, rationality, infinite knowledge, and unbounded love. Sorrows, poisons, and hatred are creations of humans themselves. The other animals are not so blessed and privileged. In spite of this, they follow the laws of nature. Only mankind defy His laws with the help of his ability to reprogramme their subconscious mind and intellect, which He has otherwise given for the purpose of purification of human consciousness and finally for achieving liberation. The major cause of natural calamities is the exploitation of nature. Some natural calamities are for ensuring the safety of our planet, and some are the balancing acts of God.

'He created this beautiful universe, including our planet. Ordinarily, He has provided everything that we needed. He has no intention to damage it. We exploit His graceful treasures with greed and for sensual pleasures and thereby face the consequences. We are unable to manage our Mother Earth properly by ensuring peace and harmony but try to invade other planets. Today, we have already landed on a meteor after travelling billions of miles [on 7 August 2014, a space station landed on a meteor for the first time]. On the other hand, in several places, we are bombing to kill our own species just to satisfy our egoistic natures. The consequences of all our destructive acts are conveniently being phrased as acts of God and termed as destiny decided by Him. The apparent advantages of such exploitation may be enjoyed by only a handful of people in this world. They forget that the same consequences are to be borne by the entire mankind. We perceive the existence of God as a matter of logic when He comes as huddles with His spiritual laws to prevent our unlawful acts. Whereas when we are in deep trouble, both physically and mentally, we start praying to Him for help. Otherwise, on most of our visits (with a few exceptions), we use His holy residence as meeting places to just settle our social commitments and personal interests.

'Lord Ganesha is the wisest god. His eyes are small so that He can concentrate. His ears are big so that He listens more. Having a flexible trunk means being more adaptable. These are in general the qualities of an intelligent person.

'Dussehra and Diwali are two of our major festivals. You must have seen the deities, which are worshipped during those festivals. The goddess Durga has ten hands with a weapon in each. She rides on a lion, and there is a devil under Her feet, whom she has captured and killed with a spear. She has four children: Saraswati (the goddess of learning), Lakshmi (the goddess of wealth), Lord Ganesha (the god of knowledge and wisdom), and Lord Kartikeya (the god of defence). People believe that the full family of Durga goes to earth once in a year for four days from Kailash, a mountain in the northern part of India, where she lives with her husband, Lord Shiva. She blesses mankind with mental strength to fight against evils within.

'The story goes like this: Lord Brahma once was very pleased with a devil because of the impeccable dedication showed by the devil towards Him. He blessed him with a boon that no man on earth or a god in heaven could capture and defeat him. After some time, the devil became a powermonger. He started exhibiting his immunity by harming others in his kingdom. Later he lost his balance and started destructing the kingdom of the gods and goddesses. The gods then went to Lord Shiva for a solution to the problem as they were unable to stop the devil. Shiva advised them to invoke the goddess Durga and empower her with all their strengths and weapons. The devil only had immunity from a god but not from a goddess. Accordingly, they invoked the goddess Durga. She captured the devil and destroyed him.

'This ancient story depicts the need of capturing our bad habits, which are like demons. If allowed to grow, they ultimately become the cause of our destruction. The goddess Durga needed ten hands, five organs of actions (karma), and five organs of wisdom (gyan) to capture a devil. The long human history of the world demonstrated again and again that many powermongers misused their powers given by common people. Those poor people were exploited repeatedly. But such demons could not prevail over the justice of God in the long run. Eventually, they got their punishment in due course.

'Festivals of various forms, continuing from generation to generation have always remained the key to happiness for the common people of the world. Such festivals serve two purposes in general:

1. It gives messages to the believers and in turn to the societies to remain in the proven and right paths for a better living. This also depicts that, in our mind, the evil intentions, bad habits, greed, anger etc. reside as our enemies. To become happy and peaceful, we need to control such indomitable enemies with the blessings of God.

2. It served as an opportunity for common people to forget their differences, sorrows, hardships in life and to enjoy together. Such celebrations act as a vent for letting out the contaminated and accumulated feelings out of their minds before those outbrust. Festivals also provide opportunities for various working classes of people to earn in exchange for their skills.

'As I explained earlier, India is no more a rich country. The common people have frustrations and poverty in their lives. To get relief from such miseries of their day-to-day lives, they celebrate many festivals. Indian people by tradition have more patience and perseverance, and they can tolerate more hardship without revealing aggressive demonstration of their frustration in their minds.

'The Indian civilisation is 75,000 years old. The governing by-laws of Indian societies had been prepared by ancient rishis, saints, and wise people in consideration of all prevailing conditions of the country. Those by-laws had been documented by such people over the ages in the Puranas, Vedas, Upanishads, the epics, Bhagavad Gita, etc. This must be similar to the history of all other civilisations of the world. The universal laws governing the state of minds and intellects of human beings, are the same for all. They all had equivocally advocated that a balance in all important aspects of life is needed to remain happy. Discipline, forgiveness, love, values, sense of justice, respect, honesty, truthfulness, etc. are the basic human virtues. These virtues are required to be cultivated in our minds and intellects.

'For preaching the masses, those wise people chose simple stories, poems, phrases, gospels, etc. over the ages. Such golden rules, known as dharma, eventually became the true religion of India. The essence of dharma is actually the ways and means of living a good, righteous life. It clearly advises the dos and don'ts of life. The teachings will remain true and valid forever. The wise people dedicated their whole lives to discover the golden rules of God, the relationship of human beings with Him, and the intricate science related to the body, mind, and intellect. They revealed the deep mysteries of birth, death, the purpose of human life, and life beyond death. They documented the constituents of the universe and its nature, the behaviour of our planet, and the effects of the sun, the moon, and other nearby planets on human lives. Their findings had been amazing and are considered to be the basic data for advance studies. Today's scientific research is being done on such revelations for further clarities and explanations.

'In India, the saints (rishis) did researches on such matters and documented them in stories, gospels, phrases, epics, etc., which the common people could understand easily. The Vedas, the Upanishads, the Ramayana, the Mahabharata, and the Bhagavad Gita are some examples of such holy creations. Even now, grandmothers and grandfathers narrate such stories to their grandchildren to develop their morals.'

'Yes, Uncle! My grandma and mummy too tell me stories from such books. I know many stories from the Ramayana and the Mahabharata,' the young boy responds enthusiastically.

'You must have heard from your parents that those stories describes the ideas of many complicated scientific inventions and applications. The Ramayana and the Mahabharata, which are the two famous epics of India, vividly describes modern aircraft, rockets, artesian wells, the concept of underground water, test tube babies, television, concept of atoms, molecules, anatomy of human beings, sophisticated weapons, complex defence system, supersonic carriers, transponders, complex human relations, the relationship of BMI (body, mind, intellect), reincarnation, operation on the human body, concept of ideal schools and colleges, an ideal education system with most modern administration and management systems, electricity, modern construction methods, and what not.

'On the other hand, with more and more modern inventions, we are challenging the predicaments of nature and God. The more we are trying to make the world materialistic by satisfying our sense organs and by unfolding the hidden treasures of God, the more destructive sides of such inventions are also getting exposed. We with our natural instincts have also started misusing the ill and destructive side effects of such inventions. Due to the egoism of some people, we are now sitting on a heap of such destructive weaponries, which are capable of destroying our beautiful planet in no time. We have been overexploiting the beautiful gifts of nature, which can cause severe catastrophes in the near future.

'Still we are not satisfied. We have now started invading other planets with the intention of extending our areas of exploitation. Scientists are trying to overcome our mortality. In the process of our madness, we disregard our own noble qualities, noble ways of living, purpose of lives, and finally, the golden rules of God. As a consequence, we invite more diseases, conflicts, miseries, and unhappiness in this world.'

The priest expresses his mixed feelings on the uncontrolled and improper usage of scientific advancements. He, at the same time, admits that science and technology have done many good services to societies. It has given immense benefits by enriching knowledge and by providing comforts of living at new heights. The world virtually has become a small village. People have become more social and have become closer.

The boy, on the morning of the sixth birthday of his brother, visits the priest to take his blessings. They have saved some money which they want to donate to the temple. They hand over the money to their uncle. He is very pleased and says that people have become less generous nowadays to donate for such a purpose, which has caused hardships in running the temple. He becomes very happy to realise that these two boys have donated their entire money which they have saved for a good cause selflessly.

The brothers start discussing on their way back home the lessons they have learned recently from their priest uncle:

- Physiologically, the external body and some parts not visible from outside like the heart, brain, kidneys, liver, blood, etc. These all together constitute the gross body. To see those, we shall have to expose our skin, flesh, and bones.

- Mind and intellect are the two vital components. They remain invisible but actually drive us and are known as subtle bodies.
- As per the spiritual explanation, our body comprises following five sheaths:
    - food sheath (annamaya kosa)
    - vital air sheath (pranamaya kosa)
    - mental sheath (manomaya kosa)
    - intellectual sheath (vignanamaya kosa)
    - sheath of eternal bliss (anandamaya kosa).

- Liberation from sorrows and misery is the purpose of human life. To achieve the same, the intellectual sheath needs to be improved.
- Science can only try to explain what we can experience and perceive. Only a very small part of God's activities are visible, like the tip of an iceberg. Therefore, the jurisdiction of science is limited up to the tip only.
- God is the supreme being, who determines and executes everything that happens.
- Wise people and saints, through their concentrated knowledge and experience of the universal truth, translated the golden rules of God into simple stories, epics. We should follow their teachings for good governance of our societies.
- The golden rules of God are applicable alike to all His creations without any exception.

5

Philosophy and Maturity

The two most important days in your life are the
day you are born and the day you find out why.

Mark Twain

The cycle of nature rotates slowly but ceaselessly, following
her universal law. The sun rises and sets; the moon and stars
seem to appear in the night sky and disappear during the
day. The rivers continue to flow with tides and ebbs, the
spring comes after the winter, the birds sing, snakes go into
hibernation, clouds sail in the sky, it rains, snow covers the
mountaintops and then disappears. People come and go, but
her cycle goes on forever.

With the advancement of time, the elder brother has
grown up and has stepped into his adulthood. The younger
one has reached his youth. Their association with the priest,
the simplicity of their grandmother, the love and care of
their parents, and the guidance of their sister have helped
them to grow with high core values.

The elder one has become a very emotional
and generous person with excellent qualities,

like painting and playing musical instruments, whereas the younger one has a strong liking for studies and knowledge. He has a deep sense of imagination and has inquisitiveness for spiritualism. They have a very strong family bond, having concern for one another. Their lifestyle has been very simple, without the exposures of unnecessary luxuries. They enjoy their lives to the fullest, indulging in simple joys, like small festivals, games, friendships, outings, special home-made foods, etc. Very often, they visit the temple and spend some time with their esteemed priest uncle.

One such day, the younger one asks the priest, 'What is the method of attaining liberation? Is it uniform for everybody? If yes, how can it be practised?'

One gradually attains tranquility of mind by keeping the mind fully absorbed in the self by means of a well-trained intellect, and thinking of nothing else. (Bhagavad Gita)

The priest becomes very happy with these questions and appreciates him. 'You have asked me very basic questions, but at the same time, these are the most difficult to practise in one's life. These questions do not arise in the minds of many people even at the last laps of their lives, when corrective action cannot be taken easily. They again start their journey on the hard and thorny paths in search of an unknown stone which they believe can turn everything into gold instantaneously with a simple touch. Alas! This never comes true. If one touches fire with one's finger, it will only burn irrespective of his status as a king or pauper, irrespective of his nationality or religion. This was true ages before and will remain the same even after billions of years as long as our planet and mankind exist.'

> Just the luminosity is the nature of the sun,
> coolness of water and heat of fire, so too the
> nature of Atman is Eternity, Purity, Reality,
> Consciousness and Bliss. (Adi Shankaracharya)

The priest continues, 'My sons, I am not a very profoundly-read person. I had only read the Ramayana, the Mahabharata, the Bhagavad Gita, some Puranas, some stories of the Jataka, a little bit of the Vedas, Upanishads, and also about the lives of old monks, priests, rishis, and the wise men of the world, who spent their lives in pursuit of the answers to the questions you have just asked me. To understand liberation one has to first understand birth, death, karma, re-birth, purification process of mind&intellect, jeev atman. Then one has to practice to purify the jeev atman. Therefore before understanding the libration, I will like to explain you all those you may have to bear with me for some time befor we reach to our final destination.

'God restricts the easy entry to His palace of eternal bliss. He veils us with His maya (magic) of sensual pleasures and egoism, in which we remain busy to find happiness, and in that process, we get lost in the desert in search of the oasis. We do not look within and beneath for what lies more valuable than precious stones, like diamond, gold, sapphire, emerald, and pearls. We hardly introspect to find out the sources of happiness, the epicentre of all our pleasures. As long as we are covered with the darkness of egoistic nature, the bright light of the soul is not visible to us. We are unable to tap into divine love, wisdom, peace, and bliss of our valuable life.

'With the influences of rajas and tamas gunas, we become blind and unable to see the ever-increasing consequences of various diseases, untimely and premature death. These take their toll on people, not only physically and emotionally, but also spiritually. The pace of life and its demands, immoral acts, divorces, crimes, etc. have caused a hypercompetitive world, which have worn us out. At times, we take an attitude of an ostrich, as if such cancerous diseases of the society will never touch us. We see dead bodies being carried in front of us day in and day out, but we never think of death. This is the biggest wonder or blunder of human life once explained by Yudhisthira, the noblest character of the Mahabharata, one of the famous epics of India. This is exactly what I had been referring to as egoism and maya of God.'

The younger one requests the priest to elaborate it a little more for better understanding.

The priest starts again, 'We generally identify ourselves with our gross body, the five sense organs, the mind and intellect. We only have some faint knowledge of our most subtle kosa (sheath), known as anandamaya kosa (bliss), and believe that we possess the soul, which is a part of God. We have this wisdom in our knowledge. The knowledge of water in any way does not quench our thirst. Similarly, knowledge alone does not fetch us happiness unless we practise to acquire the same. In reality, we from our childhood are encouraged to have a special identity in the society around us. From this desire, the birth of "I" takes place. Then we start taking pride in our own body, mind, intellect, education, accomplishments, family, status, position, power, etc. Such thoughts give rise to egoism.

'As long as we live in the blanket of egoism, we cannot perceive the beauty of creation, the purpose of life. Instead we are overpowered by it. If we keep such harmful elements close to our hearts, can we remain in peace and happiness?'

The younger one again interrupts, 'God is the creator, the supreme authority of the universe. His best creation is the human beings. In spite of it, why has He given egoism?'

'A splendid question indeed,' says the priest. 'I do not know the right answer, but within the limitation of my knowledge, I will try to explain.

'Cobra, a type of poisonous snake, lives harmlessly with its poison inside. It spits venom for its self-defence. It never uses the venom for destruction of other snakes or to prove their supremacy over the animal kingdom. The same poison is used to make many medicines. Some of those are ingredients for making life-saving drugs. Similarly, the egoism of human beings has two parts. One is good ego, and another is bad. These two egos are inseparable and therefore cannot be bestowed in isolation. The bad ego, I have explained to you before in details. I shall explain a little about good ego as well. It will be very difficult to administer the human kingdom good ego without bad ego. We must have the power of discrimination in order to differentiate good from bad, wise from unwise, and friend from foe. This reminds me of two short stories preached by Shri Ramakrishna Paramahamsa, one of the greatest demigods of India and guru to Swami Vivekananda. To explain the requirement of good ego, he used to preach his disciples these stories.'

Story I

Some cowboys used to take their cattle for grazing in a field where there was a terrible venomous snake. One day a holy man was travelling that way. The cowboys warned him about the snake and advised him not to go there. The holy man told that he knew tricks on how to capture snakes. He continued on his way. The snake attacked him with its hood expanded.

When he chanted a charm, the snake fell helpless at his feet. The holy man asked it why it did evil to others.

'Let me give you a holy name, which you should chant day and night. This will purify your mind, and you will become wise.' He gave it a holy name and went away, with a promise to see it later. The snake followed at verbatim the teachings of the holy man.

After this, the cowboys noticed that the snake did not bite any longer. They threw stones at it. The snake became a weak and helpless creature. One day, one of the boys, with a little courage, held it by its tail and started whirling it and then threw it at a distance. The snake was hurt, and with great difficulty, it somehow managed to reach its hole. After some months, the holy man came back and started searching for the snake but in vain.

He enquired from the boys, and they narrated the fate of the snake. He knew that the snake had not died as he had passed on some power to it necessary for survival. At his repeated call, the snake came out and bowed before him. He wanted to know its experience. The snake replied that, with the name of God, he was very happy.

The holy man asked him again, 'How come you have been reduced to a skeleton?'

It was hesitating to complain against those boys. After repeated insistence, the snake revealed the incident. Then the holy man replied, 'What a pity, my dear. You should have protected yourself from being manhandled by your enemies. I forbade you to bite and put your venom in anybody. Why did you not hiss and raise your hood at those who wanted to kill you?'

The preacher advised the snake to raise its hood and hiss at evildoers but not to bite them. 'Keep enemies away by showing that you know how to deal with an enemy if necessary. You have the power of resisting evil. Only, you must take care not to pour venom into the blood of your enemy. Do not resist evil by doing evil in return but make a show of resistance that you can make if needed.

Story II

Long ago, there had been a very sincere disciple of a renowned guru (master). He used to follow the preaching of his guru at verbatim. The guru taught all his students that God existed in all creatures.

One morning the students were going to take a bath in a river. Suddenly, they saw a mad elephant was rushing towards them, and the mahout (the master of the elephant) was trying to capture it. He was shouting at all the students to stay away from the path of the elephant. All ran away except the referred disciple. He remembered the teaching of his guru, who taught that God resided in all creatures. He thought, *If so, then why would it harm me?*

The elephant found him on its way, picked him up with its trunk, and threw him into the air. The disciple fell down at a distance on the ground and was severely injured. He then started doubting the teachings of his guru.

In the evening, he narrated this incident to his guru. The guru explained him, 'You did not run away from the path of that mad elephant because God resided in it? But it was also a fact that the same God resided in the heart of the mahout too. Why did you not follow his advice? Over

Ashok Kumar Chattopadhyay

and above, God resides in the hearts of the other students also, whom I taught the same lesson. They ran away and requested you to follow them, but why did you not follow their instructions?'

The priest continues his explanation, 'The guru explained to him the necessity of discrimination between good and bad for our survival. This discriminating quality comes from ego. Now as I told you, both good and bad remain within the same ego. We should adopt the good ego and discard the bad one using our consciousness. To develop the right sense of discrimination, we shall have to bring our minds under our control. Winning a battle is easier than wining our own mind. It is to some extent easier to control our minds by sacrificing and concentrating the same on the lotus foot of your perceived God. When you purify and perfect yourself completely in all respects, then only you can do away with your egoism in the name of your God, who remains invisible. Then one does not require any deity or any other physical form or even any formal practices. As such, a person identifies himself completely with God, then gets power within to protect himself from all evils.'

The younger one exclaims that he understood the phenomenon of ego and its maya clearly now.

The priest confirms, 'So now you have understood that to achieve success in life, we need to train our minds. Our final aim in life should be to go beyond the cycle of birth and death, thereby liberating ourselves from our sufferings and pain. This is only possible by human beings. The process is slow indeed, but we must patiently practise as preached by our ancient sages, seers.

'We, from our childhood, follow the teachings of our school teachers, college professors, seniors, and bosses. We, while studying, never try to reinvent the complex scientific formula. We depend on the findings of the great scientists and proceed further for other inventions. In that process, we have reached other planets located billion miles away from our Earth. But in general, we are not willing to walk a little distance, as per the advice of our wise people, to get closer to the real treasures of God. We are prepared to run a rat race in our lives for acquiring materialistic pleasures and end up with broken hearts and injuries, like camels continuing to chew the thorny plants and bleeding perpetually.'

> There are only three events in a man's life; birth, life and death; he is not conscious of being born, he dies in pain, and he forgets to live. (Jean de la Bruyère)

The priest goes on, 'The spiritual practice makes us happy in life at a very slow pace but surely shows the results from its very initial stage itself. For practising spiritualism, one need not abandon his family or need not live an isolated life away from society or need not compromise his professional life or family life either. On the contrary, if practised properly, the benefits start accruing in all areas of our lives, including professional career. It will not only enrich our inner world, but it will also enrich our outer world and make us more efficient.'

The younger one again interrupts and questions, 'If that is so, then why do the saints, rishis, priests leave their families and go to jungles or mountains or other isolated places to practise spiritualism?'

The priest is embarrassed; in fact, he has expected this question from the younger one. He replies, 'The great scientists of the world did not leave their families. They also lived the lives of common people. Yet they could achieve their goals. They apparently looked mad on their outside appearances to others. The common people gave the least importance to them until they became famous for their great inventions. They actually walked through the paths showed by the great saints and wise people—only their goals differed. But all such missions and visions eventually led them to the ultimate goal.

'My son, the scientists I talked about, they lived in our societies but still remained at a distance from the greed, need, and sensual pleasures of life. Many of the greatest scientists never even went to high schools, did not wear party suits, and they yet achieved their goals with the help of their trained minds and intellects. Our impure thoughts obscure and darken our minds. Internal or external disturbances can make us weak both physically and mentally. Our ignorance can cloud our consciousness.

'The real scientists, spiritual gurus, true reformers of our society sacrificed their lives for the purpose of finding the truths of life. They had taken extreme steps to discipline their minds by withdrawing themselves completely from the materialistic world. They practised to live for others. As you have many subjects which you can study in a university to get a degree, similarly there are many ways to get a degree from His own university. Some reach there through the road of karma, some through love and affection towards God, some by attaining great knowledge, some through extreme devotion, and so on, but all the roads lead us to Him.

'As of now, I have been citing examples of the benefits of walking on the path of dharma or the absolute truth. It is, however, very easy to demonstrate the consequences of an unbalanced life. You may have been reading in the newspapers every day, listening from radios, and watching in the television about immoral acts, destructive activities of terrorists, bad habits of taking drugs, spread of new diseases, warmongering, extremely selfish acts, uncontrolled rivalries, disgraceful behaviours of people, divorces, child abuses, sleeplessness, accidents, depressions, and so on. Some of these happened in earlier days as well, but over time, the degree of it has reached a very alarming level. People are overexploiting the physical gifts of nature.

'Some sections of people, however, started realising the devastating effects of it and wisely became the whistle-blowers. New international protocols and laws are being made and are being implemented throughout the world. But more-intelligent exploiters are finding the loopholes of such protocols and laws for their commercial benefits. However, with the persistent efforts of the media and the whistle-blowers, there is a general awareness in the society. People have started realising slowly the effects of such exploitations in the name of commercial benefits. Scientifically developed high-yielding food items—like vegetables, fruits, fishes, chickens, etc.—are being processed with chemical fertilisers and pesticides. Too much application of fertilisers may show some initial benefits but spoils the fertility of the soil permanently. Apparently, such people are ignoring the bad effects of their actions. There is a need of a paradigm shift in the society. There is a serious need of introspection by us to discriminate between good and bad.

'We see ghosts in the street side lamp posts and avoid it, and in the same way, we carefully avoid the spiritual path. This happens because of our ignorance. If we open the windows of our minds, we shall surely see light entering it, and the long-prevailing darkness will be gone in a few moments.

'Stephen R. Covey, in his very popular book *The Seven Habits of Highly Effective People*, had described one of the seven habits as sharpening the saw. This habit is the habit of discrimination. It is about the need of introspection about the results of our actions and taking continuous corrective measures. We can reach perfection in our lives by following this process.

'In general, all people of the world are physiologically similar. Our sense organs, feelings of love and happiness are the same in spite of our different sizes, colours, education, and knowledge. If someone does not activate or use a particular faculty, it may become ineffective with passage of time. Let me give an example. If a baby immediately after birth is kept in darkness for a considerable time, there will be serious impairment of its physical vision. Similarly, if we do not develop our minds and intellects at an appropriate time, there may be impairment in the development of healthy ego. Therefore, for development of a good ego, one has to be trained from childhood by one's parents, teachers, relatives, and friends. The training should include lessons on love, compassion, knowledge, skill, moral, and behavioural sciences.

'There is a need for a culmination of the laws of spirituality and science since both are required for an ideal and balanced life. As such, there is not much difference between spirituality and science. The acts of God, explained by some acceptable people of the society or by demonstrations using special instruments or universally perceived by human sense organs, which are repetitive in nature, are considered to be within the domain of science. Laws of nature—with respect to our body, mind, and intellect—follow a particular pattern. We are all physically built with the same energy, having the same minutest invisible particles in the form of blocks with similar behaviours and manipulative properties. The most subtle energy that drives our minds and intellects is known as the spirit or atman. Atman, being energy, cannot be destroyed or created or burnt or damaged with any weapon. It has no colour, no smell. It cannot be seen. It is pure. After death, it leaves the body and remains as an integral part of the infinite universe.'

> The Atman, the sun of knowledge that rises in the sky of the heart, destroys the darkness of the ignorance, pervades and sustains all and shines and makes everything to shine. (p. 121, quote n. 67, Atman Bodh)

The younger one sharply replies, 'If that is so, then why do we all look different? Why are our characteristics different? Why are our minds and intellects different?'

The priest explains that to understand the homogeneity of atman and its nature, he will give them a simple example. Pure air we feel everywhere around us, but we cannot see it. It does not have any odour or shape. If we take three differently shaped pots in our hands, the air inside the pot will seem to have three different shapes. If we break those pots, the air inside gets mixed with the air surrounding us. The pots are made of clay, having different shapes. Clay is a component of earth. It is given different shapes by human beings, then hardened in fire. After breaking, it gets converted into earth again, which does not have any shape. Depending on the shapes and their uses, we give them different names. But those names, shapes, colours are physical appearances only and non-permanent in nature, like our physical body or shape, whereas the air is similar to atman.

Air is everywhere around us—in our garden, in the sweet smell of flowers, in the forest, in the smell of sandalwood, in the mountains with its freshness. And the same air is also found surrounding the dirty waste bins, spreading foul odour. It is our choice where we will take the air from. The same is the case with atman. It is our choice indeed. How will we shape it? How shall we use it? Therefore, we need to look within before making the choice. It is believed that human birth is indeed a culmination of several births. Even with the grace of God, billions of sperms having the potential of human life, race towards the ovary, but only one or two will get the chance to cross the final line in meeting the egg. Even after the qualifying round, it has to face several challenges for about ten months inside the mother's womb before it can see the light of the outside world. Thereafter face other challenges of life. Therefore, human life is indeed very precious. Human beings are very unique from other species, for our ability to manipulate, modulate, self-introspect, and communicate directly with God. We also have the power to discriminate, dissect, rationalise, and invent. With all the above qualities in place, if we try to explore ourselves and our relationship with God, the benefits will be immense. So shall be the loss if we do not do so.

Learning is a lifelong process. It never ends, but its start is always with a first step. We need to switch on the headlights of our car to start with, drive a short distance within the range of its visibility, and then continue this process until we reach our destination. To begin with, it will be very difficult to sit down in a fixed place with an empty mind for even a few minutes. Once we get accustomed with this practice, for a longer duration, we can focus our minds on our desired thoughts. The focused mind is a very powerful tool. If we sit and introspect with this tool, removing the dirt lying within becomes possible. With the corrected mind, we can purify our intellect and can finally visualise our atman, which is nothing but pure joy and bliss.

God has given us the following six abilities as hidden treasures, which we need to utilise properly. They are:

- *shama*—inner silence and calmness
- *dama*—self-control
- *shraddha*—trust and respect
- *uprati*—ability to rise above things by not being afraid
- *titiksha*—equanimity and inner strength
- *samadhana*—ability to remain focused on the goal.

The system of purification is similar to any other physical system. If we try to play a simple musical instrument, to start with, we will generate only noise. After practising for several years, one can play such immaculate notes that the audience is mesmerised. There is no shortcut to it. Others cannot do it on somebody's behalf. Only an experienced teacher can help us in our progression.

At the initial stage, there is a need for a favourable environment in terms of company, surroundings, reasonable physical comfort, and isolation from other activities, which are required for sensory gratification. After some period of practice, such restrictions may not be required. It is just like the formation of curd. The curd will not form if the milk is not kept under ideal conditions. Once the curd is formed, it will not lose its shape or revert back to milk. After planting saplings in a farm, a guard is put around it so that it is protected from goats and cows. But once the plant grows into a big tree, even an elephant chained around it cannot damage the tree. Therefore, during spiritual practice, one should remain in touch with the good teachers and keep wise company who can expedite the process.

Then the priest observes that the elder brother looks anxious. He asks, 'What is the matter?'

The elder one replies that the method which he just explained must be very difficult and is a long-drawn process to reach the ultimate goal.

The priest promptly advises him that he doesn't need to pursue it; it is not necessary to become a saint. But even small progress will fetch proportional benefits in day-to-day life, including one's professional field. This process of small, small improvements is used in the industry for achieving quality products, which is popularly known as kaizen in Japan.

Many aged and elderly persons go to the temple. They sit down in the evening and discuss the problems of their family lives. They at times express the dissatisfaction and miseries of their lives. Some speak about their ill health, and some complain about their relationship problems with their grown-up children. Our miseries, pains, and fear of death in old age occur because of our ignorance and lack of practice of the good principles in life. Does such practice help them to solve their problems? On the contrary, it increases exponentially. One cannot change the world but can change oneself for improvement, which may in turn trigger the world for a larger benefit.

In our early days, we remain busy pursuing our external needs in life—studying, earning money, running after worldly pleasures, bringing up our children, and so on. In this particular phase of life, we are controlled to some extent by our conscious mind (to an extent of 10 to 20 per cent), and the rest depends on our subconscious mind. When we grow old, the controlling power of our conscious mind comes down to 1 to 2 per cent. During our old age, the subconscious mind starts driving us completely. Most of our thoughts and behaviours are overpowered by the subconscious mind.

If the same remains unclean, then the outcome may be one or a combination of the following:

- fear of losing vitality of our body
- loss of glory or beauty (appearance)
- loss of attention of others even at home
- fear of ageing
- fear of retirement
- abnormality in behaviours and interactions
- tendency to depend on unnecessary medicines
- fear of betrayal and loss of respect
- fear of death
- going into depression.

If we want to get rid of these, we shall have to address our minds from a younger age. There is no other shortcut method or magic to escape from such consequences.

The younger one endorses the view of the priest and discloses that he has noticed similar indications in the behaviour of their grandma in recent days. Their grandma is slowly becoming childish. Her behaviour has become inconsistent in the last year. But she is still stable and loves them.

An agitated mind has been proven to be the cause of our major illnesses. We must know our mind, its strengths and weaknesses, from an early age so that when we enter our professional lives, we are well aware of the complexities which we might face. We carry out the SWOT (strength, weakness, opportunities, threats) analysis before investing money in any venture but very seldom practise it while taking decisions in our own lives. Meditation, introspection,

Ashok Kumar Chattopadhyay

adoption of universal good practices, and a balanced lifestyle are the keys to a successful and happy life. Then the priest stops the discussion and advises his beloved disciples to go home and think about the day's discussion.

The two of them look at each other, then slowly get up and start walking towards their home. In the evening, they share their learning with their sister.

- The governing laws of God are applicable eternally and equally for all.
- As you sow, so you reap your harvest.
- The maya (magic) of God pervades every realm and veils the sources of absolute happiness, like uncut diamonds.
- The mind, unless trained, can be our worst enemy. Happiness is a state of mind.
- The birth of 'I' or 'self' is the root cause of our misery.
- We must adopt good ego and discard bad ego.
- Teachings of conventional schools and colleges remain incomplete if spiritual science is not learned. The ultimate truth lies within, which needs to be discovered. Mind and intellect should be trained and addressed for smart living.
- The process of searching for God commences by disciplining the gross body and then the subtle body.
- God's energy pervades all the realms; it cannot be destroyed. It has no colour, no shape, and no odour. This is the most subtle part of the universe and resides within the human body, known as spirit or atman.

66

- At old age, the subconscious mind fully overpowers the conscious mind. In order to remain happy in old age, the removal of negativity from our subconscious mind is necessary. The purpose of our precious life is to purify our BMI and achieve liberation to make ourselves free from the cycle of birth and death.

6

Death in the Family

> When you came you cried and everybody
> smiled with joy; when you go smile, let the
> world cry for you.

> Rabindranath Tagore

Days, weeks, and years pass. The beautiful seasons of nature
rotate fast yet slow for some unhappy creatures. The children
of this family are growing up well with high character ethics.

It is a full moon night; the winter has spread its cold
wings with fog around. A full-moon night has its own
charming beauty, and both brothers and their sister are
enjoying the beauty from the rooftop of their house. The
reflection of the moon is shining on the surface of the pond.
The cold breeze of pre-winter is threatening the tall trees
with a fear of loosning their leaves. The temple stands with
its head held high between their house and the pond as if it
wants to exhibit its pride of having captured God inside and
retaining the sole right of His manifestation. Some priests
strongly believe that God cannot be invoked or worshipped
without them as if it is their sole and patented right.

The younger brother first breaks the silence and says, 'Our priest uncle is very nice and wise too. He calls himself not a very well-read person, but it does not seem so. He has taught us the concept of SWOT analysis, which is part of management study. I feel he is a very well-read person. He has assimilated the complex concept of God and science and can explain it in very simple words to others. It appears he has deep knowledge of science as well.'

The elder sister stops him and asks about his preparation for the entrance test, which will ensure his admission to a good engineering college. He replies, 'I am prepared for it.' But after listening to the sermons of the priest uncle, he has started thinking about the real purpose of life.

The elder one quickly responds, 'Do not forget about good ego, that one needs to become worldly and that one needs to be wise to serve the society properly.'

All three of them are engrossed in the discussion when suddenly their mother cries loudly that their grandmother is not feeling well. The younger one says, 'It has become a regular habit of grandma. She loves to take medicine and believes that it can keep her alive forever.'

Their father asks them to come down immediately. The younger one then understands that it must be serious; otherwise, Father would not have intervened.

No sooner have they come down than Father directs the elder brother to call a doctor immediately. They find Grandma gasping for air; she is struggling to breathe. She has almost lost her voice and is whispering. Their mother is utterly perplexed and is looking blank. Father is trying to assist her in breathing. She weakly calls their sister close but is unable to raise her hand. She tries to communicate with her eyes. A little stream of tears roll down her cheeks. Their father immediately places her head softly in his hands. In no time, before anybody can realise it, a feeble gurgling sound comes out from between her lips, then slowly she closes her eyelids forever. The elder brother returns with the doctor uncle, who resides next to their house, but before he can do anything, Grandma is no more.

Tears come out of their father's eyes, which the children have never witnessed before. Mother along with their sister starts crying loudly. The elder brother also starts sobbing. Only the younger one sits down quietly beside Grandma and softly rubs her palm. He has no idea of death. This is the first occasion he has witnessed the death of a beloved member of his family.

He starts remembering all his childhood memories with Grandma, who has loved him unconditionally. Slowly he starts feeling an ache close to his heart, and a stream of uncontrolled tears starts rolling down his cheeks. His elder brother joins his mother and sister and tries to console them.

Few hours later, the birds starts singing, the sun rises, and the stars and the moon disappear as they did every day. The bell for the morning prayer at the temple starts ringing, the milkman delivers milk to the houses around, and the cattle starts grazing. The only exception is, today Grandma is not going to wake up from her eternal sleep. Her chanting of the morning prayer will not be heard any more as her voice has been choked forever.

The neighbours slowly arrive in their house to pay their last respects and to give company to the family. The room is filled with the heavy air of death. The ambience inside becomes very gloomy. But it slowly starts lightening up with the presence of the well-wishers, friends, and neighbours.

The younger one says to himself, 'Only now I realised the importance of having good friends, relatives, and neighbours around.' The boy can see that their priest uncle has also arrived and is trying to console all the family members. Slowly the relatives also reached to pay their last respects to Grandma before her last journey.

The younger one, sitting beside the dead body, starts to realise more about the importance of atman. He starts thinking about where their Grandma came from, and where she will go now. Is it really her last journey? Who was Grandma—the body, the soul, or the combination of both? Nothing has been lost physically; only the invisible soul has left the body. Physically, she has stopped breathing, her heart has stopped pumping blood, all the organs have become non-functional, all physical responses are missing, and the body has started cooling down abruptly.

He has also observed the strange behaviours of people around; they are hesitant to touch the dead body of their beloved grandma. He realises that even the holy people after their death left behind only a physical mass, which is considered unholy and impure and needs to be disposed quickly and safely. It reminds him of the advice of the priest uncle that when we are alive, we give utmost importance to this mass instead of the atman. He remembers the poem he read in high school written by Thomas Gray, which read:

> The boast of heraldry, the pomp of power,
> And all the beauty, all the wealth e'er gave,
> Awaits alike the inevitable hour, the paths
> of glory lead but to the grave.

Some more time pass. The priest uncle performs the rituals, and the body of their grandma is taken out of their home for the last rites. This is apparently the end of a life.

The elder brother tells the younger one, 'See the paradox? When you were born, you were crying, and all of us were laughing with joy. Today Grandma is on her last journey. She is smiling, and all of us are crying. Grandma had been a nice person who had established the bond in the family. She loved everybody at home. She had concern for all the relatives, friends, and our neighbours too. Our parents respected her from their hearts and valued her opinions on various domestic matters. She lived a good life. Suddenly, her demise has created a vacuum in the family. The first experience of death in some one's family makes a very deep impression on one's heart. We are fully consumed by the grief of separation from our beloved ones. This raises many questions about death, about the possibility of transmigration and reincarnation, about the rituals followed by family members for some time.'

The two brothers and their sister sit on a bench outside the temple because they are not suppose to enter the temple premises for a period of two weeks. Traditionally, at the end of the mourning period, a simple feast is arranged. All relatives and friends are invited to attend the same. Some ceremonial prayers are performed by the family members along with a priest.

Seeing them sitting on the bench outside, the priest of the temple comes forward to console them. They want to know why all the rituals are necessary after the death of somebody. The priest replies that he will not be able to answer correctly as he did not find any logic in many of those. The priest confesses that he can only guess. These systems have been followed by the Hindu families from the very early days in the country. There is a set of similar rituals in other religions too, in India and abroad.

Maybe the old orthodox society has made the rituals for the following reasons:

1. to divert the minds of the affected family members
2. to stabilise the soul of the dead person.

The priest says that he shall try his best to explain his statement as logically as possible. 'I have already explained to you that happiness and sorrows are different states of mind. It is the mind that registers the above feelings first and then activates other organs of the body. If someone is injured externally, there shall be a need for immediate treatment. First, we try to stop bleeding from the injury, and then we apply medicine for healing. Initially, the process of healing is fast, but later it takes some time to cure completely. Similarly, the death of a very close person creates a deep scar in the minds of close family members. There is an immediate need for first aid. Simply, the presence of good friends, neighbours, and relatives and their consolation act like first aid. Subsequently, the rituals keep the affected people busy, and their minds get occupied with other responsibilities. Time is the greatest healer, which heals the scar slowly over time and then finally hides the scar in one's memory.'

7

⟶⟫⟩⟨⟨⟵

Science and Spirituality

The life of the dead is placed in the memory
of the living.

Marcus Tullius Cicero

Slowly memories of their grandmother take a back seat
in the busy schedule of their thoughts. But her influence
prevails among the family members in deciding many
important matters.

In the meantime, the elder brother, after completing
his degree, joins a bank. The younger one is almost on
the verge of completing his degree in electrical engineering
from Jadavpur University in Calcutta. He is a day scholar,
which helps him to remain at home while studying. Their
sister is continuing her postgraduate degree even after her
marriage. She lives with her husband not very far from their
parents' house.

Their father is about to retire from service. Their sister
often visits their parents and joins them on all occasions
and celebrations.

The priest uncle has become elder but still remains very agile, probably because of his disciplined lifestyle. Even now, they visit the temple almost on a regular basis.

One day, the younger brother asks about the family of the priest uncle. He remains reserved for a while, and then he reveals that he belongs to a well-to-do family. His father expired at an early age. He wanted to become a scholar in life but ended up eventually as a priest of this temple. Since then he has remained there as its caretaker. He also added that he has remained unmarried.

The younger brother again says, 'Uncle, on various occasions, you have discussed many things about birth but never on death. Please tell me something about it.' The priest assures him they will discuss this subject the day his sister is present. She knows more about physiological death.

Even though the priest lives within the four walls of the temple, he is quite well read. He goes to the community library almost on a regular basis. He loves to read technical books and journals but also remains engrossed in spiritual books as well. He has acquired very good knowledge from the epics, Bhagavad Gita, Vedas, Puranas, and life histories of holy persons and saints and their teachings. Overall, he is a knowledgeable and helpful person. But whenever somebody asks him about his personal life, he mostly avoids discussing it. Everybody in the society believes that he is a very wise person. This impression he has created because of his impeccable behavior with everybody, irrespective of wealth, religion, status, and caste. In fact, he himself practises whatever he preaches.

He always advises the younger brother, who is very dear to him. 'Read as many good books as you can, books based on the various aspects of life and the material world, so that your knowledge is complete. Knowledge helps us to improve our intellect and good ego.

'Studying in a good institute is the first step to building a successful career. The university gives us reasonable knowledge on the subject. Thereafter, one has to acquire knowledge from the practical experiences of life, accomplishments, mistakes, and also from teachers, elders, spiritual guides, and from association with good people. Then we need to know how to discriminate between good and bad, how to reject the bad things in life. It is very important to develop communication skills for understanding the behaviours of others so that one can become worldly and wise and can manage situations better. Finally, the most important thing is to practise and live a balanced life.'

> There is no real excellence in this entire world
> which can be separated from right living.
> (David Starr Jordan)

'We must win over ourselves first, and only then should we try to win over others. Both of you have the right basic ingredients. Now develop yourselves and go for a personal victory first so that you are successful in life.' The priest then requests them to go back home as he needs a little rest.

Both of them return home. It is a holiday, and they want to give company to their parents. Their mother asks them where they have gone.

They reply, 'To the temple.'

'Why at these early hours?' she asks.

'To spend some time with the priest uncle.'

She praises the priest for his generosity and wants to know the subjects of their discussions.

The elder one summarises it for her:

- One must know and determine one's real purpose in life.
- One should be worldly wise in life.
- As you sow, so you reap.
- There are rituals to stabilise and purify the mind.
- Both character ethics and personal ethics are required to become successful in life.
- First, one must achieve private victory, which opens the gate for public victory.

The younger boy concludes their discussions, saying, 'Mama, I understood from what the priest uncle said that spiritualism and science need to shake hands. I think science is that small part of spiritualism which people can explain in terms of theories and formulas.'

This book now takes a different direction, towards its ultimate journey, to its final destination—whether reincarnation is a myth or a science.

8

A Solemn Mission

Man is made by his belief. As he believes, so
he is.

Bhagavad Gita

The two brothers and their sister, in evening of the Guru
Purnima on 12 July 2014 (an auspicious full-moon evening),
prepare their mission statements and ask the priest to see it.

The statements read:

1. Today, on 12 July 2014, we two brothers and sister,
    keeping the image of the Lord Ganesha (the god
    of wisdom) in our hearts, with a humble prayer
    to Goddess Saraswati (the goddess of learning),
    and finally, under the lotus feet of Maha Kali (the
    goddess of power), take a solemn oath that we
    shall study and gather knowledge on the process of
    reincarnation with the aim to explain it scientifically
    for the benefit of mankind.

2. We shall give our sincere efforts to complete this research work on or before the next Guru Purnima in August 2015.

3. We pledge that while working on this subject, we shall not hurt the sentiments or belief of any person, community, religion, or nation.

4. We, to the best of our knowledge, shall not infringe on other proven or patented theories on this subject if there are any. However, there could be some references to published papers, books, journals, information from the Internet or matters available in the public domain.

5. We do not intend to and shall not involve ourselves in any kind of dispute or litigation, knowingly or unknowingly, to establish our findings.

6. The subject of the process of reincarnation, to the best of our knowledge and understanding, does not have any direct conflict with God's activities. We also believe that the Lord is supreme and that we do not have the competency to gauge Him or His activities. It is He who has created this infinite universe, and it is He who controls it.

7. In spite of our best efforts, if any word, sentence, phrase, text, content, findings, examples, comparison, quote, etc. used by us in our report causes any concern to anybody, that may kindly be considered as unintentional. We apologize for it at the outset.

8. We admit that we are novices on this subject and have very limited knowledge. We do not intend to challenge any existing theory on this subject, whether published by other authors or available in the public domain. Over and above all, we shall

ensure that our report will not in any way override any such theories or teachings. We fully believe that whatever has been narrated in the holy books or whatever has been explained or proclaimed in the teachings of the wise people and saints are the absolute truth on the subject matter.

9. Our work is merely an endeavour to bring out the possible scientific explanation of the process of reincarnation.

10. We need blessings of thee.

The priest carefully goes through the statements and comments, 'You have really grown up and become mature. You have demonstrated your firm commitments through these mission statements.'

They reply that they are prepared and have come to their guru (teacher) for his guidance on their research work. They confess their total ignorance on spiritual matters. They confide in him that they have always lived within the cocoon of the wisdom of their priest uncle. Their mission cannot take off and shall never be successful if it is not led by their priest uncle.

Their priest uncle thinks for a while and says that he wants assurance from them that during their journey, they shall follow the complete mission statements verbatim. All of them agree and reconfirm at once. The uncle further continue and tells them that he has been waiting for this day for a long time, and he conveys his acceptance to become a member of the team for this noble mission.

They sit down together in the prayer hall for a while and pray quietly for acquiring strength and concentration of mind. Uncle explains that to execute any project, there is a need to identify the scope of the project and a proper plan to move forward.

They collectively decide to implement this task following the given plan of action:

1. Look for the current available information on the subject.
2. Collect the revelations and theories available in the holy books.
3. Take into consideration the findings and opinions of the wise and saintly personalities of the world.
4. Find out more about the accepted (general) concepts of reincarnation in the society.
5. Describe the physiological body and its constituents.
6. Describe the relationship among the body, mind, and intellect (BMI).
7. Describe the process of physiological birth.
8. Describe the process of physiological death.
9. Work out the principle of human intelligence.
10. Analyse the closest and most similar proven scientific processes of birth and death.
11. Compare birth and death closely.
12. Use feedback technique to eliminate any possible differences.
13. Compare the statements of accomplished teachers and saints.
14. Establish the principle of transmigration.
15. Take into consideration the crossroad between religious thoughts and the principle of science.

9

Transmigration

When the Aggregates arise, decay and die, O
bhikkhu, every moment you are born, decay
and die.

Gautama Buddha

The Present Position and Belief on Transmigration

There has been no direct scientific proof of transmigration
other than the demonstrations and some physical evidences
given by people who claimed to have remembered many
incidents of their previous lives. In some cases, the
phenomenon of reincarnation has been inferred from
birthmarks from previous lives, from the recollections or
knowledge from previous lives, from the visualisation of
events like near-death experiences, etc. duly verified by the
responsible people of the societies.

The collection of case histories by Dr Ian Stevenson of
the University of Virginia, USA, is the highest in this regard,
which includes about three thousand cases. Based on his
case histories, he established the truth of the occurrence of

reincarnation. There are many books on this subject, mostly spiritual, which have described reincarnation based on the realisation and understanding of the respective authors or from their direct or indirect experiences. They have claimed that, as per their knowledge, there are no globally accepted scientific explanations available on the process of transmigration. However, there are doctrines written down by many great minds in favour of reincarnation.

The priest says that he has tried to assimilate some of the doctrines and theories left behind by some of the great minds of the world. He at times has wondered about the different opinions and the repertoire of expressions and beliefs on this subject. Some atheists, even if they tend to believe in God, discard the concept of transmigration due to the lack of convincing scientific explanation.

If people are asked, 'Have you ever seen God?' most of the replies are no! If they are asked again, 'Do you believe in God?' most of the answers are yes. Therefore, it is not always necessary to see to believe. We cannot see air but can feel it. The effectiveness of the gross physical body along with its five sense organs is very limited, much inferior to those of many other animals. But we still rely mostly on our sense organs rather than believing our superior and unique subtle body.

As a matter of fact, human beings just only discovered the unknown laws of God those exist already.

> The secret of creativity is knowing how to hide your sources. (Albert Einstein)

The human mind and consciousness cannot be adequately measured through the existing scientific tools or means. At present, only some possibilities can be explored. Science has now significantly advanced with its theories of quantum physics; it may be a matter of time before the curtain is raised from the ancient concepts of the soul and its journey through reincarnation. But if the scientists decide to close their minds with the belief that there is no existence of a soul and transmigration or reincarnation, they will not be able to reach any plausible theory on this subject.

The essence of the work of the brothers, their sister, and the priest is to give the scientific community of the world some food for thought.

The existence of God and the existence of atman or soul still remain a matter of argument, waiting for universal acceptance. But the fact remains that many inexplicable matters or happenings can be explained based on the existence of the atman or soul. Science, spiritualism, and religion can cross-fertilize with one another, inspiring new ideas that may finally culminate into a synthesis that goes beyond our present understanding of this subject.

In the seventeenth century, Rene Descartes—the eminent academician, philosopher, mathematician, and scientist (1596–1650) of France—divided everything of this universe into two realms: *res extensa* (matter) and *res cogitans* (mind). He called the first part as classical science. The second part was named as mind, which was not considered as a respectable subject of study by the scientific society in those days. The subject of reincarnation was considered to be a part of res cogitans and remained as a subject of no interest to the scientists.

Ancient Indian philosophers believed that at the very beginning of creation, the sound of *om*, the first and original vibration, divided the unity of the divine universal energy. Two powers emerged from it:

1. *purusha*—original consciousness
2. prakriti—primordial nature.

In the triad *aum* (*om* is pronounced as *aum* while chanting), the divine energy is united in its three elementary aspects:

1. Brahma Shakti—the creative power that manifests the universe
2. Vishnu Shakti—the preserving power that sustains the cosmos
3. Shiva Shakti—the liberating power that brings about transformation and renewal.

Prakriti is the eternal stream of divine energy and is part of the divine being. In a progressive sequence, three gunas and five *tattvas* (elementary principles) emanate from prakriti. These form the basis of manifestations of all gross and subtle forms. The five tattvas are earth, water, fire, air and space. The three gunas are sattva, rajas, and tamas.

Without some external influence, the tattvas cannot unite. For unification of two or more tattvas, gunas are required. They are the primordial forces that have an effect on physical and astral planes and can influence us physically, psychically, and spiritually. The tattvas that combine to form the physical body in which the soul lives again disintegrate on our death and return to the cosmos. The soul then continues to wander, waiting to find a new body where it can take a new form again under suitable conditions.

If we can successfully analyse and synthesise the process of rebirth, like it is done for any other electrical or mechanical process, and convert it into an equivalent system which is similar to transmigration and can prove that both are similar, then it shall be more convincing to both scientists and spiritual people. It will be a unique disclosure of the most fascinating hidden treasures of God. By doing so, we shall be able to give the message to mankind that reincarnation is no more a myth but a reality. The people who do not believe it and justify only materialism may undergo a paradigm shift and adopt the concept of continuous improvement of their minds and intellects. These efforts will surely be of immense benefit to all societies.

The Revelations and Preaching in the Holy Books

On the subjects of atman or soul, birth, and death, the Bhagavad Gita has remained an authentic source through the ages. Any discussion or analysis remains incomplete without reference to the Bhagavad Gita.

The Bhagavad Gita states the following about the atman or soul:

> There has never been a time when you and I have not existed, nor there be a time when we will cease to exist. As the same person inhabits the body through childhood, youth and old age, so too at the time of death he attains another body. The wise are not deluded by these changes.

> The end of birth is death; the end of death is birth: this is ordained! And mournest thou, chief of the stalwart arm! For what befalls which could not otherwise befall? (chapter 2, verse 20, translation)

The soul is never born and never dies at any time, nor does it come into being again when the body is created. The soul is birthless, eternal, imperishable, and timeless, and it is never terminated when the body is terminated.

The soul is indestructible, incombustible, insoluble, and unwitherable. The soul is eternal, all pervasive, unmodifiable, immovable, and primordial.

The priest says, 'Since our subject of interest is reincarnation and transmigration of the soul, we must first try to understand whether it has a universal acceptance throughout the world. If not, what are the reasons for it? In India a large majority of people believe in transmigration. I have collected some information regarding the global acceptance of this concept, which I would like to share with you.

'A large number of Christian populations may not believe in reincarnation and transmigration of the soul. They believe we are born once and then disappear forever upon death. Therefore, they tend to live a more materialistic life. In my mind, local environment may influence the lifestyle of people. The Christian population is mainly dominating the Western part of the world, where the natural resources are more, and they are relatively rich and have less population. Therefore, they can afford to be more materialistic than the people of the Eastern world. In spite of the same, there is a mixed perception about the belief on rebirth in the Western world. I say this after looking into the differences in their mass behaviour vis-à-vis the teachings of their saints and wise people.'

The priest gives some examples in support of his statement.

Origen has stated, 'Is it not more in conformity with reason that every soul for certain mysterious reasons is introduced into a physical body in accordance to its rewards and past activities?'

Goethe has remarked, 'I am sure that I, such as you see me here, have lived a thousand times and I will have to come again another thousand times.'

In the Bible, book of St Mathew (chapter 17, verses 12 and 13), Jesus says, 'Verily I say into you that Elijah has already come and they recognize him not; but have done with him whatever they wanted. Likewise the son of man shall suffer also due to them.'

In Shakespeare's *Hamlet*, there is a reference to the spirit of Hamlet's father appearing before Hamlet and narrating to him how he was killed by his own brother.

The eminent scientist Aldous Huxley has written in his religious treatise *Evolution and Ethics*: 'None but the very hasty will reject reincarnation on the grounds of inherent absurdity. Life the doctrine of evolution itself, that of transmigration of the soul has its root in the world of reality and it may claim such support as the great argument of analogy is capable of supplying.'

Professor Lutoslawsky has said, 'I cannot give up my conviction of a previous existence before my birth and I have the certainty to be born again after my death until I have assimilated all human experiences, having been many times male and female, wealthy and poor, free and enslaved; generally having experienced all conditions of human existence.'

Henry Ford stated, 'I adopted the theory of Reincarnation when I was twenty six. Religion offered nothing to the point. Even work could not give me complete satisfaction. Work is futile if we cannot utilize the experience we collect in one life in the next. When I discovered Reincarnation it was as if I had found a universal plan I realised that there was a chance to work out my ideas. Time is no longer limited. I was no longer a slave to the hands of the clock.'

As for the Mohammedan culture's take on transmigration, in the noble Quran, chapter 2, verse 28 states, 'How can ye reject the faith in Allah?—Seeing that ye were without life, and He gave you life; then will He cause you to die, and will again bring you to life and again to Him ye return.'

Chapter II, verse 154 states, 'And say not of those who are slain in the way of Allah. "They are dead." Nay they are living; though ye perceive (it) not.'

Chapter 71, verses 17 and 18 states, 'And Allah has produced you from the earth, Growing (gradually), And in the End He will return you into the (earth), And raise you forth (again at the resurrection).'

Chapter 20, verse 55 states, 'From the (earth) did we create you, and into it shall we return you, and from it shall we bring you out once again.'

Siddhartha Buddha has said, 'Through many a birth wondered I, seeking the builder of this house. Sorrow full indeed is birth again and again.'

Katha Upanishad (ii. 19) states, 'If the slayer thinks that he has slain, or if the slain think that he is slain, both of them know not that soul can neither slay nor be slain.'

Jainism and Sikhism do believe in reincarnation, similar to Hinduism.

Julius Caesar recorded: 'The principal point of their doctrine is that the soul does not die and that after death it passes from one body into another.'

The Chuang Tzu states, 'Birth is not a beginning; death is not an end. There is existence without limitation; there is continuity without a starting point. Existence without limitation is space. Continuity without a starting point is time. There is birth, there is death, there is issuing forth, there is entering in.'

Kabbalah in Judaism teaches, 'The Soule of Moses is re-incarnated in every generation.'

Guru Granth Sahibji 126 states, 'When the body is filled with ego and selfishness, the cycle of birth and death does not end.'

Guru Granth Sahibji 325 states, 'As long as the tongue does not chant the name of God, the person continues coming and going in re-incarnation, crying out in pain.'

10

Present Proof of Reincarnation

I am not afraid of death because I don't believe
in it. It's just getting out of one car, and into
another.

John Lennon

Experiences of Great and Wise Men

1. Experience of Dr Ian Stevenson

He devoted forty years to the scientific documentation of
past-life memories of children from all over the world. He
had more than three thousand case files. Dr Stevenson was
a medical practitioner and had many scholarly papers to his
credentials. He was the former head of the Department of
Psychiatry at the University of Virginia and was the director
of the Division of Personality Studies at the same university.

2. Experience of Dr Michael Newton

He is a renowned hypnotherapist from USA. He worked on the subject of reincarnation and has documented information worth fifty years of client sessions—subconscious memories of their past lives and even memories of the time in between the two lives. His book *Journey of Souls* reveals many case studies which supports the reality of reincarnation.

3. Experience of Dr Eben Alexander (MD)

He is an eminent neurosurgeon at the Brigham and Women's Hospital at Harvard Medical School in Boston. His book *Proof of Heaven* vividly describes his personal experience with the soul when he was in a coma for seven days.

4. According to Swami Abhedananda

According to Swami Abhedananda, the soul exists beyond death. Swamiji was a direct disciple of Paramahamsa Ramakrishna. He was in USA for twenty-five years (from 1897) in charge of the Vedanta Society.

5. Teachings of Swami Vivekananda (Yogananda, *EastWest*, May–June 1927, vol. 2–4)

He started writing about reincarnation with a quote from the Bhagavad Gita: 'Both you and I have passed through many births; you know them not, I know them all.'
He concluded with the following paragraph:

> It is thus that the doctrine of reincarnation assumes an infinite importance before our minds for the fight between reincarnation

and mere cellular transmission is, in reality, fight between spiritualism and materialism. If cellular transmission is the all sufficient explanation materialism is inevitable, and there is no necessity for the theory of soul.

If it is not a sufficient explanation, the theory of an individual soul bringing into this life the experience of the past . . . is as absolutely true. There is no escape from the alternative, reincarnation or materialism. Which shall we accept?

Swamiji said:

The body is dying every minute. The mind is constantly changing . . . But beyond this momentary sheathing of gross matter . . . is the atman, the true self of man, which is permanent, ever-free.

Everything in this universe is indestructible . . . You cannot take away one atom of matter or one foot pound of force. You cannot add to the universe one atom of matter or one foot pound of force.

Does the law of conservation of energy apply to consciousness? If everything in the universe is indestructible, it follows that man is immortal. How can that be true? Everyone dies! A man is but a coat upon a stick.

Dust returning to dust. But this is the fate of the body, not the soul. How do we live and transform ourselves after the body has died? We take on multiple bodies until we attain freedom or moksha.

As per Swamiji:

- Everything in this universe is indestructible.
- Knowledge comes from direct experience.
- Preservation of learning is inherent in the process of reincarnation.
- The fallacy of not thinking an idea through to its logical conclusion.
- How can we inherit the entire experience of living creatures without reincarnation?

Some More Quotes on Reincarnation by Wise People

- Rumi: 'Don't grieve; anything you lose comes round in another form.'
- Mahatma Gandhi: 'Each night when I go to sleep. I die. And next morning, when I wake up, I am re-born.'
- Kurt Cobain: 'If you're really a mean person you're going to come back as fly and eat poop.'
- Rabindranath Tagore: 'I seem to have loved you in numberless forms numberless tunes . . . in life after life, in age after age, forever.'
- Benjamin Franklin: 'When I see nothing annihilated and not a drop of water wasted, I cannot suspect the annihilation of souls . . . I believe I shall, in some shape or other, always exist. I shall not object to a new edition of mine, hoping, however, that the errata of the last may be corrected.'
- William Wordsworth: 'Our birth is but a sleep and a forgetting; The soul that rises with us, our life's star, Hath had elsewhere its setting. And cometh from afar.'

- Count Leo Tolstoy: 'As we live through thousands of dreams in our present life, so is our present life only one of many thousands of such lives which we enter from the other more real life and then return after death. Our life is but one of the dreams of that more real life, and so it is endlessly, until the very last one, the very real the life of God.'

- Socrates: 'I am confident that there truly is such a thing as living again, that the living spring from the dead, and that the souls of the dead are in existence.'

- Pythagoras: 'The soul passes into subsequent body of either human or animal . . . After undergoing successive purgation and when sufficiently purified, it is received among the gods and returns back to eternal source from which, it first produced.' (This doctrine is from Judaism.)

- Ralph Waldo Emerson: 'The soul comes from without into the human body, as into a temporary abode, and it goes out of it a new . . . it passes into other habitations, for the soul is immortal.'

- William Jones: 'I am no Hindu, but I hold the doctrine of the Hindus concerning a future state (re-birth) to be incomparably more rational, more pious, and more likely.'

- Henry David Thoreau: 'As far back as I can remember I have unconsciously referred to the experiences of a previous state of existence.'

- Trutz Hardo: He is a German philosopher and regression therapist who did extensive research work and reached a conclusion about the reality of reincarnation.

- Kubler Ross: He is a Swiss-born psychiatrist and spiritualist and, in her book *On Death and Dying*, advocated the reality of reincarnation.
- Arthur Schopenhauer: 'Were an Asiatic to ask me for a definition of Europe, I should be forced to answer him: It is that part of the world which is haunted by the incredible delusion that man was created out of nothing, and that his present birth is his first entrance into life.'
- Mark Twain: 'I have been born more times than anybody except Krishna.'
- Jesus Christ (in the Gnostic Gospels, Pistis Sophia): 'Souls are poured from one into another of different kinds of bodies of the world.'
- George Harrison: 'Friends are all souls that we've known in other lives. We are drawn to one another. Even if I have only known them a day, it does not matter.'

The priest stops here. His three companions are solemnly silent and are looking at the priest for starting a discussion on the subject. The priest says, 'I shall tell you one more quote to clarify the purpose of our meeting: "There are two ways to be fooled. One is to believe what isn't true; the other is to refuse to believe what is true" [Soren Kierkegaard].'

The priest has collected the golden ideas from the priceless works of great people from different eras and from different spheres of society who had indoctrinated in favour of reincarnation. He wonders how there can still be a difference in opinions on this subject.

Antoine Henri Becquerel, a French physicist, along with Marie Sklodowska Curie and Pierre Curie, discovered radioactivity in 1896, and all of them got the Nobel Prize in 1903. Albert Einstein, a German and the most influential physicist of the twentieth century (1879–1955) a noble laureate, discovered the theory of relativity in 1905. Their discoveries fell under the realms of res cogitans.

A new era started thereafter by joining the two realms (res extensa and res cogitans) into a modern science, which has boosted man's knowledge, allowing it to transcend the limitations of our five sense organs and developing invisible models.

The scientists found that the two realms are not independent and cannot be studied separately, particularly the aspects of nature. Due to this, modern science got recognition to study subjects like soul, mind, and reincarnation.

Albert Einstein though was not fully convinced about reincarnation but acted as a catalyst to work on the subject with his theory of relativity, which is summarised in its simplest form below.

Mass and energy are both but different manifestations of the same thing; there is an equivalence between all matter and energy in the universe, quantifiable by the simple equation $E = mc^2$, where E is energy, m is mass, and c is the speed of light in vacuum.

Einstein summarised: 'Remove matter from the universe and you also remove space and time.'

Mass and energy are two forms of the same thing. The speed of light is 186, 282 miles per second.

Under the right conditions, mass can be converted into energy and vice versa. To find out how much energy an object has, multiply the mass with the square of the speed of light. When mass is converted into energy, it achieves the speed of light. Pure energy is electromagnetic radiation, and it moves at the speed of light in vacuum.

The formula of kinetic energy as derived is $KE = mv^2$, where KE is kinetic energy, m is mass, and v is velocity..

The square of the speed of light is 448.9×10^5 miles per hour. Therefore, a small chunk of matter can produce a large amount of energy which we cannot ordinarily perceive.

Our common sense and logic as well as the principle of conservation of energy and matter suggest that it is impossible for something to come from nothing.

The idea that something is the natural state of the world requires a paradigm shift in our thinking. There has always been something—that is, it has been existing eternally. So living beings does not come from nothing. If so, what is that something?

The process of transmigration involves that something in addition to the body, mind, intellect, soul, media, and the transformation mechanism. If all the above subjects can be properly understood and analysed, we may perhaps throw some light on the mystery of God.

'Transmigration must be a subtle process, which apparently cannot be measured with our known and conventional instruments. For ages, it has been described as a connection between heaven and earth. Our ancient rishis [saints] used to describe it as transportation and transformation of energy.' The priest says that he has seen some scientific gadgets that use similar wireless transportation and transformation technique.

Hearing this, the younger brother promptly responds and narrates his experience in using a Murphy Radio in his childhood. He tuned it to his desired radio stations by adjusting a knob. An indicator shows the accuracy of the tuning. When the width of the mercury column becomes very thin, the clarity and volume of a particular broadcast is at its maximum.

This is similar to the operating system of modern television and radio. He explains that there are transmitters in the radio stations and that the radios have receivers. Music or voice or picture is converted into electric signals, then the same is superimposed on electromagnetic waves, which are transmitted in the form of energy. Those waves reflect or refract back from the atmosphere (ionosphere) of the earth. A radio unit at home acts as a receiver. At a particular combination of electrical parameters, like resistance, inductance, and capacitance, maximum transfer of the transmitted energy takes place in the radio. Exactly at that location of the tuner, that particular channel can be heard clearly.

The priest includes some additional clues by further clarifying that a radio transmitter consists of some masses comprising of various electrical and electronic components packed in an outer casing. The music or picture is fed into it, the box converts the music or picture into subtle electromagnetic wave, which cannot be perceived by our five sense organs. It then travels several miles and reappears in a similar-looking receiver as music or pictures. The gross body of the radio is also covered by an external box which is like the outer shell of the human being. The components inside the radio function like our internal organs. It has a control knob, which functions like our minds.

The radio works only if it has electric power. The radio ceases to function immediately after the withdrawal of electrical power. Similarly, our body ceases to function immediately after withdrawal of the life force (prana) from our body. The radio has the inherent capability to reproduce sound energy, which is captured by its antenna.

'Don't you all feel that it has some similarity with transmigration of the human soul?' the priest asks.

The younger one—like Archimedes of Syracuse, an ancient Greek mathematician, physicist, engineer, and astronomer—started shouting, 'Eureka! Eureka!' He has become very excited and starts saying, 'Uncle, perhaps we can successfully make an attempt to explain reincarnation scientifically.'

The priest smiles at him. He loves this boy because of his enthusiasm and inquisitiveness. He proposes to them to make a meaningful and acceptable paper for all classes of people, including the scientific community. Therefore, this subject needs to be studied more deeply so that all aspects of reincarnation are analysed properly and put in a sequence in a manner which cannot be refuted logically.

They have already discussed that modern science accepts that matter and energy are interrelated. It is not mandatory any more to prove all phenomena of nature inside the laboratory. There are other ways to prove such phenomenon scientifically to the society—through irrefutable logics.

One such basic principle has been suggested by Jeremy Hayward of England, a PhD in physics. He described how to deal with a new theory:

1. Study the relevant phenomenon.
2. Formulate the new theory.
3. Use the theory to predict observations that we should be able to make if the theory is correct.
4. Look for the predicted observations.

Richard Philips Feynman (1918–1988), an eminent physicist in USA, is known for his work in the field of integral formulation of quantum mechanics and the theory of quantum electrodynamics, and he is a Nobel laureate in physics in 1965. He described the process in details. He actually further simplified it by combining the first two steps into one and formulated it, as given below:

> If the observations made in the last step do not agree with the predictions of the earlier step, the proposed step is not acceptable. If they agree, the theory becomes acceptable. If more and more observations show agreement, the theory receives stronger scientific acceptance. Once a theory becomes scientifically accepted by this test it remains so, unless someone finds reliable new data to prove its unacceptability.

The priest then concludes, 'My friends we shall have to walk through these steps with all our observations of the complete phenomenon of reincarnation and then formulate a theory first, and then we have to predict the observations.

'It is truly a multidisciplinary task, and fortunately we have the team comprising of a physiologist, an electrical engineer, a commercial person with a logical mind, and also a person with some knowledge of spirituality and other general subjects. Let us join our hands together and plunge into the knowledge and experiences of our respective specialisations.'

They decide to meet again in the temple the next Sunday. After they disperse, the priest starts thinking about the two brothers. How nicely and slowly they have shaped up since their childhood. They have grown up as balanced persons. They have stable minds and have the ability to control their minds and bodies with their intellects. The priest feels that he has been a bit selfish by influencing them from their childhood.

He himself has held this concept of rebirth for the last fifteen years and has tried to discuss the same with many people, but they have not cooperated. These two boys and their sister have been brought up in an environment suitable for working on this subject. He feels that the exact phenomenon of rebirth, if accepted by the society, will put an end to the exploitation of innocent people. Particularly, the diabolical acts of children due to misguidance can be reduced considerably.

The young children are being used in the front line of subversive activities by being assured of false hopes that their lives in paradise will be on roses and shall remain like that forever. They believe in God, which is good, but those poor people are ignorant about His manifestation. They must understand that God exists in harmony, peace, love, and compassion—not in battlefields or terrorism. If at all He appears in the battlefield, it is only to re-establish the justice and law set by Him for this unique planet.

The sister is very much impressed by today's discussion. She has got a spark to work on the subject in which physical body plays an important role. The younger brother also appears to be very excited with this subject of transmigration.

The elder brother says, 'My role shall be that of a critic and an umpire.'

They decide their respective roles they will play. The sister requests the younger brother to elucidate the background of the mission since she does not know the earlier events.

Her brother summarises it for her:

- Can we prove reincarnation scientifically?
- To understand the purpose of life.
- Build a balanced and successful life.
- Following universal law of God, is spiritualism.
- The human body has two parts—the gross body and subtle body.

- God is omnipresent and omniscient.
- According to the Bhagavad Gita, Param atman or universal soul is infinite and cannot be created or destroyed.
- End of birth is death, and end of death is birth.
- A huge majority believes in rebirth. But there is still a segment which opposes this belief.
- There are similarities between radio waves or electromagnetic waves and transmission of life energy.
- The purification of mind and intellect is required for realisation of God.

11

⟫⟩⟨⟪

Humble Appeal to the Valued Reader

IGNORANCE is without gaining Knowledge
& Knowledge is gained without IGNORANCE.

Charleston Parker

You are the most important person for us. But our request is, one should remove the prejudices from one's mind about reincarnation while reading this book. Kindly read this book with an open mind. What we mean is, we are going to make a journey into a domain of new perception; it may influence you logically, and you may start believing in rebirth. It is always good for us to know what we know and also what we don't know as both are important.

The picture in the next page is a good switch for swinging one's perception. It is a very famous and old model of the Harvard Business School. If you can locate in it a beautiful lady of sixteen, then you may ignore the image of the lady in her eighties. But in the very first instance, if you discover an eighty-year-old lady in this photo, then you may take some time to discover the lady of sixteen in it. You have a strong logical mind. Please keep it open while making this journey with us into the realm of the mysterious act of God: reincarnation. When we end our journey, you may have a paradigm shift in your beliefs.

We do not suggest changing the religious beliefs or opinion of the reader nor his traditional perceptions and practices. This book is about a possible scientific explanation of the process of reincarnation.

The teachings of noble people of the world have always proved to be correct. They have realised the truth themselves. Discourses are generally developed, keeping in mind the understanding abilities of common people. Their objective was to make the society more disciplined so that people can remain happy in our beautiful planet. This book aims to highlight the process of reincarnation. Since the subject is not very clear to the believers and also to the non-believers, there is no intention of hurting anybody's sentiment.

12

⋙⋘

Beginning of the Search

If you can't explain it simply, you do not understand it well enough.

Albert Einstein

One week appears to be a long time for the two brothers and the sister to contain their excitement. Their priest uncle have given them very important assignments. They have remained busy for the whole week for data collection, reading books, and surfing all possible sites on the Internet.

On Sunday morning, they complete their breakfast and prepare to leave. In fact, the sister arrived the previous night. Their mother asks where all of them are going so early in the morning. She thinks that they are going for an outing.

They reply, 'Mama, we are going to our temple to meet the priest uncle for a detailed study on some scientific aspects of the Bhagavad Gita.'

She becomes happy and says, 'It is always good to remain in good company.' Their mother is a very God-fearing lady. She spends considerable time in the day to perform puja and *regular prayer*.

All of them assemble in the prayer hall and sit down on the floor, which is cool and comfortable. The priest welcomes them and offers some prasad (sweets).

The sister starts first, 'Why do we need to prove the process of reincarnation to the people? Haven't they already heard of similar instances happening in various parts of the world? There are people, particularly children, who have recalled their memories from previous births, and the veracity of such incidents had been verified and validated by concerned authorities. Then why are there still non-believers?'

The priest pacifies her and explains, 'Some people do not believe since there is no scientific explanation of validating the process. The process of biological birth of a child can be seen physically, death is also visible, but the process in between death and birth is not visible in the cycle. 'It is on this process that we shall have to focus to obtain a scientific explanation.'

The sister again responds, 'Water can be seen, but water vapour cannot be seen. Again when it returns back as rain, it can be seen. Then isn't it correct to say that it is a cycle of water to vapour and back to water again? If yes, then there should not be any difficulty in accepting that rain is transmigration of water.'

The priest answers, 'You are absolutely correct in your explanation. But go back to the history of mankind when the behaviour of water—the phenomenon which leads to the formation of steam, ice, water vapour, etc.—was not known to mankind. They had no knowledge of thermodynamics, and men used to believe that rain was an act of God. When science was able to explain the processes, which could not be seen or were not visible, they were universally accepted.

Similarly, we have to explain the cycle of rebirth scientifically. Only then will our mission be successful.'

'Yes, Uncle, I fully agree with you,' says the younger brother. He claims to have researched all possible sites on the Internet to find out any universally acceptable theory on this subject, but he could not find one.

The elder brother adds that his research work in libraries ever since their grandmother expired has been in vain. There is no definite explanation available on the process of reincarnation.

The priest again continues, 'Let us take this unknown process as our project, and let us try to establish the science behind it. We may identify all the elements and events involved with the transmigration and try to analyse each of those closely using the lens of scientists, technologists, and spiritualists. Study each of those separately and also in combination. Finally, conclude the steps as suggested by Jeremy Hayward or Richard Phillips Feynman.

'The events and elements related to transmigration are:

- gross body or physical body
- subtle body
- birth of human beings
- death of human beings
- soul or atman
- cosmic energy and its layers
- God time and man hour
- purification or modification process of soul
- migration of energy and its accumulation
- correction or modification process if any
- transmigration energy of energy from unknown place to the womb of mother
- reincarnation or transmigration or rebirth.

'We may consider each of the events and elements as a black box. Before we embark on this journey, we shall visit each of those black boxes closely enough to understand their constituents, responses, outputs, and how they are interrelated or interdependent.

'We shall try to establish the above as far as possible— physiologically, scientifically or technically, and spiritually. We shall take into consideration only human beings because we are more complex than any other living beings.'

13

Physiological Body

Free the child's potential, and you will transform
him into the world.

Maria Montessori

The Physiological Body

It consists of the following parts:

- bone marrow: about 4 per cent of total body mass
- bones and cartilages: about 206 bones in an adult
  human body
- vital organs: heart, lungs, liver, kidneys, intestine,
  brain, spinal cord, stomach, etc.
- outside structure: head, neck, trunk (including
  thorax and abdomen), arms, hands, legs, feet, hair,
  skin, nails, eyes, nose, tongue, ears
- systems of the body: nervous system, muscular
  and skeletal system, circulatory system, respiratory
  system, digestive system, integumentary system,
  urinary system, reproductive system, immune

system, lymphatic system, endocrine system, and sensory system.

A fully grown body has over 37 trillion cells, and each cell has tiny particles, which are moving continuously and generating an electric field. These cells keep on disintegrating and getting replaced simultaneously till old age. The body consists of elements like carbon, hydrogen, nitrogen, oxygen, calcium, iron, phosphorus, potassium, and sodium. Water makes up about 65 per cent of the human body and plays an important role in most of the chemical reactions occurring in the body.

There are about four kinds of macromolecules which are found in our body—carbohydrates, lipids, proteins, and nucleic acids. Carbohydrates provide energy to work. Lipids store extra energy and also act as building materials for the cells. Proteins serve as building blocks for cells and speed up chemical reactions in the body. Nucleic acids carry instructions to each cell regarding how to perform a particular function. The cells of the human body are living units. Each of those cells consume food, gets rid of wastes, and grows. Most of the cells are capable of reproduction.

Tissues join the various parts of the body. These also cover and protect the body's surface as skin. Muscle tissues help us to work, and finally, nervous tissues carry signals and act as the communication bridge. Some special tissues form the heart and pumps blood throughout the body.

Since our subject of interest has a deep connection with the brain, we will study it in detail.

The human brain has three basic divisions.

- The cerebrum: This is the largest part of the brain. It is the centre of intelligence and reasoning.

- The cerebellum: It is situated at the back of the skull. It is responsible for maintaining the balance of our body and also keeps our body posture in check.
- The medulla oblongata: It is the part of the brainstem that is situated between the pons and the spinal cord. It deals with the involuntary functions such as breathing, heart rate, and blood pressure.

The functions of the brain are very complex and dynamic in nature. It is believed that memories in the brain are stored as chemical structures in a neural network, information represented as a specific set of synaptic connections. The functioning of the brain depends on the electrical signals passed by the neurons and by the influence of various neurons transmitting elements, which can cause various types of uneasiness to the physical body.

The cerebrum consists of two cerebral hemispheres connected to the corpus coliseum, which helps the left side of our body to know what the right side is doing and vice versa. It is a very important function as most of the sensory organs and the motor nerves control on the left side of the body is connected to the right hemisphere of the cerebrum and vice versa. The cerebrum has again four sections known as frontal, partial, temporal, and occipital lobes. The frontal lobe is responsible for planning, judging, solving problems, motor function, language, social behaviour, and spontaneity abilities. The partial lobe integrates the information collected by the sensory organs and assists our manipulative and discriminatory abilities. The temporal lobe is responsible for our spatial perception and auditory processing ability. The occipital lobe is our visual processing centre. The cells in the lobe are placed as a spatial map of the retinal field.

Writing, speaking, and logical abilities are controlled by the left side of our brain. Three-dimensional vision, musical sense, pattern recognition, holistic and reasoning abilities are governed by the right side of our brain.

The functions performed by the brain along with the central nervous system is known as the mind as per physiological terminology. The mind is the storehouse of our information. Some information is learned and gathered, and the rest is inherited as part of our genetic constitution. However, the mind is not a physical object. We shall study it more while discussing the subtle body.

The physiological body has deoxyribonucleic acid, which is commonly known as DNA. It is the hereditary material in human beings. An adult human body has about 37 trillion cells. Every cell of a person's body carries the same DNA. It is found in the nucleus of the cell. It is because of DNA that every species gives birth to the same species. It contains the genetic instructions. The DNA segments carrying this genetic information are called genes. Each cell carries a complete set of instructions about how to make other cells, their components, and their subcomponents. This set of instructions is called genome, which is made of DNA. Every human being has two genomes, which we receive from each of our parents. A sperm cell has only one copy of a genome, and the other one comes from the egg cell. During fertilisation, the sperm cell and egg cell join to make a cell containing the two genomes. This cell has the complete set of instructions to construct the genetic make-up of a person. Therefore, DNA is the most important component of our bodies. Nucleic acid, together with proteins, is the most important biological macromolecule.

Within cells, DNA is organised into long structures called chromosomes. During cell division, these chromosomes are duplicated in the process of DNA replication, providing each cell its own complete set of chromosomes.

The information in the DNA is stored as a code made up of four chemical bases: adenine (A), guanine (G), cytosine (C), and thymine (T). Human DNA consists of about 3 billion bases, and more than 99 per cent of those bases are the same in all human beings. The order, or sequence, of those bases determines the information available for building (and maintaining) a living being, similar to the way in which alphabets are arranged in a certain order to form words and sentences. An important property of DNA is that it can replicate or make copies of itself. Each strand of DNA in the double-helix structure can serve as a pattern for duplicating the sequence of cells. This is essential when cells divide because each new cell needs to have an exact copy of the DNA present in the parent cell.

Their sister provides some information to the younger brother, which is very important for him to know as an electrical engineer. She says that Dr Martin Blank, PhD (1957), the ex-president of the Bioelectromagnetics Society, worked at both Columbia University and University of Cambridge, and he has compared DNA to what electrical engineers refer to as a fractal antenna. A fractal antenna can pick up a range of frequencies across the EMF spectrum. There are two additional features of DNA that fulfil the requirements of a fractal antenna—electrons present in DNA conduct electricity and the fact that DNA is coiled within the nucleus.

Dr Blank has shown a slide listing the diameter sizes of the coils present within a single DNA molecule:

- double helix = 1 nanometre
- chromatin fibre = 10 nanometre

- solenoid = 30 nanometre
- hollow tube = 200 nanometre.

Each of these different coils responds to a frequency on the EMF spectrum, which explains why our DNA responds to such a wide range of frequencies.

In a nutshell, the human body is equipped with fractal antennas present inside each and every cell, which responds to the entire range of frequencies on the EMF spectrum.

The brother further explains that it is a very small dimensional antenna having higher bandwidth and 'antenna gain'. Its physical shape is not like a typical antenna. Its shapes are very funny and irregular. It looks small, but because of its shape, the perimeter is very large. It has a very wide bandwidth. Because of its fractal shape, it works like a virtual combination of capacitors and inductors. This is the fractal antenna with different resonances, which can be chosen and adjusted by choosing the proper fractal design. Electrical resonance may not be directly related to a particular scale size of a fractal antenna. The physical size is not related to its resonant or broadband performance. In a conventional antenna, length determines frequency or wave length.

But in the case of the fractal antenna, this rule does not apparently apply. In reality, these antennas remain shrunken, and because of their different physical shapes, they happen to have different resonant input impedance. Our mobiles have fractal antennae inside. In short, DNA can act as a fractal antenna due to the shape of its helical structure and a wide bandwidth, with different resonant input impedance.

The younger one continues to explain that the human body is a powerhouse and can generate power and transmit electrical signals through the nervous system. It generates electromagnetic field within and around the body, and the fluids present in our body act as the electrolyte. He says that they shall go into more details when they discuss the subtle body.

14

Spiritual Gross Body

The main facts in human life are five: birth,
food, sleep, love and death.

E. M. Forster

The priest patiently hears the constituents of gross body
explained by the brothers and sister. Then he responds that
he knows that the gross body consists of only seven basic
ingredients: bone marrow, bones, flesh, fat, blood and other
liquids, dermis, and epidermis. It has following basic parts
legs, thighs, chest, arms, back and head.

The above parts are together packed and moulded into
a form, which is the most beautiful creation of God. It is the
residence of our all I-ness and my-ness and the associated
consequential ego, happiness, pains, miseries, etc.

The gross body is made up of five *tanmatras* or tattvas
(subtle elements): ether, air, fire, water, and earth.

The process by which the subtle elements of the body
become part of the perceivable gross elements is known as
panchikarana in Vedanta, which in scientific terms is known

Ashok Kumar Chattopadhyay

as pentamerous or self-division and mutual combination. It is explained below in the given chart:

Spiritual Gross Body

Stage	Eather	Air	Fire	Water	Earth	Description
1						Tanmatras each in itself
2						Tendency to divide into two equal parts
3						The split is complete
4						One-half remains intact, the other splits into four
5						Each half married to four bits borrowed from all others

In the first stage, the tanmatras remain intact. In the second stage, they show a tendency to divide into two halves. Each divides into two parts in the third stage. In the following stage, one-half of all the five elements remain intact, while the other half gets divided into four equal parts. Thus, under the column ether, we have in its fourth stage half a tanmatra remaining intact and the other half getting divided into four equal parts, each constituting one-eighth of the original one.

In the fifth stage, each half tanmatra combines with one-eighth tanmatra of all other elements, constituting one unit of gross element.

This process is called panchikarana. Out of the gross elements, the physical body is formed. Our sense objects of sound, touch, form, taste, and smell are constituted of

118

nothing other than the subtle tanmatras of the rudimentary elements.

The sense objects are innocent tanmatras but later, in other forms, become the sense organs of the gross body. Steam cannot bind water even though both are the same element in their subtle and gross forms respectively.

The Gross Body

For human beings, the gross physical body is the vehicle through which it contacts the world of objects. If a person is not conscious of his gross body, he will not be able to perceive the world of objects around him. The physical body is a residence of the mind. Birth, decay, and death are the inevitable and essential properties of our gross bodies. It has five sense organs—ears, eyes, nose, tongue, and skin—which help us to gain knowledge of objects around us. The organs of speech, hands, legs, anus, and genitals are the organs for action, which help the body to perform the basic acts of survival.

The gross body becomes active when it combines with the systems known as prana, which means manifested life energy. Prana expresses itself in the various physiological functions, such as prana (perception), *apana* (excretion), *vyana* (digestion), *samana* (circulation), and *udana* (thinking).

These are the vital energies of life, which decay and finally cease to work at the time of death. Prana is a layer which acts as an adhesive between the gross body and the subtle body. The sense organs establish connection with the subtle body through prana.

The gross body grows and develops, taking energy from food, so it is known as the food sheath (annamaya kosa). It is influenced by the food we eat as well as by the external environment. Over this is the sheath which acts as a link between the gross body and subtle body, which is known as vital energy sheath (pranmaya kosa). The above two *kosas* have already been explained earlier in detail.

15

The Subtle Body

> The power of God is with you at all times;
> through the activities of mind, senses, breathing,
> and emotions; and is constantly doing all the
> work using you as a mere instrument.
>
> Bhagavad Gita

The priest states, 'It will be better for you to understand the subtle body in continuation to the spiritual explanation of the gross body. Let me explain first, and then we shall hear about the subtle body physiologically and scientifically.'

He explains about the five organs of action (hands, legs, speech, anus, and genitals), plus the five organs of perception (eyes, ears, nose, skin, and tongue), plus the five pranas (perception, excretion, digestion, circulation, and thinking), plus the five elements (ether, air, fire, water, and earth), plus the discriminative intellect, ignorance, desire, and action together constitute the subtle body.

The five elements in their mutual combination cause the material formation of the world of objects; the very same elements form the subtle body. The reference of discriminative intellect is part of intellect as explained earlier in the discussion about BMI. The ignorance of the universal truth is called *avidya* or nescience. The effect of avidya manifests as desire, and out of desire, the result is action.

The body, which is made up of thoughts and their functions, is composed of the five subtle elements which have not yet undergone the process of mutation. This body and its desire, as suggested by intellect, becomes the conditioning of the self to create an ego. Past impressions condition the present thought patterns. This subtle body is responsible for our various experiences like pleasure and pain. When we function completely through our subtle body, we start dreaming. We function through both the gross body and the subtle body while we are awake. When we are in deep sleep, both the gross body and the subtle body remain inactive.

The above stages are merely conditioning of our intellect, whereas pure consciousness (which is the pure energy) remain uncontaminated. The atman thus remains untouched in all states of our consciousness and experiences. It is not at all involved with our pleasure, sorrow, pain, etc. Shri Sankaracharya, one of the greatest sages of Hindu religion, had described this phenomenon. Like the tools of a carpenter are his instruments, the subtle body is an instrument for all activities of the atman. Therefore, the atman remains completely unattached from all human experiences or feelings. It is just like pure light; pure light cannot be perceived. It is perceived only when it falls on an object and reflects back from it, and we become conscious of that object.

Similarly, when the consciousness reflects back from an object, we become conscious of its presence. The moment the object is removed, its reflection on consciousness disappears. When the mind is agitated, the reflecting medium is disturbed; the reflection of light appears to be hazy. As soon as the mind is quiet, the intellect becomes brighter. Pure atman is ever blissful, and there is no sorrow in it. We get a flavour of it momentarily after getting up from a deep sleep. Mind and intellect can be reprogrammed in an effort to get back to our real consciousness—the atman, the state of pure bliss which exists in each of us.

The sister says that there have always been differences between scientists and spiritualists on the topic of the functioning of the mind. Scientists have tried to prove that the mind is an act of the brain. Mental events are not always similar and simple like the brain events, but they are related to the brain in a complex and subtle way. Till date, the human mind and consciousness are better understood following the processes prescribed by the wise people of ancient days rather than the neural activities described by the scientists. Some scientists have concluded that the mind is not at all a part of our physical body; it is subtle in nature and not a mere chemical activity in the physical brain. It is, however, responsible for generating patterns of thinking processes and commands energies having different frequencies for different patterns. It can also influence and reprogramme the existing ones.

The younger brother opines that the mind, intellect, and consciousness mainly have some electrical functions. The chakras are located at different centres of the body as powerhouses of cosmic energy, which can be activated for attaining certain powers. The chakras are like valves located at each intersection of three major stems along the spinal cord known as *nadis*—*ida*, *pingla*, and *sushumna*. Each chakra contains fabulous power and can be activated or stimulated by physical and mental techniques. The chakras can be understood as specific nexus points along the subtle wiring system of the body. These are energy points; they are apparently an unknown mystery, but these can be stimulated through concentration, regular meditation, and also by chanting certain notes having specific frequencies.

Chakras are therefore centres of subtle energy located at different parts of the human body. There are seven chakras located at the perineum, sacrum, solar plexus, heart, throat, brow centre, and crown of the head.

The priest starts explaining the different divisions of the subtle body present within us, which are:

- The mind: It has three parts—the conscious, subconscious, and unconscious mind. The subconscious and unconscious minds are together known as *chitta*. It is part of our thoughts and feelings that we are aware of. The brain acts as an interface between it and the physical organs.
- The intellect: It is responsible for our decision-making and reasoning ability. The brain acts as an interface between it and the physical organs.
- The subtle ego: It is part of the causal body, the final vestige of the nescience (ignorance), which helps us realise that we are different from God.
- The soul or atman: It is the god (universal energy) who resides within us and is our true nature. It is the main component of the subtle body, which can neither be created nor destroyed. It is purest in nature and remains unaffected by any actions of human beings; it always remains in the state of absolute bliss.(But can be conditioned as can be done to water and air as explained before)
- The subtle body: The above four components constitute our subtle body, which leaves our physical

body at the time of our death. This vital energy, which is released at the time of death, goes back into the universe.

- Nescience: Other than our soul, everything happening around us is an illusion. We are seeing what we are conditioned to see, and it is as good as magic being shown by a magician. It is the root of our miseries, attachments, and unhappiness.

- The jivatman: The atman, conditioned by impurity, is known as the jivatman. God's ray of light or energy, which exists in all forms of matter in this universe, is called the paramatman. The paramatman is pure, just like a seed of a tree containing all the qualities of that tree; similarly, the atman carries the qualities of the paramatman.

Jivatman, the individual soul, is the reflection of the atman of an individual. Just like waves emerge from the ocean and form different shapes and finally mixing with the ocean, in the same way, jivatman emerges from the atman, and after undergoing a long process of development and gaining experience returns back to the atman. It is different from paramatman or God because it is conditioned by ego. Once the impurities are removed from the jivatman, like dirt is removed from water, it attains enlightenment. *Satya* is the truth, *chit* is the consciousness, and *anand* is the bliss. Together, they constitute the essence of the divine self, which dwells within everybody.

> Where can we go to find God if we cannot see him in our own hearts and in every living being. (Swami Vivekananda)

16

Science of the Subtle Body

> Seek ye first the kingdom of God, and everything shall be added unto you.
>
> Swami Vivekananda

The younger brother informs them that the psychodynamics of our minds is an electromagnetic structure. It is similar with the electrical process of cause and effect. The consciousness determines our vibration (amplitude and frequency together), consisting of energy in terms of amplitude and time in terms of frequency.

> The universe consists solely of waves of motion . . . there exists nothing other than vibration. (Walter Russell)

Multiplication of frequency and amplitudes is thought of in relation to the ascension process. All things are energy; these bodies containing energy are becoming more attuned and are reaching a higher vibration rate due to the dynamic energetic force of the universe. Extending and expanding vibration rates occur in nature, and we, being a part of the same, are also capable of ascension.

There are known quantitative frequencies that have been measured to show the body–energy connection.

Audio:	20 hertz to 20,000 hertz
Ultrasonic:	100 kilohertz to 10 megahertz
Radio Frequency:	150 kilohertz to 1.5 megahertz
High Radio Frequency (RF):	1.5 megahertz to 40 megahertz
Very High Radio Frequency (VHF)	40 megahertz to 100 megahertz
Ultra-High Radio Frequency (UH)	over 100 megahertz
Human Body cell frequency:	1.52 megahertz to 9.46 megahertz
Upper limit of human hearing:	15 kilohertz

As per the 'Symposium of Biological Effects' by E. Stanton Maxey, MD (1977): 'Biological systems are influenced by the terrestrial electrical environment like magnetic field, electric field. Electromagnetic brainwaves (0.1 to 30 Hz) occur at frequencies those of terrestrial and the Schuman resonance. Our decision making abilities are subordinate to alpha, beta, gamma (.01 to 5 Hz) theta (4–7 Hz) and delta (0.1–4 Hz) brain rhythms with their related states of consciousness.'

> To know the mechanics of the wave is to know
> the entire secret of Nature. (Walter Russell)

Nerve impulses are electrical energy signals. They create an energy field around the body and electromagnetic energy waves that can travel outside the body. Our nervous system is constituted of a network of cells called neurons, which transmit information in the form of electrical signals. Billions of nerve impulses generated by the neurons create a magnetic field around the human body. This magnetism is induced to other bodies surrounding us. It can be felt when we are close to some people. We feel good with some and bad with some others.

During the festival days, like the different pujas, Christmas, Id, and other occasions, people just forget their miseries, differences, enmities and enjoy the celebrations together. This happens because of synchronisation of positive thoughts, or in other words, due to matching resonances of thought waves which influences the hearts and mood of all present there. Indian *kirtana* (a type of folk music) is also a similar example.

The fundamentals of life are based on electrical fields of energy. Everything in our planet contain electric charges that interact with other energy fields (Haisch et al. 1994, Hunt 1996). Human beings are not only biochemical beings but are also energetic and informational beings that interact and communicate on a constant basis both among themselves and with their external world (Oschman 2003). In essence, human beings are simply a network of energy that functions as a unit within a large sphere of energy.

The more a wave pattern manifests a tangible structure, the more slowly it changes, like our tissues, organs, etc. If the same is less, then changes are fast (for example, the intangibles, like our moods, thoughts, etc.) because wave patterns hold the accumulation of all the information that they have encountered. They provide the body with the ability to remember how to look and act, to remember past events, and to remember how to perform different tasks (M. C. Taggart 2002). Wave patterns give a logical and complete explanation about the ability of the body to manage multiple and complicated tasks instantaneously in different parts of the body. Some types of human energy can travel long distances at very high speed. Metaphysics explains that energy as magnetic energy is manifested as life force, vital force, and human aura.

Each of us emits unique energy patterns. The typical electrical frequency of our brain activity is between 0–30 hertz, muscle frequency is about 225 hertz, and heart is about 250 hertz. We radiate energy having frequency between 100–1,600 hertz.

It may appear that this energy is very feeble, but it radiates throughout the universe, and therefore, we broadcast our essence in the cosmos. The Earth is moving around the Sun, which in turn is whirling around the Milky Way, and our galaxy is zipping through the universe.

The universe is an ocean of energy full of lashing waves. Throughout the universe, energy is received and transmitted through radiations. We receive and transmit spiritual, psychic, and physical energies proportionate to our intellectual and spiritual capability. We can tune ourselves to the universal energy frequency for experiencing spiritual and psychic pleasure. There are chakras of energy that are physical and spiritual in our bodies, as explained already. When kundalini, the conscious energy, moves through the chakras, our level of consciousness changes.

The younger one stops and confesses that he knows only this much about the subtle body. The priest is very happy with the information given by the younger one.

The elder brother has attentively heard the complete presentation. He summarises the discussion on the physiological body and the subtle body of human beings.

- The physiological body of a human being is comprised of bone marrow, bones, vital organs, outside structure, and other systems. The finer parts are cells, which further contain smaller particles.

- The cells disintegrate and get replaced up to old age.
- The body consists of many chemical elements.
- Nucleic acids carry instructions to each cell, telling them how to function.
- The brain acts as the central control desk in the human body.
- The functions of the brain along with the central nervous system are known as the mind.
- DNA is the hereditary material of the human body.
- DNA acts also as fractal antenna in the human body.
- The subtle components of the gross body are ether, air, fire, water, and earth.
- The process of panchikarana (self-division and mutual combination) is where the subtle elements convert into the gross body.
- The gross body becomes active when it comes in contact with the prana.
- The prana acts as an adhesive between the physical body and the subtle body.
- The subtle body causes our various experiences.
- Pure energy or paramatman or *the universal energy* remains uncontaminated and unattached. It always remains in a state of happiness and bliss.
- The physical body has some energy centres, which can be stimulated to improve the status of our consciousness.
- Atman contaminated by impurities is known as jivatman. The impurities can be removed.
- The universe consists solely of waves of motion.
- The fundamentals of life are based on electrical fields of energy.

- Each human being emits unique energy patterns, which radiate throughout the universe, and our essence is broadcasted in the universe.
- We receive and transmit spiritual, psychic, and physical energies, which are proportionate to our intellectual and spiritual capability.

17

❧

Birth of a Human

The two most important days in your life are the day you are born and the day you find out why.

Mark Twain

The priest states, 'Your sister has discussed the physiological process of birth with the elder brother in details when the younger one was born. But let us again discuss the matter in brief for our project and also for a better understanding.'

The sister responds immediately as it was her subject of specialisation. She starts explaining the process of birth.

In human reproduction, a live birth occurs when a foetus, whatever its gestational age, exists inside the maternal body and subsequently shows any sign of life—such as voluntary movement, heartbeat, or pulsation of the umbilical cord—for however brief a time span and regardless of whether the umbilical cord or the placenta are intact.

The process of physiological human birth can be divided and described in the following stages: fertilisation; development of the foetus leading to the formation of heart, lungs and brain; prenatal development; and finally, conception.

The life of an embryo begins when a male spermatozoa makes contact and fuses with a woman's egg. An embryo is an unborn young. It cannot survive on its own in its early stages of development. It is human in nature, and it grows in a woman's womb. As per biological definition, an embryo is a multicellular diploid eukaryote at the initial stage of development. It is developed from an ovum that has been fertilised by a sperm.

Out of several millions of sperms released after ejaculation, only one lucky sperm can enter and reach the egg. The rest die within forty-eight hours. The struggle for survival starts from that first stage itself. Getting through the outer membrane of the egg is itself the first challenge. Once the sperm crosses this hurdle, the process of fertilisation begins. After fertilisation, it is only a single cell which quickly multiplies. Thereafter, it latches on to the wall of the uterus and starts growing. In the very first month, its head, trunk, and little arms and legs start forming. At the end of nine to ten months, the baby is fully developed and ready to see the light of our planet.

During the developmental stage, it gets nourishment from the mother's body through the umbilical cord, which is disconnected at birth, and then the baby starts taking oxygen on its own and starts taking food externally for its nourishment. The gross body then starts growing due to cell divisions (mutation process) and mutual combination, as explained earlier while discussing the gross body.

A fully grown man has about 37 trillion cells. Every cell of a person's body has the same DNA, which carries the instructions and information from its parent or original cell. Every person has two genomes: one from the father and one from the mother. Our DNA acts also as fractal antennas right from the sperm and egg stages of the father and mother respectively. Therefore, every cell in the human body is capable of transmitting and receiving electrical signals.

The sister has concludes, 'I hope this much will be enough for the purpose of our mission.'

The priest uncle responds gladly, 'Yes! You have touched all the important information that should be known to us for studying our subject matter.' He then continues to explain the birth of a human spiritually.

Views of some noble persons and holy books:

> Our birth is but a sleep and a forgetting:
> The soul that rises with us, our life's star,
> Hath had elsewhere its setting,
> And cometh from a far. (William Wordsworth)

> The new Birth is, then, a sovereign act of God by His spirit in which the believer is cleansed from sin and given spiritual birth into God's house hold. It renews the believer's intellect, sensibility, and will to enable that person to enter the kingdom of God and to do good works. The Old Testament saints were born again when they responded in faith to God's revealed message; New Testament saints, when they respond in faith to Jesus Christ. (Carl B. Hoch Jr)

> Verily We created man from a product of wet earth, then placed him as a drop (of seed) in a safe lodging, then we fashioned the drop into a clot, then we fashioned the clot into a little lump, then we fashioned the little lump into bones, then clothed the bones with flesh, and

then produced it another creation. So blessed be Allah, the Best of Creators! (Quran 23:12–14)

It is he who has created you from dust then from a sperm-drop, then from a leech-like clot: then does he get you out (into the light) as a child: then lets you (grow and reach your age of full strength; then lets you become old, though of you there are some who die before, and lets you reach a term appointed, in order that you may learn wisdom. (Quran 40:67)

According to the Bhagavad Gita, birth and death do not have much significance to the universe. The atman is all pervading. It is like an ocean of energy. Our physical life is like a bubble in the ocean. They appear and disappear, but their constituent remains the same. Human beings are created from the energy that is atman when they are born, and when they die, they disappear like bubbles in the ocean of energy. The process is the same for everyone. They differ in their outward appearances, mental attitudes, intellects, wisdoms, etc. Their actions make them different. The cycle of birth and death continues. As discussed, the quality of the energy may be different due to conditioning of the energy by us. Human beings are born with similar kind of energy in different forms and qualities depending upon their karma. Each of us holds energy, including electrical energy, having different magnitudes and frequency. We have been blessed by the God with a special favour that we can manipulate the quality of the vital energy that determines our destination. If we wish, we can get liberation from the cycle of physical birth, and death and can remain in the inert form.

The priest says, 'Human life is therefore a unique creation of God. The process of birth, as your sister has just explained, is so precise and complicated that no one other than God can create this manufacturing unit.'

The younger one applauds the priest uncle for his wise explanation and claims that he has got a very vital clue for the better understanding of reincarnation.

18

Death of a Human

The fear of death follows from the fear of life.
A man who lives fully is prepared to die at any
time.

Mark Twain

It was now the turn of the sister to give a presentation on this subject. She stands up and starts explaining on the request of her younger brother. The priest says, 'Oh no, my dear! Please sit down and explain.'

She follows the instruction of the priest uncle and continues with her presentation. She starts, 'The definition of death for human beings is a bit complicated as its legality can be challenged at different circumstances by the close ones of the deceased.'

'Death is defined as the stopping of all the vital functions of the body, including the heartbeat, activity of the brain, and breathing.' With the development of several medical equipment, like artificial lungs, heart machine, and artificial vital organs of human beings, it has become increasingly difficult to formulate a universally acceptable definition of death.

'For our purpose, the following definition is sufficient. Death is the irreversible cessation of all the following:

1. cerebral function, usually assessed by EEG as flat line
2. spontaneous function of the respiratory system
3. spontaneous function of the circulatory system.

'Being medically dead is irreversible. The body starts decomposing immediately after death. People are very sceptical in declaring death. After death, the body is cremated or buried by most of the people. Hence, it becomes impossible to revive it physically.'

The younger brother questions his sister, 'What happens to the electrical signals and electrical activities of the body after death?'

His sister answers, 'A graphic record of brainwaves representing the electrical activity occurring in the brain, which is used especially in the diagnosis of seizures and other neurological disorders, is captured by the instrument known as the electroencephalograph. This instrument shows a flat line when a person dies. Usually, it is observed for four to six hours before declaring a person dead, along with the readings of other instruments. In our brain, the electrical transmission and signalling activities are performed by neurons.

'My brother has asked me a very difficult question regarding electrical functions of the brain after death. It is true that all active electrical functions of the body stop after death even though researchers found that some brain cells could be kept alive for some time passively.'

The priest then states, 'The atman of a human being is the simplest form of energy. It resides inside our body until we die. During our lifetime, we remain busy to satisfy our physical bodies, and after death also, people become very sceptical to declare the death of a human body. If you ask me, spiritually, death is nothing but the separation of soul from the body. When prana seizes to support the body, there remains none to hold the soul within the body. We know what prana is. Its absence establishes physical death.

'Death means forgetting one's last life. It is a state of permanent sleep. One forgets everything about the present relationship with the body. When we die, our physical body comprising of ether, earth, water, fire, and air decomposes, and the gross materials return to the destination. Hindus burn the body after death. After burning, what remains physically is the ash. Ash is another form of earth. The Bible says, "Dust thou art, and unto dust thou shalt return." Christians and Muslims bury the dead body. After death, the spirit or atman conditioned by mind, intellect, and ego leaves and goes to a resting place from where it migrates to another body to enjoy or suffer according to one's karma.'

The priest gives them some views about death by some communities.

> As a person gives up old and worn out garments and accepts new apparel. Similarly the embodied soul giving up old and worn out bodies verily accepts new bodies. (Bhagavad Gita, chapter 2, verse 22)

> When death comes to one of you, our messengers (angels of death) take him (his soul) into their custody and they do not neglect in doing so. (Al-An'am 61)

When a Christian dies the person's soul is transported into heaven to be with Christ. (Apostle Paul)

The priest concludes that our physical bodies are made of trillions of cells; those cells die and regenerate, and the cycle continues. We undergo numerous changes right from our childhood until we die. So the physical body is not permanent, and death is the final destination of our physical body. Our spirit or atman is imperishable; it remains forever in the form of energy, which can neither be created nor destroyed.

19

Soul/Spirit/Atman/Ruh

The whole universe is one in the Atman. That Atman when it appears behind the universe is called God. The same Atman when it appears behind this little universe, the body, is the soul. This very soul, therefore, is the Atman in us.

Swami Vivekananda

The priest says, 'The subject about the soul or spirit and its words are more closely related to spiritualism rather than science—although science also agrees, on principle, the presence of the same universally. Let me take the lead for this deliberation.'

He gives them the opinions of different communities about it.

The soul is indestructible; the soul is incombustible, insoluble and unwitherable. The soul is eternal, all pervasive, unmodifiable, immovable and primordial. (Bhagavad Gita, chapter 2, verse 24)

The Quran describes the origin of the soul in the creation of human beings.

> So when I have made him complete and breathed into him My spirit (Ruh), fall down making obeisance to him. (Quran 15:29)

The Christians describe it as:

> The LORD God formed man from the dust of the ground, and breathed into his nostrils the breath of life; and man became a living soul. (Genesis 2:7)

> The dust returns to the earth just as it happened to be and The spirit itself returns to the true God who gave it. (Ecclesiastes 12:7)

Majority of the world's population believe in the existence of the soul. Even though some differ in opinions, according to them, the soul is a matter of personal belief. As such, science may not deal with this subject because it works mostly with visible things, whereas the soul is a subtle object. Some people have had near-death experiences, which they could not explain scientifically. Such incidents and the experiences of people have led them to think that there exists some kind of energy beyond our conscious knowledge.

Science, as per the priest's knowledge, cannot explain the phenomenon of consciousness. As such, in his opinion, science only discovered the facts which already exist in this universe. Soul is a similar truth that needs to be unveiled more clearly by scientists.

Scientists believe that the brain functions because of neuronal firings and synaptic transmissions. Functionally, neurons are not so simple. In each neuron, millions of tubules coherently vibrate in megahertz frequency range, providing functional capability of 10^{15} operations in a second.

- Dr Stuart Hameroff (MD) and Dr Deepak Chopra (MD) explained the phenomenon of consciousness after death and the interconnectedness among living beings and the universal consciousness, which we know by the names of spirit or soul or atman.
- Dr Robert Lanza (MD) has expressed that there exists a vital life force independent of the physical body.
- Dr Eben Alexander (MD), a Harvard neurosurgeon, claims that heaven exists after being in a week-long coma in 2008.
- Dr Francis S. Collins (MD and PhD), the director of the Human Genome Project in Rockville, Maryland, has reaffirmed that information embedded in DNA proves the existence of God.
- Dr Stuart Hameroff, professor emeritus at the departments of anaesthesiology and psychology and the director of the Centre for Consciousness Studies at the University of Arizona, and British physicist Sir Roger Penrose opined that the essence of the soul is contained inside structures called microtubules (present within the brain cells). They described that our souls are more than just the interaction of neurons in the brain. They are in fact constructed from the very fabric of the universe and may have existed since the beginning of time.

As per John McCannon in *Barron's AP World History*, 'Every living creature has its own individual soul, known as Atman. However, the material world is an illusion (maya).

143

It causes suffering and prevents the individual soul from perceiving or being connected with the World soul. The goal of existence is to rejoin one's Atman with the Brahman, allowing oneself to be absorbed into perfection.'

A large majority of the human population believes in the existence of the soul and that the human body is the abode in which the soul resides.

Shri Sankaracharya explains that atman is the self that knows the functions of the entire gross body. It remains unaffected from any of the worldly feelings and emotions. The pure consciousness always remains aloof from all the material pleasures of the world. It is pure just like sunlight; it can be perceived only when it falls on an object. But whenever we identify an object and relate with it, our ego arises. It is because of our ego that we at times feel happiness or otherwise. The atman is ever blissful and joyous and unperturbed by any worldly conditions.

> We believe that every being is divine, is God. Every soul is a sun covered over with clouds of ignorance; the difference between soul and soul is owing to the difference in density of these layers of clouds.

> Even the lowest of the low have the Atman inside, which never dies and never is born, immortal, without beginning or end, the all pure, omnipotent and Omni present Atman. (Swami Vivekananda)

Consciousness, in simple terms, means 'the sensory awareness of the body, the self, and the world'. Newborn infants also demonstrate consciousness through their reactions to external stimuli even though maturation takes place over a long time. Even today, consciousness remains to scientists a key puzzle which they are yet to solve.

According to Searle, it can be explained as 'inner, qualitative, subjective states, and processes of sentience of awareness'. Modern science treats it as a global neuronal workspace (GNW) model.

The priest concludes from all the above opinions that atman or spirit exists. It cannot be mass; it is surely in the form of energy which is pure and exists in the entire universe. It is the most subtle form of energy. It can be perceived only when it reflects on objects. It resides everywhere in every form depending upon the quality of the format. It corroborates the theory of conservation of energy by Albert Einstein, which is accepted universally.

According to the law of conservation of energy, energy cannot be created or destroyed, but it can be transferred or transformed from one form to another. This also proves the property of atman as described in the Bhagavad Gita.

The following is the conversation of Albert Einstein and Rabindranath Tagore in Berlin in 1930:

The scientist asked, 'Do you believe the divine is isolated from the world?'

The poet said, 'Not isolated. The infinite personality of mass comprehends the universe . . . The truth of the universe is human truth.'

The scientist said, 'Then I am more religious than you.'

The three students are dumbfounded by the stunning explanation of their priest uncle. The elder brother volunteers to summarise their discussion on the existence of atman.

- Our DNA acts as fractal antenna, which enables our cells to transmit and receive electrical signals.

- The birth and death of the physical body do not have any effect on the soul because the soul is imperishable. Atman is immortal, inert, indestructible, insoluble, incombustible, unwitherable, eternal, and all pervading. Human beings die when all the vital organs of our body stop working and the vital energy departs from our body. From the spiritual perspective, death occurs when the soul leaves the physical body.

- A large majority of people believe in the existence of atman.

- Universal consciousness exists; individual consciousness is a part of it, which is veiled or coloured by the perceptions of the material world. But the atman or soul remains unperturbed by these.

20

Cosmic Energy, Ionosphere, and Other Layers of Earth's Atmosphere

I believe that there is some mysterious ray pervading the universe that is fluorescing to it. In other words, that all its energy is not self-constructed but there is a mysterious something in the atmosphere that scientists have not found that is drawing out those infinitesimal atoms and distributing them forcefully and indestructibly.

Thomas Edison

The elder brother asks the priest, 'Uncle, I have been observing you from my childhood. You always told me that you never went to any school or university for formal education, but how could you acquire such vast knowledge on both spirituality and science?'

The priest smiles and answers, 'Many great spiritual persons, philosophers, and scientists had not gone even to high school or university, but still they acquired knowledge and taught us. I am a very ordinary person trying to understand the subject of reincarnation and its relation with science. I told you that I invest my afternoons in libraries to learn the subjects related to our mission.'

Without asking any further questions, the younger brother starts sharing his knowledge on cosmic energy and its layer.

On 3 February 1941, just few months before his death, Rabindranath Tagore wrote:

> This gigantic creation is a fireworks display of
> Suns and stars across the skies on a cosmic time
> scale. I too have come from the eternal and
> the imperceptible Like a spark in a tiny remote
> corner of space and time. Today as I entre the
> final act of departure, the flame weakens,
> The shadow reveals the illusory character of
> the play.
> And the costumes of grief and happiness begin
> to slacken. I see the colorful costumes
> Left over by hundreds of actors and actresses
> across the ages Outside the arena of the theatre.
> I look up only to find
> Beyond the backdrop of hundreds of extinguished
> stars
> Nataraj, silent and lonely. (Akash Bhora Surjo
> Tara)

It appears the ocean is infinite to us because of the apparent unending volume of water. In reality, it is not so; the volume of water is finite. Similarly for us, the cosmic world appears to be infinite as we cannot perceive beyond that. Perhaps the limitless God sits beyond such boundary of cosmic energy but provides the energy in which our world has manifested.

The following are said about cosmic world content:

All of my investigations seem to point to the conclusion that they are small particles, each carrying so small a charge, that we are justified in calling them neutrons. They move with a great velocity, exceeding that of light. (Nikola Tesla, 10 July 1932)

All the wonderful cosmic manifestations are existing by the Supreme will of God, and all of them are subordinate to that Supreme will. (Bhagavad Gita 9.6)

Energy cannot be created or destroyed; it can only be changed from one form to another. (Albert Einstein)

The energy in various forms—like cosmic, electromagnetic, etc.—exists everywhere in the universe. It is in the space among galaxies, planets, materials, humans, and even molecules. It acts as a bond which keeps the universe balanced and in order. This is our life force as well. It is very essential for us; it is even required for the expansion of our consciousness. It is a type of energy that pervades all spaces throughout the cosmos.

Nikola Tesla claimed, 'This new power for the driving of the world's machinery will be diverted from the energy which operates the universe, the cosmic energy, whose central source for the earth is the sun and which is everywhere present in unlimited quantities.'

The Earth's ionosphere has a very close relation to the mission of the brothers, their sister, and the priest. Ionosphere is the atmosphere of our planet, which is ionised by the cosmic and solar radiation. This layer extends approximately 70 to 1,000 kilometres from the surface of the Earth. Relatively, this area is closer to the Sun and is therefore exposed to high energy from cosmic rays and the Sun. Atoms of this layer get stripped of one or more of their electrons, and the area becomes positively charged. The ionised electrons then start behaving as free particles.

Ionosphere is important for us as it helps radio wave propagation to distant places, including satellites. A simple diagram of this is presented below.

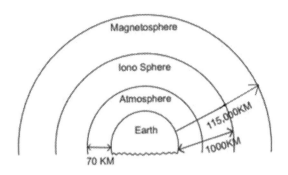

The ionosphere has three layers known as the F, E, and D regions (D being the closest and F being the furthest from the Earth). In F region, the electron density is highest.

The Earth has a magnetic field which reaches up to 115,000 kilometres into space. This layer prevents most of the particles from the Sun carried by the solar wind from hitting the Earth. The Sun and other planets have also their magnetospheres.

The magnetosphere is a mix of free ions and electrons from both the solar wind and the Earth's ionosphere and is confined by electromagnetic forces that are much stronger than gravity and collisions.

The lowest part of the Earth's atmosphere, encompassing a distance of 10–12 kilometres from the surface is known as troposphere. Stratosphere starts from a distance of 10–12 kilometres from Earth, followed by the mesosphere. It is in stratosphere that the incoming solar radiation forms the ozone layer, which is very important for our earth.

The atmosphere is divided into following four layers based on temperature:

- Troposphere: 0–12 kilometres
- Stratosphere: 12–45 kilometres
- Mesosphere: 45–85 kilometres
- Thermosphere: 85–100 kilometres

Energy is transferred between the Earth's surface and the atmosphere via conduction, convection, and radiation.

- Conduction is the process by which energy is transmitted through direct contact with the neighbouring molecule.
- Convection is the process by which energy is transported by groups of molecules from place to place.
- Radiation is a process where transfer of energy takes place without the involvement of any physical substances. It can transmit in vacuum. An example of this kind is the travel of energy from the Sun to the Earth by means of electromagnetic waves. The shorter the wave length, the higher the associated energy with it.

The air varies in its chemical composition at different altitudes, and various chemicals absorb different wavelengths of electromagnetic radiation. Wherever there is the right combination of selected chemicals and an abundance of radiation of a type that those chemicals are good at absorbing, the atmosphere absorbs a lot of energy. On average, about 342 watt per square metre of energy reaches the top of the Earth's atmosphere.

Exosphere is the outermost layer of the Earth's surface. In this layer, atoms and molecules escape into space, and higher-altitude satellites orbit our planet. A particle of electromagnetic radiation is known as a photon. It spreads in the form of a wave.

'I have been using frequently the word *electromagnetic wave*. Let us try to understand what it is.' The younger brother continues his explanation.

Electromagnetic waves cause charged particles, such as electron, to move up and down. These waves have both electrical and magnetic properties and can travel through solids, liquids, gases, and vacuum spaces at the speed of light.

Electromagnetic waves are characterised by wavelength and frequency. The wave length is the distance between two successive wave crests or troughs as shown below:

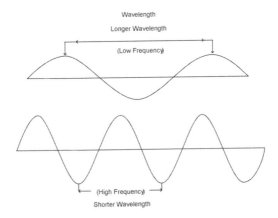

Frequency is measured by the number of wavelengths that passes through a point in one second. It is measured in either cycle per second (c/s) or hertz (Hz). The shorter the wavelength, the higher the frequency, and vice versa.

Atmospheric electricity just above the surface of the Earth is negligible, whereas if we go up, it increases. The air above the surface of the Earth is positively charged, and Earth's surface is charged negatively. In addition, due to friction among clouds, static electricity is also generated, which at times gets discharged to Earth as lightning.

The atmosphere in different regions is often found to be at different local potentials (electric potential is the amount of electric potential energy that a unitary point charge would have when located at that point), which may differ from the Earth by as high as 3,000 volts within 100 feet. The electrical conductivity of the atmosphere increases exponentially with height.

We may see differently the Earth's atmosphere. It is made up mostly of nitrogen and oxygen molecules. Light wave has its associated electric field, which disturbs the electrons of the molecule, causing them to oscillate just as the electric field oscillates. Each molecule then becomes a tiny antenna, which re-radiates and scatters the light from the Sun. The simplest form of antenna is a dipole antenna; it looks like a thin wire. For effective radiation, the length of the antenna should be longer for low frequency and shorter for a high-frequency energy transfer.

At any given time, each ionosphere's layer has a maximum frequency at which radio waves can be transmitted vertically and reflected or refracted back to Earth. This frequency is known as critical frequency, which is different for different layers.

There has been continuous electrical influences on Earth and, by and large, in the universal atmosphere. For relevant understanding of the issue, the explanation will be restricted to the Earth's atmosphere. There is a tremendous effect on the atmosphere of the Earth, including the ionosphere, because of the alternating current (AC) and direct current, which operate at the speed of light. The electromagnetic and electrostatic map of the Earth's atmosphere and on its surface is being dynamically changing moment to moment because of the various sources of energy distributed all around, including lightning discharges, thunderstorm, optical emissions, precipitation of magnetosphere electrons, radioactive emissions, change of electron density, etc. As already explained, the Earth's atmosphere has layers of various gases, which are being retained by the high gravitational pull of the Earth. With all these activities, there always remains a coupling between the Earth and its atmosphere.

Earth and its different layers of atmosphere act as different types of capacitors, which are distributed all around. The surface of the Earth acts as a negative plate if we consider a single capacitor (Earth as one plate and the atmosphere as the other one). Therefore, electrical energy can be stored with different parameters (like frequency) at various locations of the atmosphere depending upon their properties.

'Now, for my sister, I would like to explain very briefly how a capacitor functions and its working principle.' The younger brother then talks about the capacitor and its functions.

A capacitor can store charge and can release charge under favourable conditions. An elementary capacitor is made up of two metallic plates (any conductor of electricity) separated by dielectric media or material (which is a weak insulator but can be polarised by applying an electric field).

If voltage is applied across the two plates, an electric field is created. Positive charge will collect on one plate and negative on the other, which works like a battery. When the capacitor is charging, the current will pass through it until it is fully charged (saturated), then no more current will pass through it in that direction. Therefore, if we apply direct current (DC) across the plates, then it will just get charged and then stop working. But if we apply AC, then it continuously gets charged and discharged and will continue working.

The word *resistance* is very familiar. By using resistance and capacitance in electrical or electronic circuits, the circuit frequency can be made sensitive. That is, depending upon the parameter of the resistance and capacitance, a particular frequency or a range of frequencies can be allowed to pass through the circuit, or in other words, the energy with the other frequencies can be filtered. One point should be remembered: the energy that acts or passes within the human body is mostly AC in nature; therefore, the body capacitors effectively function within human beings.

In an electric circuit, there is one more important component known as an inductor. A simple inductor is a coil made from the wire of an electrical conductor. If current is passed through it, the coil generates a magnetic field which opposes the current flow. We have understood that a capacitor opposes voltage; similarly, the inductor opposes current. Both of them can store energy and release selectively when AC is applied across it. As for explaining the role of resistance, it always opposes the flow of the current in an electrical circuit. In Earth's atmosphere as well as in the human body, these three electrical components—resistance, inductance, and capacitance—are working continuously.

The sister asks how inductance works in the human body. The younger one promptly replies, 'Since the inductor opposes the flow of the current, it means it opposes the flow of electrons. It becomes hot and glows because of the heat.

My sister, when you get angry but cannot express it, your face also shows such a glow or a blush. I hope now it is clear to you how inductance works in our body. Actually, the question of my sister is very good. Incidentally, our sister has explained about some coil-like internal components that exists in our body. The inductance principle can always work upon such coils.'

The priest says that it is now his turn to speak on this subject, but he acknowledges that the younger brother has mesmerised them all with his informative and impressive lecture. The priest then starts speaking about the perceptions of the spiritualists on this subject.

They have understood that there is an unlimited resource of electrical energy in the universe, on the Earth's surface, and within humans. In absolute terms, spiritualists describe the universe as having the following seven layers: earth, water, fire, sky, air, the total energy, and false ego. Each of those are related with a chakra lying within us.

> Subject to the control of the supreme personality within us of Godhead, the sky allows outer space to accommodate all the various planets, which hold innumerable living entities. The total universal body expands with its seven coverings under his supreme control. (*Srimad Bhagavatam* 3.29.43)

The Quran explains it as given below:

> It is He who created everything on the Earth for you and then directed. His attention up to heaven and arranged it into seven regular heavens. He has knowledge of all things. (Quran 2:29)

Incidentally, scientists of today also considered the following seven layers of Earth's atmosphere: troposphere, ozonosphere, stratosphere, mesosphere, thermosphere, ionosphere, and magnetosphere. The seven heavens surrounding our planet are Sun (Sunday), Moon (Monday), Mars (Tuesday), Mercury (Wednesday), Jupiter (Thursday), Venus (Friday), and Saturn (Saturday). Each day of our week is dedicated to each heaven.

According to the Hindu Puranas, the seven heavens are Satyaloka, Tapaloka, Janaloka, Maharloka, Savarloka, Bhuvarloka, and Bhurloka.

Similarly, in Judaism the seven heavens are Vilon, Raqi'a, Shehaquim, Zebul, Ma'on, Makhon, and Araboth.

The layers of Earth's atmosphere, with respect to other planets, have significant interferences with our planet. We can physically feel the same. The occurrence of the tide and ebbs, the disturbances on radio signals, the body aches during full-moon and new-moon nights, the mood swings on various seasons, weather conditions, etc. are all examples of the same. Astrologically also, it is believed that the planets have constantly affected the human body and its life force.

In the priest's mind, in the atmosphere, the accumulation of energy takes place in a local area first, and then depending upon the property of the atmosphere, they accumulate in a bigger area, then go to the final destination. It is similar to the movements of clouds. Charged particles of the same polarity, frequency, etc. accumulate in a specific region.

Gita (chapter 9, verse 21) describes that there are two broadly classified main layers where jivatman accumulates. One is the Chandraloka, and the other one is Brahmaloka. The paths (margs) to reach the above layers are known as *pitryana* and *devayana*. Those who go to the former return back to the earth in accordance to their karmic cycle, and those that go to the latter do not come back to the earth. Such souls get further purified there and eventually unite with God.

The younger one opines that there are not much of differences between the findings of ancient saints and present scientists. The only difference is that the saints realised the truths by rousing their inner wisdom without the help of any external apparatus, whereas present scientists find them with the help of apparatus and acquired knowledge.

The sister volunteers this time to summarize.

- The universe is full of wonders and appears to be infinite.
- Cosmic energy exists everywhere; it has maintained the balance of the universe and acts as life force for us.
- Earth's atmosphere has the following seven layers: troposphere, ozonosphere, stratosphere, mesosphere, thermosphere, ionosphere, and magnetosphere.
- Due to solar and cosmic radiation, the ionosphere gets ionised.
- Ionosphere plays an important role in the functioning of radios, televisions, and other medium of broadcasting. Energy is transferred between the Earth and its atmosphere through conduction, convection, and radiation.
- Continuous electrical activities happen in our planet, its atmosphere, and the human body.
- Each molecule in the atmosphere acts as a tiny antenna.
- Every layer of the Earth's atmosphere has its own critical frequency. Earth and the layers of its atmosphere also act as capacitors.

- A capacitor can store energy and continuously work with AC. It can filter and can selectively choose energy with a specific frequency. It resists voltage build-up.
- An inductor can do the same, but it resists current build-up.
- Spiritually also, there are seven layers in the atmosphere of Earth.
- All planets in our universe exist in equilibrium and interact with each other in some way or the other. This phenomenon is experienced physically as well.

21

God Time and Man Hour

Who among us has never looked up into the
heavens on a star lit night, lost in wonder at the
vastness of space and the beauty of the stars?

Jeb Bush

'The topic about God time and man hour is a subject of
philosophy and can be better explained by our priest uncle,'
says the elder brother.

The priest smiles and starts speaking, 'Timelessness
is beyond our concept and perception, although it is true
that man has only created time for his convenience and
thereby had invited many troubles. Every day, from morning
till night, the time clock haunts us. We wake up to the
sound of the alarm clock every morning. The big ball at
the Times Square reminds us of the start of every new year
and simultaneously the lament of the bygone year and the
steady process of ageing. The clock determines the time of
our painful retirement from services and eventually from
our lives, even though it has some definite merits. Other
than humans, all living beings do not have time, so they

may be relatively happier than us. It may be wise to first see what the wise people said about it.'

The priest gives them examples of the religious and philosophical understanding of God's time.

The Bible describes it as:

> For a thousand years in your sight are but as yesterday when it is past, or as a watch in the night. (Psalm 90:4)

The Quran proclaims:

> They challenge you to bring forth that torture [in hell] and Allah will not break His promise; a day of your Lord [paradise/hell promise] is like a thousand years of what you count. (Quran 22:47)

According to Bhagavad Gita:

> Those who know Brahma's day which comprises the duration of four billion three hundred and twenty million years and his night also the duration of four billion three hundred and twenty million years are knower's of day and night. (Bhagavad Gita, chapter 8)

The priest continues, 'It is therefore very difficult to perceive the gap between the concept of God's time and our time. In fact, for all purposes, God's time is considered infinite. We explain our time in terms of year, month, day, and hour. God's time is expressed or measured in terms of yuga. The Satya Yuga lasted 1,728,000 years. He counts by dynasty yuga for His assessments.

'Think that we are sitting with God somewhere in His palace, trying to locate our planet within our universe. We just cannot locate it as it looks like a quark.

'We become impatient that God does not listen to our prayers even after several years. Now imagine in His kingdom how small our physical existence is and how small are a few years of the Earth or a few hours of human life with respect to the universe! If we think perspectively, His response to our prayers is practically instantaneous.

'Therefore, God's response to our karma is always immediate in spite of our insignificant physical presence in the universe. Earth is only 4 billion years old. God's time is infinite, and we live for a very small duration in one lifetime.'

The summary of the discussion in this chapter is as follows:

- God's time span is infinite and cannot be measured in terms of man hour.
- He is the creator of the universe and is very kind. He responds to all our prayers spontaneously.
- His systems never fail.
- Our life is just a flash in time.
- A timeless mind can perceive God better.
- The universe has no time, which cannot be measured in finite terms but only in events.

22

As We Sow, So We Reap

A man is born alone and dies alone; and he experiences the good and bad consequences of his karma alone; and he goes alone to hell or the supreme abode.

Chanakya

They decide to disperse for lunch and meet after two hours. When the sister enquires about his food, the priest replies, 'I will only eat some fruits today, which I have in the temple.'

After they have left, the priest quietly enters the temple of the goddess Kali, sits before Her, and starts praying with folded hands, 'Divine Mother, I have been performing puja [prayer] every day before you ever since I have come to this temple. I have tried my best to perform my duty to the best of my ability, sincerity, and devotion. I walked on the path of spiritualism as per my best understanding and faith. I am supposed to be unattached with the material world while serving you in your temple. You have given me this rare opportunity of serving you and your children selflessly. I confess before you that I cannot remain fully unattached to the outside world. Slowly my associations with the two brothers have developed into a fatherly affection.

'We all have started researching on the process of reincarnation. This subject, to my knowledge, has not been unveiled by you in a definitive and scientific manner even though majority of the people of your world believe in transmigration or reincarnation. We are exploring this realm, but not with any ulterior motive. We are only trying to reveal one of the simplest and greatest processes of yours scientifically so that the faith and belief of your devotees in you will remain unwavering. Some of your children have forgotten the karmic cycle and the principle of "as we sow, so we reap", which has cast a shadow of unhappiness in our world. Everything is known to you in this universe, including the events which will happen in future. My humble confession is that the three persons who are involved with me know nothing about your apprehension of any possibility of exploitation, which the society has been doing in past.

'If you consider it to be improper, please punish me alone. As you know, this has been my plan for a very long time. I have influenced them to take initiative in this mission. I am praying for you to please pardon them as well as me. If you find our work beneficial for the human race, then kindly bless the two boys and their sister and let this mission serve its purpose.'

23

❧❧❧

Purification Process of the Soul

Knowing yourself is the beginning of all wisdom.

Aristotle

All of them return to the temple, bringing some fruits for their uncle. They have also brought a flask full of tea so that a long break during the discussion could be avoided. Their uncle becomes very happy upon seeing their preparations and sincere efforts.

They decide that the leading role in the subject of the purification of the soul will be taken up by their uncle. The specific issues or processes relating to physiology will be explained by their sister, the younger brother will explain issues which require scientific explanations, and the elder brother will play the role of an umpire. He will resolve any argument by hearing all sides and settling the matter mutually acceptable to all.

Soon they are all engrossed in the discussion.

The priest explains, 'We have observed in our previous sessions that the gross body, mind, and intellect are interlinked. Actions of the three—in isolation and in combination—condition and influence our minds, which enables us to feel emotions like happiness or pleasure. We become the victim of our avidya (ignorance) unknowingly. Majority of the world population is suffering due to the lack of peace and to the instability of the mind. They are searching for happiness in shopping malls, homes, palaces, wealth, relations, power, religions, temples and other places of prayers, and failing which, they are not even hesitating to explore court rooms, police stations, drugs, wars, subversive actions! But seldom do they take the time to introspect where the key of all solutions and eternal peace lies. This perhaps is the greatest mystery of God in this modern and advanced world. On the other hand, there are some people who are ever happy and satisfied even in this world of apparent misery and evil. Misery cannot even touch them. Such strangers remain happy irrespective of their situations, wealth, poverty, etc.

'Others feel that the expressions of happiness of those poor people are hypocrisy and are external masks worn by them to hide the problems in their lives. Sufferers do not even try to find out the key to their happiness. An intelligent person shall surely not hesitate to ask them this life-changing or live-saving question. I am sure that the answer for those acclaimed people will be, "The source of happiness is within you," like how the lamp of Aladdin, veiled and unattended, lies in one's heart. Please discover the magic lamp within you through the process of introspection. The dust is required to be removed by oneself, as Aladdin had done for his lamp, to make life more meaningful and happy. The good news is that God has given this ability to each of us, and that is why we are His crowned creations. If someone is a victim of unhappiness, he is advised to simply follow the proven footprints of the wise people, which will lead to the island of happiness. I am an ordinary, humble, and unknown person trying to show you a route to your dreamland. I have understood with my very limited knowledge and perception that there is no other alternative or a shorter route to reach there because that is the only route map to liberation left behind by all the great personalities and saints of our planet. Our endeavour shall be to trace the route with a compass for the satisfaction of scientists, who believe it to be a more dependable and accurate instrument.

'I must introduce the drivers of the vehicle. You, the younger brother, and your sister have all the required qualifications and licences to drive the vehicle. Your elder brother has a standard and accurate compass, which he will use from time to time to calibrate our GPS. I am only holding the redundant map in my hand to help and guide you, the drivers. If you are ready, we may now start our journey.

'All of us get angry for some reason or other. It happens due to events or incidents which do not match up to our expectations or which we simply do not like. After some time, our anger subsides. The reverse is also true. In both cases, we generally do not notice what happens at the physical level. At times, we do not intend to become angry, keeping in mind the problems of our blood pressure. But the moment we are exposed to unwanted situations, we get excited unknowingly. All these happen actually in our mental level. Our conscious as well as subconscious minds do not want to hear matters which they are programmed to be unhappy with. The moment they decipher that the signals are not in their favour, they revolt or express their displeasure through physical gestures.

'Apart from all other physical problems, our breathing rate increases immediately, which we hardly observe. We can very easily feel it if we deliberately try to observe the same with concentrated mind. As soon as the cause of unhappiness is withdrawn, the mind starts stabilising. After some time, our breathing rate becomes normal. Controlling our conscious mind is easier than controlling our subconscious mind, which controls us predominantly at old age. This happens because of the deeply written tracks we have inherited from our previous actions and habits. What is the solution then? We know that the pure atman or soul does not take any active part in anything; it only observes. The subversive practices of the mind and body spread some dust on it. The next superior layer of the mind is intellect. It is required for understanding the games and habits of the mind and for taking corrective measures for cleaning the dusts so that we always remain happy, which is our normal nature. Before I talk about the process of purification, let your sister tell us something about our physiological behaviour.

Their sister is an emphatic listener. Initially, she is hesitant to say anything but finally responds, 'Commonly, anger makes our blood boil, ears burn, teeth grind, fists clench, muscles contract, facial expression change, etc. This kind of physical behaviour occurs because of disturbances in the physiological level. In our brain, amygdale is the component that deals with our emotions. As we get angry, chemicals like cortisol, adrenaline, and noradrenalin surge through our bodies. The amygdale gets activated. The time between a trigger event and a response from the amygdale can be a quarter of a second. But within that time, blood flow increases in the frontal lobe, especially in the left side. As we have explained earlier, the left side is the reasoning and logical side of the brain. It tries to understand the cause and effect and then tries to neutralise the effect quickly. Some neurologists say that within two seconds the reaction is balanced. There is a common saying that if you suddenly become angry, count to ten, and the anger will subside. The people who are habitually angry may lose this regulator. They may not produce acetylcholine, a hormone which balances the more severe effects of adrenaline. Their nervous systems are continuously subjected to stress, finally leading to a weakened heart and stiffer arteries. This causes damage to the kidney and liver in addition to high sugar and cholesterol levels. It may also cause depression and anxiety. The risk of coronary artery disease and heart attack goes up by two to three times than a normal person.' The elder brother asks in what way this subject is related to re-birth. The priest responds,' one must understand and relate the relationship of mind body and intellect first within oneself physically, and then only the subtle aspects of the same can be appreciated better. As such one of the purposes of our research work is to evolve a simple cleaning process of jiv atman.

The priest states, 'Look, after knowing all these bad effects in the physiological level, tell me why we should not address this problem. This not only damages our physical health but also damages our mental and spiritual health. Similarly, all our bad habits, if they become chronic, can impair our God-gifted healthy systems. While on this subject, I would like to involve our younger friend to throw some light on electrical or electronic rectifier, filter, and feedback system.'

At once relating to the situation, the younger brother starts explaining about the topic.

The name *rectifier* suggests that it corrects some unwanted element in the electrical system. A simple rectifier changes an alternating current (AC) into a pulsating direct current by eliminating the undesired negative half cycles of the alternative voltage. Diode, an electronic component, is used for this purpose. Its inherent characteristics provide only a one-way path for the electric current to flow. It only allows the positive half of the AC to flow. However the output of a rectifier alone is not stable, it contains ripple. To make it ripple-free, electrical filters are employed at the output of the rectifier. To make it a complete stabilised source, negative feedback system is put in conjunction with the filter.

The wave shapes of AC input to the rectifier and the pulsating direct current output look:

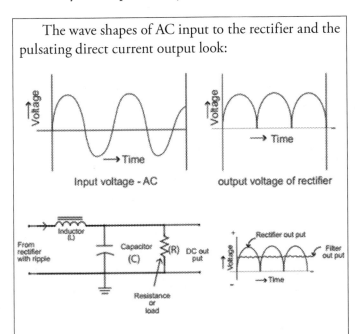

The output of the rectifier is not yet stable. The pulsation in amplitude in the output voltage of the rectifier acts as ripples or impurities. To remove such impurities, an electrical filter circuit is used. A simple filter consists of choke coils (inductor) and capacitors. A capacitor, as per its electrical property, opposes any change in voltage applied across its terminals by storing up energy in an electrostatic field whenever the voltage across the terminals tends to fall.

Therefore, some of the unwanted energy pulsations can be stored in the electric field of a capacitor, and the capacitor can then be allowed to discharge between current pulses. In this process, the fluctuations in the output voltage can be reduced.

An inductor, on the other hand, opposes any change in the magnitude of the current flow through it by storing energy in a magnetic field when the current through it tends to increase and by taking energy away from this field to maintain the current flow when the current through the inductor tends to decrease. Therefore, if it is connected in a series with the rectifier output and load, abrupt changes in the magnitude of the current through load and voltage across are minimised. A series choke or inductor has insignificant resistance to the passage of a direct-current (DC) flow as it offers a very high impedance to the passage of fluctuating current.

If the rectifier output is provided with a parallel capacitor and a series inductor in conjunction, the output of the filter will be almost ripple-free. But for very sensitive equipment, a complete, stable, and ripple-free supply or input is needed for which feedback circuit is employed in addition to filter. The feedback control system is an important technique very commonly used in modern electrical and electromechanical systems. It helps in improving the performance and correcting the output of many electrical networks. It is mostly used in processing signal quality. Simple analogue feedback control circuits can be made using individual or discrete components, such as resistors, capacitors, etc.

There are generally three types of electrical systems commonly used for control and signal. One is the open-loop system, and the others are the close-loop system and feedback system.

An open-loop system is simpler and easier, but it cannot correct or compensate the outside disturbances and the input impurities due to variations in circuit parameters. The demerits of the open-loop systems can be eliminated by introducing the feedback system. In a feedback system, a sample is taken from the output of the signal and then compared with the input or any desired standard signal or source. The difference is used to modify the effective input to get the desired results.

The simplest block diagram looks like the one shown here. This system has some advantages over the open-loop system.

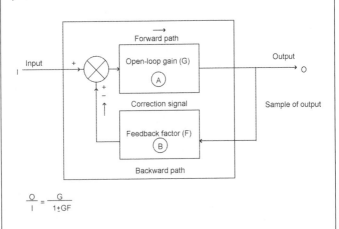

$$\frac{O}{I} = \frac{G}{1 \pm GF}$$

Signal distortion of the receiver can be reduced. The frequency response, gain, and bandwidth of a circuit can be controlled precisely. Circuit characteristics can be made unaffected by operating conditions, such as temperature, pressure, and voltage variations.

There are again two kinds of feedback systems—one is positive, and the other is negative feedback system. Both are used depending on certain conditions.

Say A is an amplifier. The input signal is required to be amplified with best quality without any disturbances or noise. One small sample is taken from the output. The sample is taken into the feedback circuit, where it is compared with the required quality signal. Here, a net correction signal is generated, which is then fed to the input of the amplifier to nullify the noises. As a result, the quality of output signal is substantially improved.

We have all the electrical or electronic components in our physiological systems. At any given condition, such components in isolation and in combination act as rectifier, filter, and feedback system to filter the impurities, ripples of our jivatman, the source of our subtle body. The connections are established by our mental body. Otherwise, the rectification of the mind, intellect, and jivatman will not be possible. It is beyond dispute that God has given us this supreme ability of rectification. In our brain, the amygdale does the same function. In fact, all our vital systems do have a similar feedback system. In the modern management system, similar feedback loops are used for improvement of the quality of management.

Life on Earth is about 4.5 billion years old, and modern man is about 200,000 years old. The perfect system which was used to manufacture human beings 200,000 years ago still remains the template for all modern engineering. Who else could be the creator of the universe and its beautiful species if not God?

Before the discussion on the feedback system of the mind, there should be a discussion about the power of the mind and the demerits of the open-loop system.

In the 1960s in New York, a worker on a Friday was working inside a cold storage van. He got delayed to complete his work. While going out, the door of the van got closed and latched. He cried from inside for help, but nobody could hear him. It was a weekend. Others had left the shop early. The system of the van was such that if the door latch was closed, the refrigeration cycle would start. The fellow inside had nothing but a pen and the log sheet. He got scared and started feeling cold. Out of fear, he started writing his experience on the log sheet and continued until he froze to death.

The next Monday, when people came and opened the door of the van, they found his dead body. His autopsy report confirmed that his death was due to freezing. But what was most surprising was that the cooling system of the van was actually faulty. On the contrary, the blower fan was found running, which meant that it had continuously supplied air inside since the door got closed. The worker did not die due to scarcity of oxygen. Doctors, after further examination, declared him dead due to heart failure even though all the symptoms of death were similar to freezing.

Later on, a panel of doctors concluded that he died because of his mental simulation on the consequence of the closed door as he was aware of the working mechanism of the van. The ill-fated fellow wrote his imagination in the log sheet until he died. He became focused with his mind and started imagining the various effects of freezing on the human body. His body responded accordingly until he actually died.

A focused mind works like a laser beam. Concentrated sun rays through a magnifying glass can cause a jungle fire. Under the same sun, one can take a sunbath while cosily sitting beside a sea beach.

The mind is a tool which can be utilised for immense benefit of mankind, and at the same time, it can also cause destruction as well. It all depends on how we use it. Who controls the use of the mind? It is controlled by the programme engraved very deeply in our subconscious and partially by our intellect. I have already told you that the conscious mind can be directed and controlled very easily by our intellect. But for rewriting the subconscious program, one has to take the help of the sharp feature of intellect and introspection. God has also given this power to human beings only, then why should we not use it?

For changing a deep-rooted bad habit, one has to first take a firm resolution with unshakeable conviction. Start the remedial measure by withdrawing fuel into it. The mind vehemently opposes the process during the first three weeks and then slowly becomes tired, and finally, after ninety days, it becomes tranquil and surrenders. But to erase the programmes completely from the subconscious mind, it may take some more time.

What actually happens within us?

1. Intellect decides to change the habit of the mind by the power of discrimination (*viveka*)
2. It provides an input signal to the mind.
3. The mind processes the signal and corrupts it with its own programme.
4. The output functions are observed by the intellect. It discriminates over a feedback system through a backward path.

5. After discrimination between the desired quality of signals as required by the intellect and the output quality, it sends again a corrective signal input to the mind. The mind now responds to the corrected input signals and again corrupts it but this time with lower spike or intensity.
6. By repeating this process again and again, the mind's programme gets corrected.
7. It starts functioning as desired by the intellect.

In this process, the body, mind, and intellect take part. However, our soul remains inert but exposes its own quality because of the removal of dust from it. The inherent quality of atman is eternal bliss. Therefore, purification of the mind with the help of our intellect is essential for the realisation of the self.

The word *introspection* is often used. This is the actual process of the feedback loop. Introspection is the tool, as shown (B) in the diagram. What is it? It is the eye of our intellect. It senses the actions of our mind. How can it be practised?

Sit down preferably in a quiet and comfortable place. The sitting posture can be adjusted as per the comfort of the individual, but the spinal cord should be straight and erect. Close your eyes, stop your normal movements, and start observing the quality of your breathing with the eye of your mind. Make sure that you don't inhale or exhale one breath without keeping track of it. As a beginner, you can observe how vehemently your mind reacts to this. Within few seconds, the mind will start running here and there. Simply observe as a keen observer. Do not involve yourself with the game of the mind. But remain alert and go on observing it. The next mischief will be done by your mind by causing discomfort to your body. You will start feeling uncomfortable with your sitting posture. Let your tool witness this. If you feel uncomfortable, change your posture, but be aware of each and every action.

If we are successful in this exercise cycle of ninety days, then we can overcome a major hurdle. Thereafter, we shall have to practise continuously. Within a short time, you will start liking the mental exercise.

Once we discipline the mind, it becomes reasonably focused with its concentration. A concentrated and focused mind slowly becomes a tool like a laser beam. With a sharp mind, we can now concentrate on the different parts of our internal physical body to observe their normal functioning. This is how we can prepare for deep meditation. For sharpening the mind, it is necessary to slowly withdraw it from sensual objects as it has a normal tendency to get attached to those.

At this stage, for early result it is essential to follow the rituals prescribed by the saints and wise men. Develop very high faith and devotion to gods or goddesses of your choice. Faith and belief immensely helps in cleaning and sharpening the mind and intellect. Once intellect achieves its short goals, it becomes interested to achieve further long-term goals. By walking on this path of purification, one can reach the final destination as set.

> It is easy to talk on religion, but difficult to practice it. (Paramahamsa Shri Ramakrishna)

This is the reason why the Hindus worship multiple gods and goddesses. The Hindu culture is much more diversified. People of different states have different beliefs, different languages, different lifestyles, and different food habits.

The ancient wise men advised the people to follow any demigod of their choice but to follow the principle as explained because the purification process is universal. It is the inherent property of human beings. This is the creation of God, known as dharma to the Hindus, dhamma to the Buddhists, religion to the Christians, Islam to the Muslims, and so on.

> God can be realised through all paths. All religions are true. The important thing is to reach the roof. You can reach it by stone stairs, by wooden stairs or by bamboo steps or by a rope. You can also climb up by a bamboo pole. (Paramahamsa Shri Ramakrishna)

24

❧❧❧

Physiological Responses during Meditation

Meditation is the soul's perspective glass.

Owen Feltham

Their sister clarifies that even though she has not been practising meditation, she can relate to the responses of the physiological body during the process of meditation. She reveals that she has recently acquired some knowledge about the effects of both natural and external electromagnetic forces on the human body, which she would like to share with them all.

The word *vibration* is very important with respect to physical responses.

- What are vibrations?
- Vibration is the oscillatory motion of various bodies.
- The response to a vibration exposure is primarily dependent on the frequency, amplitude, and duration of the exposure.

- Free vibration takes place when a system oscillates due to the action of internal forces only.
- Forced vibration is caused by the action of external forces.
- When the external frequency matches with the natural frequency of a system or body, the phenomenon of resonance occurs. This causes large oscillations.
- It has been discussed earlier that human beings emit electrical energy outside the body, having different frequencies which are induced on other bodies and vice versa. These vibrations influence one another.

The frequencies of such emissions vary with the state of mind. We have experienced this while praying in the temple. The environment becomes pleasant because of collective positive thinking, which has a specific range of frequency.

- Our DNA can transmit bioelectrical energy within a wide range of frequencies, and there is an exchange of photons between different organisms as well as within the human brain, which can transmit energy at a frequency of 72–90 megahertz.
- Human body can transmit energy at a frequency of 62–68 megahertz.
- The study reveals the effect of positive and negative thoughts on our frequency. Negative thoughts lower our frequency by about 12 megahertz, and positive thoughts enhance the same by about 10 megahertz. Meditation and prayer raise the frequency by 15 megahertz (according to Dr Robert O. Becker, MD).

- The mind and body are deeply connected. Leading a disciplined and balanced life immensely helps one's physical and emotional health.
- The physical or natural frequencies of human beings are very low. Since life began, the Earth has been surrounding and protecting all of us with a natural vibration of 7.83 hertz, which is the same as *aum*, which is chanted by rishis for stabilising the mind. There are four types of physical human brainwaves. Their inherent frequency ranges and effects on human beings are listed below:

  1. Beta waves: These range between 13 to 40 hertz. This state is associated with a state of deep concentration and visual sharpness.

  2. Alpha waves: These range between 7 to 12 hertz. This state is associated with relaxation. The resonant frequency of Earth's electromagnetic field lies within this range, popularly known as Schumann resonance (SR), which is 7.83 hertz. It was discovered by Dr W. O. Schumann. It is the gateway for entering into a deeper state of consciousness.

  3. Theta waves: These range between 4 to 7 hertz. It is associated with an elusive stage, where the ambience of an extraordinary realm can be experienced. It is also known as the twilight stage. It increases our creativity, reduces stress, and provides special perception skill. At this stage, the body sleeps but the mind remains awake.

4. Delta waves: These range between 0 to 4 hertz. It is associated with deep sleep. It is very essential for the healing processes of the mind and body.

The internally generated resonant frequency of Earth is 10 hertz, as discovered by Tesla, whereas Schumann resonance (SR) is electromagnetic oscillations. The Earth's global electric circuits play through the space in the ionosphere as waves in plasma. The ionosphere is a very good conductive region of cosmic plasma.

The mental antenna can function as a variable tool of transmission or reception in the exchange of extrasensory information. If tuned with SR, it may carry such bio-regulating information to distant targets.

The HAARP (High Frequency Active Auroral Research Program) project of USA and the Woodpecker Project of Russia have targeted weather manipulation and mind control.

In 1973, Miller, Webb, and Dickson described DNA as a holographic projector (embryonic holography) and that is when genes encode and express themselves via light and radio waves or acoustical holography. Delocalised interference patterns create blueprints for our body's space–time organisation. It acts like a biocomputer. Our biosystems are sensitive to natural and artificial magnetic fields. Our DNA, brain ventricles, and cellular structures in the human body may operate as antennae for detecting and decoding such global and local extra-low-frequency signals.

The very structure and organisation of living tissues can be regulated by DNA. Even subtle currents can reach deep into the genetic and consciousness control mechanism. Schumann's resonance forms a natural feedback loop with the human mind and body. This feedback pulse acts as a driver for the brain and can carry information. The functional process can be altered, and a new pattern of behaviour can be induced through the brain's feedback networks.

If we intentionally generate alpha waves and go into resonance with the Earth's frequency, we naturally feel better and refreshed due to environmental synchronisation.

Alpha wave biofeedback is considered a conscious self-regulating technique, while the alpha frequency bi-natural bit stimulation is a passive management technique where cortical potentials entertain to or resonate at the frequency of an external stimulus. Through the self-regulation of specific cortical rhythms, we begin to control those aspects of consciousness associated with the rhythm. When our target is alpha, either in meditation or in biofeedback, it means entering the Schumann resonance.

Another point to be kept in mind is that the amplitude of Schumann's resonance is not constant and that it is extremely sensitive in tropical temperature. It has been observed that a one-degree rise in temperature results in the doubling of the amplitude of SR.

How can we change our vibration frequency?

1. The most effective technique to raise our frequency of energy is meditation. It happens with this technique because we try to cease our thoughts.
2. In the process of introspection and self-realisation, we shall purposefully take feedback control by taking a sample of our present thought and trying to control the input of thought into our system.
3. Laughter improves the frequency to some extent.
4. Love and gratitude enhance our transmittal frequency.

The higher are our frequencies, higher our consciousness.

Radio waves and brainwaves are both forms of electromagnetic radiation. Waves of electromagnetic energy travel at the speed of light. The difference between radio and physical brainwaves lies with their frequencies. The frequency range of radio waves is 50 to 1,000 megahertz, and that of human brain itself is 10 to 100 hertz (internal).

Robert Monroe, the founder of the Monroe Institute in Faber, Virginia, demonstrated that to reach the state of awareness, one has to remain within 5 to 7 hertz. He also found that in general the brain has a tendency to interpret imposed higher outside frequency up to 8 hertz.

The priest expresses his happiness with the information given by the sister. He says, 'Today we have walked close to our goal by several steps. There is not much difference between science and spiritualism with regard to the fundamentals of the mind and its control mechanism. For better living, one must try to keep one's mind cool, concentrated, and remaining within the alpha wave zone. But in order to achieve a higher state of realisation, one should keep the same in theta wave zone.'

The elder brother very eagerly starts summarising.

- The programmes in our minds (both conscious and subconscious) can be modified and purified, which in turn can clean the layers of dust that have accumulated on our soul.
- The apparent problems we can see externally are only as symptoms; actual problems lie within us, which need to be addressed.
- In order to stabilise the mind, we must first withdraw it from the external disturbances. Meditations help us in doing so. Using intellect, along with a

concentrated and disciplined mind, through our inbuilt feedback system can purify our soul by removing avidya or ignorance.

- A pure soul remains in the state of bliss always, and it is all pervading.

- Temples and deities help us in disciplining our minds and intellects.

- Introspection is a tool that can be used for purification of the mind and intellect.

- We have a natural physical vibration and also mind and thought waves. We transmit energy as electromagnetic waves, which travel at the speed of light.

- There are four types of physical brainwaves: beta (13 to 40 hertz), alpha (7 to 12 hertz), theta (4 to 7 hertz), delta (0 to 4 hertz).

- Schumann's resonance (SR) is 7.83 hertz, which is the frequency of Earth's electromagnetic field. If resonance occurs with human natural frequency, it gives us deep relaxation.

- We can alter or improve our mental or brainwave frequencies to reach a desired state of consciousness.

- Both science and philosophy are in agreement with each other on this subject.

25

Migration of Energy and Its Accumulation

The substance of the winds is too thin for human eyes, their written language is too difficult for human minds, and their spoken language mostly too faint for the ears.

John Muir

The priest says, 'This is the key issue of our noble mission. Let us enjoy a tea break before we carry forward our discussion further.'

The sister serves the tea and adds, 'I might not be able to contribute much on this subject as it doesn't appear to be a matter of physiology.'

The younger brother explains, 'It is more about energy and its behaviour. The soul must be a form of energy, all pervading and subtle like air. It does not have any shape, colour, and smell. It cannot be destroyed or created, which is in accordance with the law of conservation of energy, the theory of Einstein which is represented as $E = mc^2$.'

'According to modern science, the electron is no longer the fundamental particle. Researchers have separated the electron into three particles, namely spinon (it provides spin), orbiton (it provides orbit), and holon (it carries charges). A quark is an elementary particle and a fundamental constituent of matter. Quarks combine to form composite particles called hardrons, the most stable of which are protons and neutrons, which are the components of an atomic nucleus.

'There are six types of quarks known as flavours: up, down, strange, charm, bottom, and top. Up and down quarks have the lowest masses. The heavier ones rapidly change into up and down quarks through a process called particle decay. These two forms of quarks are most commonly available in the universe. Is it not similar to Siva Shakti?

'Quarks have various intrinsic properties, like electric charge, mass, and spin similar to Nataraj. Their interactions are known as fundamental forces, like electromagnetism, gravitation, etc. Elementary particles even smaller than the quark are a boson. Scientists are still searching for elementary particles smaller than the boson.

'Stephen Hawking has predicted that the Higgs boson has the potential to destroy the entire universe. At very high energy levels, it can become very unstable. But the only silver lining in that prediction is, it may be trillions of years before it happens.

'The Higgs boson field is the force within the universe which gives particles mass, and it therefore acts as the glue which holds everything together. Without it, we shall disintegrate at the speed of light. This particle is also known as the God particle. Is it not similar to Vishnu Shakti, who maintains the universe?

'It is said that there are trillions of stars clustered in 100 billion galaxies and that our Sun is like a sand particle with respect to the universe. It is now claimed by some scientists that the universe is still expanding.'

The priest intervenes at that moment and starts saying, 'Imagine how God is controlling and maintaining our universe and His kingdom. You can easily visualise the size of the Earth with respect to the universe and very easily gauge the relative size of a man thereof. Still we have the highest ego, and God has none. We defy His rules and commandments and challenge His existence. But we fail and then fall in inescapable difficult circumstances. Mostly, we remember Him then, and we visit his temple, expecting immediate solutions to our problems.

'I am sure that He wonders why there are so many problems with mankind when He has given none. On the contrary, He has given us the power of realisation, the ability to think consciously, and finally the power of introspection. We have the power of deciding our fates, making our choices, and reaching the final destination by ourselves.'

The younger brother says that he understands that God is the source of all energies. It is He who has manifested in all life forms—everything that we can see and identify and also the other way round. He has converted some into mass, and the rest has been retained as energy in various forms. The form in which He has retained our vital life energy will be explored. This is about our metaphysical energy. All forms of energy are only various forms of vibrating frequencies. Physical energy, vital life energy, and mental energy are only its various expressions in the material, physical, vital, and mental planes.

Our fundamental energy source is our soul, and this exists throughout the universe. In the atmosphere of planets, the fundamental energy transforms; some take a form that is easily absorbed by living things. Such transformed fundamental energy is called life force or vital force or prana or chi energy. The vital force or the life force has some properties similar to electricity, specially the waves and their frequencies.

Following are the similarities:

- It flows rapidly throughout our nervous system.
- It creates an energy field around our body.
- It can be transformed and transmitted at a distance.
- It can be induced to other bodies.
- It can be guided or controlled by other forces—in this case, the mind.

It is important for us to understand where the energy accumulates before they are absorbed or transformed into other life forms and what the principles of clouding such energies are? Before the clouding of vital energy can be dealt with, it may be prudent to understand what happens in this world regularly.

We are aware of global warming. It happens due to the accumulation of carbon dioxide in the atmosphere. But why does carbon dioxide—or for that matter, any other gases—accumulate in the atmosphere in the form of cloud? What causes such accumulations, and what are its effects?

It is known that the atmosphere of Earth is structured layer after layer. One of such layers, for the purpose of discussion, may be chosen as electrosphere. At an elevation above the cloud, atmospheric electricity forms a continuous and distinct element which surrounds Earth. It covers the layer up to the start of the ionosphere. This layer has high electrical conductivity and is essentially at some potential difference with respect to Earth. The electrical conductivity of the atmosphere increases exponentially with altitude. The amplitudes of the electric and magnetic components depend on season, latitude, and height. There is a potential gradient at the ground level of the Earth, and this vertical field corresponds to the negative charge on the surface of the Earth. The negative potential gradient falls rapidly as altitude increases. The positive potential gradient rises rapidly as altitude increases. Electric charge is an inner property of matter.

At the atomic level, there are three types of electric charge, which are carried by three elementary particles.

- proton (positively charged).
- electron (negatively charged)
- neutron (zero electric charge).

Atoms are in general electrically neutral. Since electrons are loosely bound, those may be easily added and removed from the atom. Ionisation of an atom is the process through which electrons are added or removed with minimum energy. If electrons are removed from an atom, a negative ion is formed, and if added, a positive ion is formed.

Mostly, Newton's law of forces is called contact forces. An object accelerates because of an applied force which is applied through direct physical contact with the object. However, some forces like gravity and electrostatic force are extended over distances even though the objects do not touch each other. The equal charges repel each other, whereas dissimilar charges attract each other through a pattern which is known as lines of force.

We know that the atmosphere of our universe, including that of Earth, acts as several capacitor banks at various levels and in layers. Each of those distributed capacitors can accumulate electric charges and acts as storage of electric energy. In the atmosphere, continuous generation of electrical activities take place. At a given condition, such a capacitor gets discharged. There are natural resistances in the various layers of the atmosphere. The path from the electrically charged point to the discharge point itself offers electrical resistance. The coils forming with the electrically conducting invisible media of the atmosphere act as inductors.

When a DC source is connected to a capacitor in a series with a resistance, it looks like:

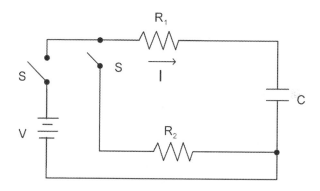

An RC circuit. R = resistance, C = capacitor,
V = battery, I = current, S = switch.

No sooner is the battery connected by switching *on* the outer switch than the initial current (I) becomes very high because the battery charges the capacitor. As soon as the capacitor gets charged up to the battery voltage, the current becomes zero. If the power source is disconnected and the inner switch is switched on, the capacitor gets discharged through the resistances shown.

If the battery is replaced with an alternating-current source in an RC circuit, what will happen are displayed in the diagram.

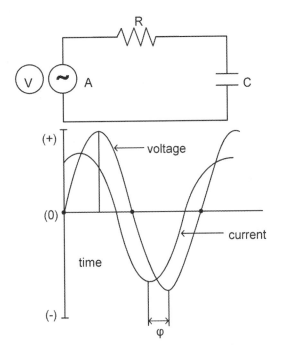

In an alternating-current source, the polarity of voltage changes at a time interval as shown in the above curve. One full cycle is from the zero (0) voltage to the positive (+) max voltage peak and then again to the zero (0) voltage and from the zero (0) voltage to again the negative (–) max voltage and again to zero. The number of cycles that occur in one second is known as the frequency of the AC system.

When an AC voltage source is connected to an RC circuit, the capacitor will get charged at the first cycle with the positive to one plate and negative to the other, and then it tends to get fully charged. The current will flow in one direction. In the next moment, the voltage polarity gets changed, as shown in the curve; as a result, the capacitor will first get discharged and then again will get charged with opposite polarity. This waveform is known as sinusoidal wave. The value of resistance and capacitance together is known as an impedance of the circuit. There is another component in the AC circuit known as the inductor. It looks like a coil made of electrical conductor. If the current flows through an inductor, a magnetic field is developed around it which tries to oppose the current. The inductance is expressed as *L* in a circuit.

A typical Resistance-inductance-capacitance circuit looks like this:

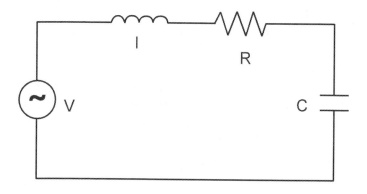

V = AC power source, L = inductance,
R = resistance, C = capacitance.

If the frequency is more, inductance becomes more, but capacitance becomes less. The effect of combined resistance, inductance, and reactance is known as impedance. In an AC circuit, electrical resonance occurs when the capacitor reactance (capacitance) and reactance (inductance) of the inductor become the same based on a particular frequency.

They are now opposite and equal and therefore nullify the effect of each other. That particular frequency is known as resonant frequency.

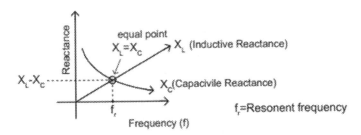

An alternator is known as an AC power source. It has its own impedance when it delivers power to an external circuit, having different impedance. Power or energy transfer takes place from the source to the external circuit. But maximum energy or power transfer will take place when the impedance of the source matches the impedance of the external circuit.

In a given circuit having fixed impedance with respect to a fixed frequency, if connected to a source of power, energy will be transferred to the external circuit. But if the frequency of the source can be varied to achieve the resonant frequency by matching the impedance of both the source and the external circuit, then maximum energy from the source can be transferred to the external circuit. This phenomenon is called impedance matching for transfer of energy from a given source (transmitter) to the external circuit (receiver). This is extensively used for transmitting and receiving radio signals. All of us have observed in our home that to get the best and clearest signal for a particular radio channel, we rotate a knob. That knob has multiple functions. It can manipulate the internal impedance of the receiver circuit by changing the values of the resistance, reactance, and capacitance (either one or in combination).

In this case, the signal is the source. By rotating the knob, we actually manipulate the impedance of the radio receiver so that matching of impedance takes place. At a specific position of the knob, the matching takes place with respect to the particular band of frequencies of the signal, and thereby maximum signal energy is received by our radio or TV. This is the fundamental principle of audio/video transmitters and receivers.

The keyword is *impedance matching.* Either by manipulating physical parameters of resistance, inductance and capacitance or by manipulating the source frequency can be achieved, which allows maximum energy transfer from the source to the recipient of the electrical/electronic systems.

The atmosphere of Earth—and for that matter, of the universe—acts as a giant capacitor. Atmospheric electricity exists because the Earth and the ionosphere act as cylindrical capacitors. The UV light from the Sun is so strong that it breaks apart molecules and atoms in the air, leaving ions (atoms with missing electrons) and free-floating electrons.

Earth's atmosphere and also that of other planets are complex electrical circuits formed with all electrical components even though these are not visible. Our communication systems utilise the inherent characteristics of the atmosphere. A simple diagram can now explain the communication waves from the Earth.

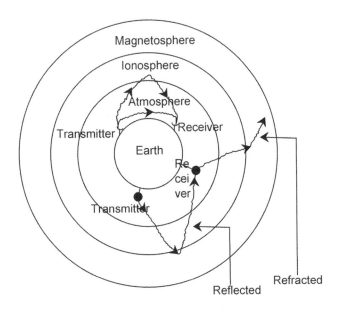

The radio waves or the electromagnetic waves generated by the antennas of radio stations can travel along the surface of the Earth. They can travel upwards and can get reflected or refracted back to Earth from the ionosphere, or they can also be refracted through the ionosphere to the magnetosphere. Part of the same can also be reflected from the magnetosphere to ionosphere as a weak signal back to the Earth.

All this possible wave propagations do happen depending upon the frequencies and magnitudes and strengths of the signals. In radio or TV communications, such surface or reflected signals are received by the receiving antennas, and the refracted waves are being utilised for communication purposes of space stations.

Summarising, the universe is full of energies of different qualities and kinds and also contains different kinds of masses. The most elementary particles are known as boson

(God particle). The entire universe is in motion. Such motion causes waves of different forms and qualities. The waves propagate from one place to another depending upon their surroundings and interactions with adjoining particles. The charged particles, as per their polarities, accumulate together. The various layers (both micro and macro) of the universe act as electrical components, predominantly capacitance, resistance, and inductance. There are sources of electrical energies around. The magnetic energy of the atmosphere in conjunction with the electrical energy always keeps the atmosphere full with electromagnetic movements and remains vibrant.

Human beings also vibrate at different frequencies depending upon our expressions and emotions. While vibrating, we always encounter resonance from both within and the outside atmosphere. When resonance occurs, the transfer of energy from transmitter to receiver becomes highest and causes higher levels of vibrations.

Electromagnetic radiation is reflected or refracted or absorbed mainly by several gases in the Earth's atmosphere. Among them, the most important are water vapour, carbon dioxide, and ozone. Some radiations pass through the atmosphere of Earth. These regions of the spectrum with wavelengths that pass through the atmosphere are called atmospheric windows. Radio waves and waves from our brains are both forms of electromagnetic radiation waves.

The radio wave signals (from radio and other wireless devices) vary from 50 to 1,000 megahertz, whereas physical human brain, depending on one's level of attention or focus, can emit waves between 10 to 100 hertz but can transmit electromagnetic energy up to 100 megahertz.

There are two principles of radio wave transmission methods, where electromagnetic energy travels from a transmitting antenna to a receiving antenna. One path is along the ground, and the other is by sky waves. The former wave travels near the surface of the Earth, and the later, one travels up and returns as a reflection or refraction from the ionosphere or other spheres beyond.

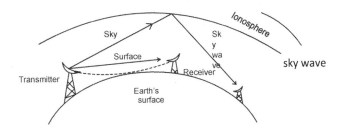

For the propagation and interception of radio waves, a transmitter and a receiver are used. Radio waves act as carriers of information-bearing signals. The information may be encoded directly on the carrier wave at the transmission end and then decoded at the receiving end, just like our old telegraphy system. It can also be impressed on a carrier wave through a modulation process at the transmitter end and then through demodulation at the receiving end. The actual information resides in the side band of the carrier wave (in case of amplitude modulation) or frequency added to the carrier wave (in case of frequency modulation) from the transmitter side, and then the reverse operation is done at the receiver side by segregating the waves.

Two very common types of such modulations are employed, which are known as amplitude modulation and frequency modulation for radio broadcasting and TV transmissions. These two systems are analogue systems. Nowadays, the digital system is used in which signals propagate as discrete voltage pulses—that is, as patterns of numbers. Before transmission, an analogue signal (sound) is converted into digital signal, which is then transmitted in the AM or FM frequency range. Voices and images are converted into electrical signals through microphones and cameras respectively. The signals are magnified through amplifiers. The amplified signal is used to modulate (superimpose) the carrier waves generated in an oscillator circuit. This is done in the transmitter. The modulated carrier wave is amplified and fed into an antenna that converts the electrical signal into electromagnetic waves for radiation into the space or along the surface.

These waves travel at the speed of light and are encountered by the receiving antenna as surface waves if within line of sight or as sky waves from the reflection or refraction from the ionosphere. The receiving antenna intercepts a part of the radiation and converts it back from electromagnetic wave to electrical signals and feeds it to the receiver. The receiver segregates the original voice or image signals from the carrier waves. It is amplified, and the noises are filtered off from the carrier and finally reproduced in loudspeaker or cathode ray tube or monitor.

The priest so far has not participated in the scientific discussions. He has been attentively hearing the presentations given by the sister and her brother. He at this point comments that there is a need to understand more clearly the science behind the working principles of the different segments of the communication system. He can see a unique similarity between the communication system and human transmigration.

He states, 'We have read in the Ramayana and the Mahabharata that written in Treta Yuga (BCE 21, 63, 102 to BCE 8, 67, 102) and Dvapara Yuga (BCE 8, 67, 102 to BCE 3, 102) respectively are some vivid descriptions of modern-type telecommunication, telepathy, test tube babies, and so on.

It is believed by modern science that human beings cannot perceive anything without prior experience coded in their DNA or genes.

'Therefore, it can be fairly imagined that some of these processes existed since ancient times. Due to the natural manifestation of human power, they slowly got depleted over time and hence was not known to the world. Modern science rediscovered these in the past two centuries.

'The matter of teletransportation (transponder) is under active consideration by scientists. This was commonly used by ancient rishis and saints, and there have been several instances of demonstrations by our rishis and ancient sages in the last few centuries. Science has opened the floodgate of the usage of electrical and electromagnetic waves formation and movement in the atmosphere of the universe, but the exact knowledge of the complex formulations are yet to be discovered. However, laboratory test results are extrapolated to predict the macroscience involved with such natural systems.

'We all have heard how mental power can perform many apparently impossible tasks. This has been demonstrated by many people, but we cannot explain the exact science behind it.

'We have been working together on this subject for a long time independently. Today being the auspicious day of God, we have been placed together in His holy temple to focus our minds and knowledge in synergy for the revelation of the science behind the incarnation of human beings. In fact, we may not be far away from this mystery.

'Before we go deeper into the subject, it may be prudent to quickly scan through the information given by your sister and brother just now.'

The priest then goes over the summary of their discussion, which includes the following points:

- The atman or soul has the properties of electrical and electromagnetic energy and can propagate as radio waves.
- The smallest particle so far known to scientists is the Higgs boson, which is also known as the God particle.
- God is the source of all energy. Our life force is like electricity.
- The atmosphere accumulates electric charges. Electrical conductivity of Earth's atmosphere increases with the increase in elevation. With different macro- and microlayers on Earth, make formation of natural distributed capacitor banks.
- In an RC circuit, if AC voltage is applied, continuous charging and discharging takes place, and current leads the voltage phase.
- In an RLC circuit, the frequency at Inductive reactance = Capacitive reactance is known as resonant frequency.
- If the power source impedance matches the load impedance, maximum energy transfer takes place from the source to the load.
- The sources of electrical power and other electrical basic components like RLC are available in nature, in Earth's atmosphere, as well as in human beings.
- For telecommunication, we need a transmitter, wave medium, antenna, and receiver.
- There are two types of radio waves—surface and sky.

- The sky wave partly gets absorbed, partly refracts, and is partly reflected from the Earth's atmosphere to the receiver antenna on the Earth's surface.
- Audio and video frequency waves are modulated by high-frequency carrier waves at the transmitter end, and again the audio and video waves are demodulated from the reflected waves in the receiver end.
- Some waves do refract from the Earth's atmosphere—say, from the ionosphere to the magnetosphere.

26

Radio/Telecommunications

Both the physicist and the mystic want to communicate their knowledge, and when they do so with words their statements are paradoxical and full of logical contradiction.

Fritjof Capra

The western sky is saffron with the glow of the setting sun. It gives a holy look to the horizon before declaring the day's end. Their sister says that she will stay over at her maternal home for another day since their assignment demands more time.

The priest starts his daily evening rituals of praying before the deities. The holy lamp, the sweet scent of incense sticks make the ambience more spiritual. Some people have gathered in the temple to take part in the regular evening prayer. They slowly leave for their homes. God, at the prevailing hour of human aggression, may desire that some people should break His code on the mystery of reincarnation, which cannot be done without His will. Perhaps He is smiling from heaven and guiding them

towards the final destination. He is a silent witness to all
their research works.

The priest prepares tea in his tea maker and offers drinks
to the siblings. The tea rejuvenates them, and the younger
brother restarts his presentation.

He explains the sections or blocks a simple radio is built
with.

Part 1: Microphone

A microphone, commonly known as mic, is an acoustic-to-
electric transducer or sensor, which converts sound energy
into electrical signal. There are three types of microphones—
electromagnetic-induction type, capacitance type, and
piezoelectric type. All these are sensitive to either a change
in electromagnetic induction or a change in capacitance or
a change in air pressure due to the vibration of a membrane
caused by voice. The output of a microphone is connected to
a preamplifier to amplify the weak signal. The phenomenon
of impedance matching for transferring maximum power
from the source to an external load circuit has already been
discussed. For some microphones, this technique is adopted.

The simple functions of a microphone are:

1. Convert the acoustic waveform into electrical
    waveform of the same shape.
2. Amplitude of the wave becomes voltage, air particle
    motion becomes current, and electron plays the part
    of air particles.
3. The current's direction of flow changes with the
    cycles of compression or rarefaction, creating an
    alternating current.

4. The flow of electrons in a conductor is resisted by the resistance of the circuit.

5. In an AC system, the current is opposed by impedance. A simple microphone looks like,

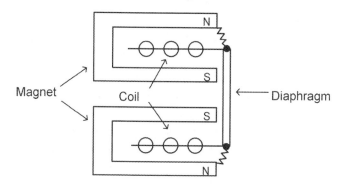

A typical microphone consists of a diaphragm placed in front of a magnet which is free to move or vibrate with sound pressure. A coil is attached with the magnet. Vibration of the membrane causes the coil to move within the magnetic field, which generates current to flow through the coil. The output of the coil is amplified for the purpose of final reproduction. Depending upon the use, the output electrical signal is amplified and filtered through electrical circuits.

At this time, the sister also shares her perception of the microphone. She says, 'There are many physiological systems that work on this principle. The simplest is our hearing system. Our ear consists of the pinna, the visible portion of the ear; the ear canal, which ends at the eardrum; and the eardrum, which is an airtight membrane. When sound waves reach the ears, the diaphragm starts vibrating, following the waveform of the sound which reaches the middle ear. The middle ear consists of a small air-filled chamber that is located medial to the eardrum. Within this reside the three smallest bones of our body, known as ossicles. They help in transmitting the vibrations from the eardrum to the inner ear. The middle ear is so constructed that it can overcome the impedance mismatch between air and water.

Sound waves enter the inner ear through an oval window, which separates the air-filled middle ear from the fluid-filled inner ear. There is again a round window, which is a membrane that finally allows for the smooth displacement of the inner fluid caused by the sound waves.

'The inner ear consists of the cochlea, which is a spiral-shaped fluid-filled tube. This is again divided lengthwise by the organ of Corti. This organ works as a mechanical-to-neural transducer or sensor. Inside this organ, the basilar membrane resides, which vibrates when sound waves enters the inner ear. This membrane is tonotopic. It is arrangement structurally, as in the auditory pathway, such that different tone frequencies are transmitted separately along specific parts of the structure. This means that each frequency has a characteristic place of resonance along it.

'Basilar membrane motion causes depolarisation of the hair cells, specialised auditory receptors, located within this organ of Corti. These cells release neurotransmitters at synapses within the fibres of the auditory nerve, which are action potentials. This is how the information of sound reaches our brainstem.

Then it is the priest's turn to explain the microphone. He says, 'It is really astonishing to understand the precision of a microphone that has been created by God while making human beings ages ago. One thing is important—this human microphone, we do not use it only for hearing. We depend on this vital instrument for discrimination of our thoughts as well. It picks up the waves of pleasure and pain that finally influence our emotions. Emotion is even important for the reproduction cycle of humans, where two souls remain in perfect synergy and create resonance for the conversion of a new soul.'

Part 2: Antenna

The younger brother starts explaining about the antenna, 'It is an electrical component which converts electrical signals into electromagnetic [EM] waves or vice versa, which are commonly known as radio waves. The antenna is installed after a transmitter or before a receiver. For transmission of radio waves, an alternating current oscillating at radio frequency is fed into the antenna, which then radiates the energy from the current as electromagnetic waves. The receiver antenna does just the opposite. It receives EM waves and converts it to AC. Radio waves carry signals as superimposed on it, which travels at the speed of light without much attenuation.

'A typical antenna consists of metallic conductors connected to a receiver or transmitter. When AC is passed through it by a transmitter, an oscillating magnetic field is created around it. The charge of the electrons creates an oscillating electric field along the elements. These varying fields radiate away from the antenna into space as moving, transverse EM field waves. Generally, there are two types of antennae—unidirectional and directional. The most commonly used antennae are whip antenna and dipole antenna. Nowadays, we see an extensive use of antennae in most of our electrical home appliances in addition to the radio and TV. Some parameters of an antenna—like gain (efficiency), resonance, impedance, and polarisation, etc.—are carefully chosen for a specific application. The resonant antenna is used for a particular resonant frequency. Impedance matching of antenna is sometimes used for maximising energy transfer. There is a special type of antenna, known as fractal antenna, which is present in our mobile phones. It is a kind that has a fractal, self-similar design to maximise its perimeter or length. It appears as the self-designed patterns of a leaf. This is very useful when a small-sized antenna is needed.'

After her younger brother, the sister starts explaining about the antenna, 'I have discussed this before, but I would like to explain it briefly once again. Every cell of the human gross body is capable of transmitting and receiving electrical signals and have identical DNA. A fully grown man has about 37 trillion cells. Every person has two genomes, one from the father and one from the mother. Our DNA acts as fractal antenna right from sperm and egg stage.

'DNA strands break and increase the stress protein levels due to EMF interactions. Scientists have considered antenna properties, such as electronic conduction, within DNA and its compact structure in the nucleus. EMF interaction with DNA is similar over a range of non-ionising frequencies, which are radio frequency and extra-low frequency ranges. There are similar effects in the ionising range but relatively more complex.

'The wide frequency range of interactions with EMF is a typical characteristic of fractal antenna, and DNA also has the same properties of electronic conduction and the shape of self-symmetrical pattern. Therefore, we can validly compare DNA to a fractal antenna. Dr Martin Blank, a professor at Columbia University and University of Cambridge, recognises that DNA, with its coil structure and sensitivity to EMF, acts as a fractal antenna. In fact, in nature, this kind of antenna is very common.'

The younger brother now starts explaining about the functions of the fractal antenna, 'While we are discussing fractal antenna in relation to DNA, I think I should provide you with some more information on small antennae and the antennae in nature.'

'The very small antennae not only involve resonance but also the magnetic and electric fields which surround the antenna. A resonating antenna becomes an efficient transmitter and receiver. Small resonant antennae in the atmosphere with huge EM fields act like long-wire antennas. The Earth's atmosphere can transmit EM waves, receive EM waves through natural antennae, and store electrical energy in its various layers.'

The priest shares his perception on the antenna. He says, 'It is really amazing to know that our DNA acts as fractal antenna. It is beyond my imagination to capture the size of a DNA and beyond my realisation how it acts as an antenna, but it does so. The atmosphere also acts as an antenna for both receiving and transmitting electromagnetic waves in addition to its ability to store electrical energy.

'The matching of impedance and initiation of resonance do occur in natural antennas as well for effective and efficient power transfer from a source to a receiver. This invisible phenomenon is occurring continuously in the Earth's atmosphere and above it. As long as the Earth exists, this will continue to happen. The poets described it as existence of life energy sailing in the sky like a glittering mass of stars and moons. Grandmas described it as an abode of all souls. The philosophers termed it as the green room of the karmic cycle. Some religious people consider it to be paradise. Scientists have looked at it for further and further exploration for ages. The common belief says that it is God's space, which may be the closest to reality as God is found in every form.'

> If you desire to be pure, have firm faith, and
> slowly go on with your devotional practices

without wasting your energy in useless scriptural discussions and arguments. Your little brain will otherwise be muddled. (Paramhamsa Shri Ramakrishna)

Part 3: Transmitter

The younger brother starts explaining about the transmitter.

This unit makes the audio and video signals suitable to transmit over long distances. The transmitter receives messages and encodes them into an alternating-current sine wave and transmits them as radio waves. The transmitter is attached to an antenna for the signals to be transmitted.

The method of superimposing a signal on to a sine wave is known as modulation. A radio transmitter is an electronic circuit which transforms electric power from a battery of electrical mains into a radio frequency alternating current, which reverses directions millions to billions of times per second. The energy in such a rapidly reversing current is to be carried by the radio waves. When it encounters another receiver antenna, the waves impose a similarly shaped radio frequency current but with less intensity in it.

A sine AC wave looks like this:

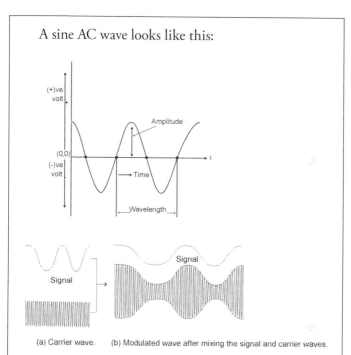

(a) Carrier wave.   (b) Modulated wave after mixing the signal and carrier waves.

In amplitude modulation, the amplitude of the sine wave (peak-to-peak voltage) changes. The sine wave produced by a person's voice is superimposed on the sine wave of the transmitter (oscillator) to vary its amplitude.

It is seen that the shape of the amplitudes of the carrier waves takes that of the signal, but the frequency of the carrier waves remain same. Therefore, the wave shape of the carrier frequency becomes that of the signal but the high frequency of the carrier remains unaltered. This high-frequency signal becomes suitable for long-distance transmission through an antenna. A radio transmitter is a device for generating radio frequency energy, which is controlled by the signals to be transmitted. In this case, the energy is controlled by the amplitude of the signal.

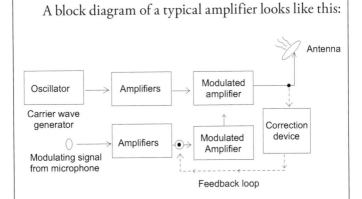

A block diagram of a typical amplifier looks like this:

Amplitude-modulated transmitter.

The performance of an amplitude-modulated transmitter can be improved in quality by introducing a negative feedback loop. A sample of an impure signal of the modulated amplifier is compared with the ideal signal. The output of the comparator is the distortion. The distortion is used in the feedback loop to correct the impurity of the output of the modulated amplifier. In this process, the signal to the antenna becomes ideal. This process eliminates amplitude, frequency, and phase distortion in the modulation and envelops and reduces hum (noise) substantially.

The transmitter output is a modulated electrical signal that is fed to the antenna, which converts it to an electromagnetic wave. It travels at the speed of light and, depending upon the antenna, propagates along the surface of the Earth or in the sky. Within the line of sight, waves can directly encounter the receiving antenna; otherwise, part of the wave can reflect or refract from the atmosphere and finally encounter the distant receiving antenna. Part of the wave may remain absorbed in the Earth's atmosphere or can travel further after refracting through the ionosphere to the magnetosphere and so on. The portion of the signal that gets absorbed in the atmosphere may encounter resonance frequency in some layers of the atmosphere and transfer energy into such sinks (capacitance or any other natural impedance). The shape of the wave, however, remains unaltered.

After her younger brother finishes the explanation, the sister explains the physiological transmitter.

Physiologically,, the human body is a micro powerhouse. It works as a broadcasting station. The body has complex electrical systems. Brain functions are predominantly controlled by electrical signals. The mind is very sensitive to frequency, which causes physical vibration. For example, fear is a heavy vibration with low frequency, whereas peace, love, and harmony cause light vibrations but at high frequency. More people become composed and attain consciousness, and the frequency of their energy level goes up. Self-worth and confidence radiate high-frequency field energy surrounding the physical body. Compassion, forgiveness transmute our energy and raise it to a high-frequency energy and vibration. Therefore, the key is, the higher the frequencies, the higher is the consciousness.

Human electrical energy is generated by a chemical process in nerve cells. Billions of nerve impulses travel throughout the human brain and nervous system. A nerve impulse is an electrical wave that passes from one end of a nerve cell to another. Each impulse is of the same size and termed as frequency impulse per second that carries information about the amplitude or intensity of the nerve signal. Neurons are the basic units of the nervous system.

Neurons send, receive, and interpret information from all parts of the body. Around our brain area itself, we have more than 100 billion neurons, and there are similar numbers in the nervous system tissues throughout the rest of the body.

Human beings have their own electromagnetic field. If electricity is passed through a metal wire, it produces an energy field around the wire, which is known as magnetic field. In a similar way, electric impulses in the brain and nervous system create human magnetic fields. There are billions of nerve impulses in the body, and these are constantly creating complex human magnetic fields. The human heart is also a source of electromagnetism. This can be detected even with the modern scientific instrument. There is a phenomenon called magnetic induction, which transfers energy from a source to another system.

Her younger brother explains it more clearly.

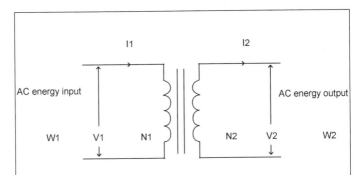

If the AC passes through the input coil, it produces an electromagnetic field around the output coil with the same frequency to the input coil and thereby causes the current to flow to the output coil also. To make it simple, the input coil's power superimposes some of its power to the output coil.

The relationships are:

$$\frac{N_1}{N_2} = \frac{V_1}{V_2} = \frac{I_2}{I_1}$$

V1: input voltage
V2: output voltage
I1: input current
I2: output current
N1: number of turns of the input coil
N2: number of turns of the output coil
Z1: impedance of the input coil
Z2: impedance of the output coil

W1 = *W2* + losses
W1: input power
W2: output power

Losses become minimum when *Z1* equals *Z2*. So output power *W2* becomes maximum when *Z1* equals *Z2*.

Impedance matching is done in an RLC circuit, and the human body also has natural RLC circuits and AC current. The frequency of the current can be manipulated with the help of the mind and intellect. Therefore, the body itself can act as a transformer and also as a radio transmitter.

During normal time, most of our energy is utilised for our day-to-day work. This keeps the electrical energy occupied in other actions like thinking, interacting, and other processes of the body for driving the vital organs.

But still some residual energy is induced by human beings around them even though the power output is very feeble. The people with very high level of consciousness and with acute control of the mind can maximise this power output and induce it on others who are in close proximity. Some of them can even transmit the same over long distances. The transfer of such energy can become instantaneous as these are electromagnetic waves that travel at the speed of light.

In our normal lives, we can even feel it. All of us must have experienced that we often feel very cheerful and comfortable in the presence of some people and become uncomfortable in the presence of some. It is indeed true that energy induced with the higher frequency of a wise man improves the frequency of their associates, and if impedance matching takes place, then the transfer of such power becomes maximum and makes us feel good. The transmission of such energy over a long distance is very much possible through the natural antenna of our body.

Such electromagnetic wave (radio wave) can travel not only through air and solid materials, but also through space. This energy is used by many people for the purpose of distant healing by generating and transmitting selective frequencies of the wave energy of the person who is applying it to the recipient or the patient.

This technique is very common nowadays. It needs practise to do so because the process demands storing extra electrical energy to transmit it over long distances. Very often, the person who transmits it feels exhausted after the act. I shall discuss later how the recipient receives the energy. This system of healing is much easier when the energy is transferred through touch, and then it works like direct connection or through surface transmission.

The priest now shares his perception. He says, 'I am spellbound to hear the presentations given by the brother and sister on the radio transmitter and its similarity with the inbuilt human transmission system. I have understood that humans can transmit their selected frequency-bound electromagnetic waves [radio waves] in the atmosphere and can also heal people. This process utilises impedance matching and thereby transfers maximum energy. I fully understand that human beings can alter the frequency and magnitude of their waves with the help of their minds and intellects.

'Now I am also able to understand that such energies can be converted into electromagnetic energy [radio energy] and transmitted over long distances, if practised. It seems your elder brother wants to say something on this subject.'

It is now time for the elder brother to give his verdict. He says, 'On principle, I agree with the presentation by my beloved brother and sister. Whatever has been said so far are scientifically proven and also have been physically demonstrated and experienced.

'I have two questions to convince myself further beyond any doubt.

1. For the transmission of audio or video signal, a high-frequency carrier wave is required. The frequency of our minds and intellects, I understand, is limited to 70 hertz. How do we modulate the same with high-frequency waves in our body, which is done by oscillator in case of radio circuits?
2. If healing a human body is possible with external energy of higher frequency, then can a simple radio oscillator be used externally?'

'Both questions are good and valid,' says the priest uncle, looking at the younger one.

The younger brother says, 'I shall try to answer the first question and our sister will respond to the second one.'

He stated that every atom in the universe has a frequency whether it is a steel structure or a grain of sand, a plant, or an organ of the body. Each cell resonates or vibrates at a specific frequency or oscillation. The body has different kinds of atoms, which contain photons, electrons, and overall, bioelectric energy that runs through it.

Georges Lakhovsky, an eminent Russian-born electrical engineer and French scientist, pointed out that all human cells are capable of reproduction and contain in their nuclei filaments of highly conductive material surrounded by insulating media. This filament, which may be the RNA–DNA complex, is always in the spiral form or helix—in other words, a coil. Therefore, each will act as a tuned circuit if its resonant frequency can be approximated by an external oscillating coil. I postulate that by exciting the nuclei with electromagnetic energy, a charge can be induced by the long-established principle of electromagnetic induction. Since each cell is an individual one and slightly different in dimensions, the excited wavelengths must be multiple and must span a broad frequency spectrum.

The existence of strong electric fields across cellular membranes is now accepted as basic fact of cell biology. (He hopes his sister will agree.) The fact is that the cells have internal electric fields. This had been demonstrated by Raoul Kopelman through his encapsulated voltage-sensitive dyes that were not hydrophobic and could operate anywhere in the cell as a nano voltmeter. Kopelman in Michigan presented his results at the annual meeting of the American Society for Cell Biology in the recent past. Daniel Chiu of the University of Washington in Seattle agrees that Kopelman's work provides proof that cells have internal electric field.

The 37 trillion cells in the body are like little wet cell batteries that operate ideally at a voltage of around 70 millie volts. The cell membrane acts as a one-way rectifier that converts the Earth's magnetic pulse into potential electrical energy which charges our cells. This energy drives cell metabolism and helps to enhance oxygenation, ATP (adenosine triphosphate, which works as primary energy units) production, overall absorption of nutrition and essential elements into the cell, and removal of wastes out of the cell. Without this energy, the cell voltage weakens, and we fall ill.

Lakhovsky postulated that all living cells have certain attributes which are normally associated with electronic circuits. These cellular attributes include resistance, capacitance, and inductance. These three electrical components, when properly configured (RLC circuit), cause the oscillation of high-frequency sine waves when sustained by a small and steady supply. The cells are influenced by both the internal and external sources of power; thus, each act as electromagnetic resonator, which is more commonly known as an oscillator. Lakhovsky revealed that not only do all living cells produce and radiate oscillations of very high-frequency waves but they also receive and respond to oscillations imposed by outside sources. The outside source of radiation or oscillations is the cosmic rays which bombard the Earth continuously. It has been observed by scientists that a cell of a healthy, normal person has a potential of 70 milli volts; of an aged person, 50 milli volts, and of an ill or weak cell, a potential of 15 milli volts.

As he finishes his answer to his older brother's questions, the younger brother says, 'I hope you have got the answer to your first question, my brother. An operating oscillator is sitting in each cell of our body.'

The sister then shares her opinion. 'Now there is no doubt that the human body acts as a high-frequency oscillator. Our cells respond to high frequencies externally impressed into our body. There is a direct relation between the voltage in each of our cell and their health status. Lakhovsky proved this with an oscillator made by him as well as by the one made by Tesla, which impressed energy with different frequencies to cure different diseases.

'This method is being used in some places, but scientists have apprehensions that the frequencies of the impressed energy, being man-made, and their effects on other organs are not yet fully established. So using this equipment is not very safe or popular. As such, human cell voltage measurement and interpretation to predict possible physical disorders are being widely used.'

The priest correlates the explanations given by the brother and sister. He says that he is happy that there has been consensus on this issue. The feedback and the induction systems has reminded him of the teachings of age-old sages.

Paramahamsa Shri Ramakrishna used to preach that for self-realisation, one needed to remain in the company of wise and self-attained people so that their good influences will have a positive impact on the seekers. Sonic waves also influence our natural frequency of mind and thought patterns. Chanting the *aum* mantra and similar other mantras as prescribed in our rituals have proved to have deep influences on our mental status. Our ancient rishis realise this phenomenon several thousand years ago, but we understood this only in recent years (and for the priest, it is today).

In the company of acclaimed persons, we can easily feel the state of happiness they enjoy in their lives. If we take feedback samples from our conscious mind and then process them with the help of our intellect through introspection and try to correct the same by discriminating, we shall get immense benefits. This is indeed the key mantra of meditation. The mind can be controlled in this process, but it needs continuous practice. This practice leads us to the gate of spiritual life for commencing the purification process of our souls. The electric waves of the mind and intellect can be compared with the modulating signal from the microphone (voice). The low-frequency signals are then superimposed on the high-frequency electromagnetic waves generated by the cells of the physical body.

Negative feedback occurs when some functions of the output of a system is fed back into the input with a reverse polarity, which tends to reduce the undesired effects in the input. On the other hand, positive feedback causes exponential growth or has a tendency to amplify. Negative feedback promotes stability and can produce equilibrium. (Negative feedback refers here with respect to polarity of signal and not conventional negativity of mind) This also occurs naturally within living organisms.

Positive feedback is used in electronic systems for boosting the gain of an electronic amplifier. The simple feedback system looks like this:

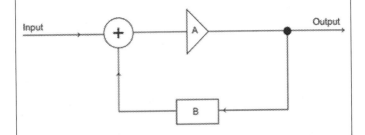

The positive feedback system in conjunction with negative feedback control is used in many electronic, chemical, and physical systems.

The sister then shares her knowledge on the feedback system. She says, 'May I now try to throw some light on feedback systems as I understand them physiologically?'

Their priest uncle says, 'Yes, by all means.'

She starts speaking, 'There are many positive feedback systems in our gross body, such as blood clotting, lactation, nerve signals, excitation and contraction, coupling of the heart, etc. When nerve signals are generated, the membrane of a nerve fibre causes slight leakage of sodium ions through sodium channels, causing a change in the membrane potential, which in turn causes the opening of channels and so on. So a slight leakage results in an explosion of sodium, which creates the nerve action potential. However, most of the positive feedback loops culminate in the release of countersignals that suppress or break the loop. I believe our uncle now must have got his answer regarding positive feedback in the human body.'

Their uncle then shares his understanding on the subject. He says, 'We have understood that the intellect and the mind are our inbuilt modulating electrical signal generators. We have within us amplifiers, oscillators, feedback systems for signal corrections, carrier wave generators, and finally, antennas in our bodies—even a single strand of hair can work as an antenna. Therefore, humans can act as the most sophisticated transmitter of electrical signals driven by electromagnetic waves into the atmosphere, and in reality, we do so. According to my understanding, through this process, we communicate with God. If we can purify our minds and intellects through the process of negative feedback, by comparing it with the real nature of our soul, it shall be possible to create resonance of our inner electrical signals or system matching with that of God. Such resonance in my opinion is the realisation of His absolute truth. If we compare the great experiences of the saintly people of the world, as expressed through their teachings or writings, we get the same message that you all have already explained scientifically.'

The elder brother agrees with the conclusion drawn by the priest.

Part 4: Receiver

The younger brother again starts with his presentation to demonstrate his knowledge of radio engineering. He says that the receiver is the most important section of the radio or video systems. It is the reproduction system. The performance output—that is, the end results—completely depends on the quality of the receiver.

Receivers in general consists of a radio frequency section, a mixer (or first detector) and local oscillator, an intermediate frequency amplifier, and finally, a loudspeaker or a monitor. A typical block diagram looks like this:

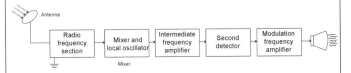

Radio receiver (amplitude modulated).

The radio frequency section provides coupling from the antenna at the input terminals of the receiver and also includes stages of tuned radio frequency amplification, which amplify the incoming signals before its frequency is changed (not shown separately).

The purposes of this section are:

1. to provide a good coupling between the antenna and the first section, which extracts maximum energy from the radio wave
2. to provide discrimination or selectivity against image and intermediate frequency signals, and since it is physically located before the mixer, it is also known as a pre-section.

The local oscillator and first detector section provide a frequency conversion system and convert the incoming signal to a predetermined fixed intermediate frequency normally lower than the signal frequency.

The intermediate frequency section consists of one or more stages of tuned amplifier having a bandwidth for the particular type of signal that the receiver is designed for. This section provides most of the receiver's amplification and selectivity. The second detector is normally a diode detector in the case of amplitude-modulated signals. It is followed by a modulation frequency amplifier to provide additional amplification and finally connected to a loudspeaker in the case of a radio or a monitor in the case of a TV.

Receiver characteristics are selected to govern the sensitivity, selectively, fidelity, and noise figure. Other qualities like power capacity, distortion, response to spurious frequencies and cross modulation effects, etc. are carefully filtered.

The sensitivity of a radio receiver is expressed in terms of voltage or power that is applied to the receiver's input to get a desired output. The sensitivity is expressed in terms of microvolts or decibels. The most important factor determining the sensitivity of a radio receiver is the gain of the intermediate frequency amplifier.

The diagram of a typical sensitivity curve is:

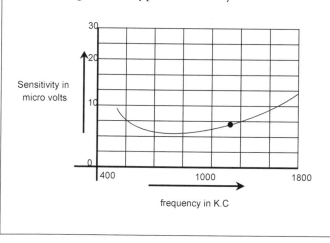

The selectivity of a radio receiver is the characteristic that determines the extent to which the receiver is capable of distinguishing between the desired signal and the signals of other frequencies. Selectivity is expressed as a curve that gives to the carrier (modulated in some standard way) the strength required to produce a given receiver output as a function of the cycles of resonance of the carrier, with the input at resonance taken as the reference. Selectivity of most receivers is determined largely by the characteristics of the intermediate frequency system.

A typical selectivity curve looks like this:

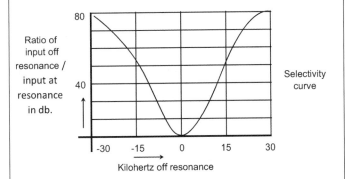

The noise figure of a receiver is a measure of the extent to which the noise appears in the receiver output. It determines the smallest power that may be received without being drowned. It represents one of the most important characteristic of receivers for high frequencies.

The antenna is coupled with the tuned input circuit to provide a substantially constant response over the tuning range of the receiver. The intermediate frequency amplifier is designed to provide a high gain per stage and a bandwidth slightly less than 10 kilohertz; the intermediate frequency is typically 455 kilohertz. Single-dial control of tuning is obtained by an arrangement that causes the local oscillator frequency and the resonant frequency of the tuned input circuit to maintain the proper relationship. The resonant circuits are typically tuned by variable capacitors.

'Oh, my brother! It appears you are taking our class on this subject,' interrupts the sister.

Her brother admits it with a proud smile and states that he has recently studied this subject so he can teach it like his professor. He acknowledges his overenthusiasm but tries to hide it by saying, 'Do you not agree with me that all the terminologies I used for the receiver—like sensitivity, selectivity, fidelity—have resemblance to conception or the physiological process of birth?'

The boy then says that all these functions have existed within human beings and can be correlated to us. He again starts to explain the simpler version of the radio receiver.

He says that, as a simple definition, a radio receiver is an electronic device which receives radio waves and extracts out the information from the same. When radio waves with information encounter an antenna, it converts the radio waves into electric current and feeds them into a receiver. It uses electronic filters to separate the desired signals from the undesired ones picked up by the antenna. An electronic amplifier is used to increase the power of the signal for further processing. Thereafter, the signal is demodulated to finally separate the audio or video signals and feed them into either a speaker or to a monitor.

A tuned radio frequency receiver consists of a radio frequency amplifier having one or more stages all tuned to the desired reception frequency. This is followed by an envelope detector, and thereafter an audio amplifier is coupled with it.

In the direct-conversion receiver, the signals from the antenna are only tuned by a single-tuned circuit before entering a mixer, where they are mixed with a signal from a local oscillator, which is tuned to the carrier wave frequency of the transmitted signal. The output of the mixer is thus an audio frequency signal which passes through a low-pass filter and into an audio amplifier. The output of the amplifier is connected to a speaker.

The waveforms of the signal input and output of an audio amplifier looks like this:

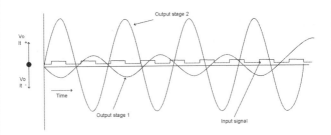

Below is a diagram of a simple AM radio block:

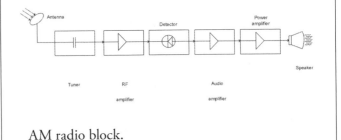

AM radio block.

The tuner of a receiver consists of an inductor and capacitor that are in parallel connection, where one of them is a variable. It creates a resonant circuit, which responds to an alternating current at one unique frequency. After combining with a detector, it is known as a demodulator. The function of a detector is to recover information contained in the modulated radio waves. The technique used for a detector is known as envelope detection. The simplest one is a diode detector. It consists of a diode connected between the input and output of the circuit, with a resistor and capacitor in parallel from the output of the circuit to the ground to form a low-pass filter. At appropriate values of the resistor and capacitor, the output of the circuit is nearly identical voltage, a shifted version of the original signal.

The diagram of a simple circuit is as follows:

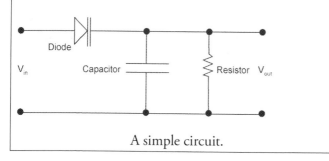

A simple circuit.

The sister then explains her understanding on this subject.

She says that the simple presentation is better for proper understanding of the radio receiver for a non-electronic person like her even though she believes now that all those electronics also reside within humans. After hearing from her dear brother, she has found that there are many commonalities between a radio receiver's process and a child's birth process. In the case of a radio receiver, the voice or picture—in other words, electrical and electromagnetic energy—is captured in an electronic box. In the case of a woman, energy (both electrical and electromagnetic) is conceived in the womb.

In some African countries, people believe the process of pregnancy begins from the time the lady starts dreaming to bear a child. In reality, our thought process has substantial influence on the process of the conception of a child. This is understood better when revisiting the physiological process of birth.

A woman has two small oval organs attached to either side of the womb, known as ovaries, which are packed with eggs. Every baby girl is born with 1 to 2 million eggs in her ovaries. The numbers decrease with ageing. During each menstrual cycle, one to three eggs start to reach maturity in one of the ovaries. The most matured egg is then released by a process known as ovulation. This is then sucked up by the opening of the nearest fallopian tube. An egg remains alive for about twenty-four hours after its release. To conceive a child, this egg needs to be fertilised by a sperm. If the egg in its journey to the uterus meets a healthy sperm, then the process of creating a new life begins.

On the other hand, only one sperm in general may become lucky to fertilise an egg.

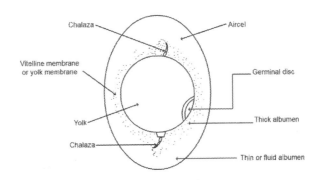

A human egg cell.

The size of an egg cell is about 150 microns. It is colourless and semitransparent.

The chalazae are two spiral bands of tissue that holds the yolk in the centre of the albumen. Chalazae look like twisted cords similar to antenna. Its structure can also form inductance and capacitance of an electrical circuit. Its spiral band can support the functions of an antenna.

The human spermatozoon looks like this:

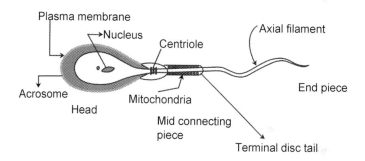

A human spermatozoon.

Sperm refers to the male reproductive cells. The human cell is a haploid, so its twenty-three chromosomes can join the twenty-three chromosomes of the female egg to form a diploid cell.

It consists of a head, which contains the nucleus; it has densely coiled chromatin fibres surrounded by an acrosome, which contains enzymes used for penetrating the egg. It has a long tail, which helps it to propel. The tail can act as an antenna during fertilisation. The sperm provides three essential parts to the oocyte (an immature ovum or egg)—the signalling or activating factor, the haploid paternal genome, and the centrosome, which is responsible for maintaining the microtubule system. It has been proved scientifically that the spermatozoa respond to an external electromagnetic field.

Sperm cells contribute about half of the nuclear genetic information to the diploid offspring. It is estimated that the DNA information in a single sperm contains about 37 megabytes' worth of data. Our DNA acts as fractal antenna, and it responds to electrical signal.

The human brain starts forming within three weeks of conception. Looking into the physiological aspects of humans and scientific aspects of the radio transmission process, it appears that there is a very close relation between the two.

The human body is capable of acting as both radio wave transmitter and receiver. Internally, the complete control systems are governed by electrical signals. Such electrical waves flow back and forth within the body. Even the elementary constituents of the physical body, our cells, are also capable of carrying electrical signals and interacting with external radio waves.

Our physical body is formed from the five basic elements (air, fire, water, ether, and earth) through a process of mutation and mutual combination. Physiologically, it is explained as cell combination and mutation. Each cell is the building block of the human body. Eggs and spermatozoa combine together, and then cell mutation takes place, similar to amplification. Is it not similar to the stages of amplification of a radio receiver at various phases? In an electronic amplifier, we cannot visualise mutation and the combination at the level of the boson or God particle or maybe at a still-subtler level not known to us. Hence, we cannot appreciate the phenomenon spontaneously.

A question may arise on what role the five elements play in forming of the physical body. Metaphysics can perhaps answer this question. The eggs and sperms are formed in the human body. The cells and the elementary components of cells consist of protons, electrons, and God particles. The egg and sperm have water, ether, earth, fire, and air in different forms—like food as a product of earth, water as a constituent of the body, oxygen taken from air for survival, fire in terms of heat, ether in terms of chemical composition, etc.

Hence, the perception of our ancient wise people can never be ignored. It is amazing how our rishis and wise people of the Earth visualized this percept or this secret of God thousands of years ago, something which science and technology discovered only in recent years.

We all have electronic components in our body, like a transmitter, receiver, oscillator, RC and RLC circuit resonators, detectors, amplifiers, both receiving and transmitting antennas, signal-carrying systems, power generators, wave generators, all desired control systems, feedback systems for purification of electrical signals, and finally, a single-tuning device, which is the mind.

Therefore, we can compare the human physical body and subtle body together to a complete communication system with both the transmitter and receiver residing in a single broadcasting station consisting of the body, mind, and intellect. Beyond us, there exists a bank of infinite giant broadcasting-cum-receiving station(s) in nature. The creator, operator, and manipulator of these stations is none other than the Almighty. In fact, the process of conception, birth, and then growing up to an adult is similar to the process of receiving antenna signal to the final power amplification of a very accurate radio broadcasting station.

The unperceived area that needs to be examined is what happens in between the transmitter and the receiver. In the case of radio communication, the transmitter is located at a place from where radio signals are generated and emitted from an antenna. The radio waves travel in the sky and get deflected in the atmosphere.

The younger brother says, 'As electromagnetic waves interact with objects and the medium through which they travel while they are travelling, they can be reflected, refracted, or diffracted. In this way, they change their direction. Mostly, interaction takes place in the ionosphere. There are various layers in Earth's atmosphere, like D, E, F-1, and F-2. When the waves encounter the layers, all stated phenomenon take place. What precisely happens in the atmospheric layer? Radio signals are modulated with very high-frequency carrier waves. Partly, the waves, depending upon their energies, get absorbed in the atmosphere. Such absorbed energy remain in layers according to their qualities. Some get refracted and are reproduced through the radio set by proper tuning. The portion which gets absorbed remains in the atmosphere in a layer where impedance matching takes place. As we know, the atmospheric layers have inherent impedances because of different layer formations. The part of the carrier waves which gets absorbed maintains the shape of signal waves. Depending upon the quality of such signals, they form layers in the atmosphere.'

The priest, taking a clue from the young scientist, says, 'I believe that our vital life energy or life force must also travel in the same way because it is the same electrical energy. We have understood the science behind our energy radiation from our physical body and the way in which electromagnetic waves are modulated. In the human body, the energy of our minds and intellects, which have fundamental waveforms and harmonics, are essentially low-frequency electrical signals. The same are modulated by the electromagnetic high-frequency carrier waves of the cosmic world or by the internal high-frequency EM waves of cells, which cause the transmission of EM energy to surround our body or to travel to a distance from our body depending on its strength.

'Have you ever noticed that under particular conditions, our energy level can reach a higher level? There are some sports which demonstrate this phenomenon—for example, boxing, karate, etc. This unperceivable power comes by bringing the frequency of the mind to resonant frequency. Therefore, it can be said that the human energy can be transformed into electromagnetic energy through the electronic and physical components of our bodies.'

At this, the priest presents two possibilities:

1. On death, the universal vital energy (with atman or soul), together with impurities, leaves the physical body as jivatman. The impurities are the imposed qualities in terms of frequencies and magnitudes being imposed by us during our lifetime. During death, the subtle body leaves the physical body for a higher energy source depending on its strength. The energy, after leaving the dead body, travels in the atmosphere at the speed of light, similar to the radio waves.

   Our internal broadcasting station, which is a receiver-cum-transmitter, is always in active mode and is continuously communicating with the broadcasting stations of the atmosphere. It draws vital energy from the specific layer to which its receiver is tuned, following the principle of impedance matching.

Through God-gifted ability, we can change the quality of our vital energy with the help of the intellect and mind. Therefore, the source and its associated quality can be chosen by us as per our desire. All our actions and reactions are then guided by the quality of our vital energy or jivatman.

2. Upon death, when the vital energy leaves the physical body (like the disconnection of a power source for a radio), it gets accumulated in a layer in the atmosphere in accordance with its quality. The higher the level of consciousness, the higher will be the frequency, and correspondingly, the higher will be the layer.

It travels to the higher level of atmosphere until the resonance occurs at some layer depending on its inherent quality. The moment it meets an energy level of resonance condition, maximum energy transfer takes place in that layer, as per the scientific law. Formation of layers take place as per the quality of energy (electrical as well as electromagnetic) in the atmosphere. Those layers of atmospheres contain the vital energy required for the existence of human beings. This is true for all kinds of species. The only difference is that the qualities of such vital energies and their locations or layers are different for different species. The diverse interactions among the five gross elements (tattvas) which forms the physical body are known as prakriti (natural forces).

The information or data of the radio signals remain in the carrier waves of the radio system. Similarly, our vital energy retains a large amount of data, which gets accumulated in layers matching its resonant conditions.

As per the law of conservation of energy, after death, the physical body is broken down into its five basic elements. The water content of the body is released as water, residue ash are left as earth or gets absorbed by earth, fire leaves as heat, air leaves as gases, and finally, the vital energy leaves as ether. Hence, the balance between mass and energy takes place.

On the other hand, the brothers and their sister have presented beyond any doubt that the human body acts as a radio receiver cum transmitter. It has all the required inbuilt electronic components.

The atmosphere of the Earth is equipped with all the required equivalent natural, electronic, and electrical components necessary for energy transmission. The natural transmitters are distributed in the entire atmosphere, like the radio stations of the Earth. The vital-energy waves with different qualities are transmitted back to Earth in a continuous process. The amazing process and steps of human birth are not unknown to us now since their sister has already explained. DNA contains fractal antenna. Sperm and egg also contain antenna. Both of them are capable of transferring or converting cosmic electromagnetic energy and radio waves into electrical energy. DNA sitting inside sperms are capable of collecting the information, memories and, even instructions required for reproduction of identical species at a focal point.

The tattvas (five elementary principles) are flowing around aimlessly in space. They are independent forces without any visible effect. If there is a concentration at one point, then something qualitatively new is produced. However, first, an assembly point must be formed so that the energy can be focused and assimilated. The sperm and egg capture the physical part of the reproduction system. The quality of the receptor or the receiver is built up as induced by the quality of the mind and intellect of the individual. The same is true for the eggs of women. But the vital difference is that the egg has another important filter, which is extremely precise, that chooses only one out of several millions sperms to enter its shell and get the blessing of a human life. One can now imagine how precious human life is. Thinking processes is finally the outcome of electrical signals being generated by the mind and intellect. The qualities of the same are unique for each thought.

A process of synergy takes place, which creates the focusing of energy between two individuals, enabling the sperm to fertilise the egg. These additional energy sources ensure the absorption of demodulated energy as per the quality of DNA of the parents. The DNA of the newly born baby depends solely on the quality of the DNA of the parents, which is the scientific principle of impedance matching and is followed by resonance.

The process of birth, death, and reincarnation is now believed to be a physiological process having two components. One part is physical, which is visible, and we can sense it with our normal sense organs. The second part is energy transformation, which remains subtle.

The priest says, 'This process of conversion of energy into mass with the help of the mind and intellect or other words by the combination of manomoya kosa and vignanamaya kosa had been demonstrated by Paramahamsa Ramakrishna by creating the physical form of Maha Kali as per his perception. There are countless numbers of such demonstrations by various saints of our beloved planet. Many saints could replicate their physical bodies at distant places by transmitting their mental energy through EM waves.

'All perceptible things of the universe are creations of God. Some we understand, and the rest we do not. Human beings are the privileged and crowned class of His creation. We remain as creatures for His excitement and entertainment. He observes the inquisitiveness and indulgences of His loved ones in our whys and hows, *my* and *mine*, I-ness and my-ness.'

27

Humble Submission

What is that we human beings ultimately depend on? We depend on our words. We are suspended in language. Our task is to communicate experience and ideas to others.

Niels Bohr

In the quest of searching the rationalities behind the teachings of the ancient wise sages and great personalities of the world, a possible scientific explanation of birth, death, and reincarnation has been placed before the valued readers.

'If the readers agree with this principle, we may proceed further to examine whether this process is valid for other aspects of gospels as suggested by the prophets, great philosophers, and seers.'

'Individual atman or spirit or soul is immortal. It cannot be destroyed, and it is part of the universal soul. It can only be given a form with external quality. Universal energy is constant and cannot be created or destroyed. It can only be transformed from one form to the other. The universe solely consists of waves of motion.'

'The soul or atman of an individual takes shape in accordance to the mind and intellect of each person. The subtle energy being held by an individual can be influenced by the mind and intellect of the individual. The quality of the subtle energy (both average and instantaneous) of individuals is determined by its magnitude and frequency. It follows the universal law of $E = mc^2$. Its elementary particle is known as the God particle because the absolute one is unknown to scientists as of now. The scientists could only solve the mystery up to Higgs boson. By altering the associated parameters of energy, it is possible to influence the quality of the same.

'Traditionally, it is explained to children that upon death, our beloved persons go to the sky and become stars and that after some time, they return back to earth. The subtle energy travels to the upper layers of the atmosphere according to its quality. It resides there until it is captured by the antenna and reproduced by the physiological receiver.

"As we sow, so we reap." It is the karmic cycle through which we undergo the various changes of our lives depending upon the manner we shape up our subtle vehicle with the help of the mind and intellect. Even though paramatman (universal energy) remains uncontaminated, jivatman is not.

'We prepare the quality of our jivatman and associated transmitter during our lifetime through our karma. Every action and reaction has its absolute frequency, wavelength, and amplitude, which influences the electrical parameters and our internal wave, thereby preparing a unique radio transmitter having a specific bandwidth. The bandwidth of our transmitter's outputs can be altered by our thoughts.

'We transmit our pure atman with harmonics created by our minds and intellects (jivatman) on the energy of a carrier wave having the carrier frequency matched for a specific layer of the atmosphere, where it is demodulated following the principle of radio wave transmission and reception. Good *karma* has specific bandwidth so does bad karma.

'Human beings are unique creatures. During one's lifetime, through the inbuilt receiver and feedback system, one can continuously improve one's inbuilt transmitter and other inherent electrical or electronic components to make our jivatman suitable to launch in the ultimate orbit of paramatman, which is pure bliss. Once the jivatman is launched in a better orbit, its return is assured in a better womb.

'By means of continuous improvements through karmic cycle, we may get liberation (moksha). The best recipients of atman (through jivatmans) are human beings, who can rapidly improve the parameters of their own receivers and transmitters for achieving improvements.

'By means of continuous improvement of jivatman, the soul may become so pure that a stage may be achieved where there shall be hardly any human beings present on Earth who have a receiver to tune the quality of energy of such a highly pure soul. On the death of such a personality, their energy may not even reflect or refract back or get absorbed in the Earth's atmosphere. It may travel to the atmosphere of another planetary system.

'The more the purification of the soul (jivatman) is done, the more the possibility of its returning to the earth through transmigration is reduced. Eventually, the liberation of jivatman takes place, and individual human life rests in eternity as jivatman dissolves in paramatman.

'All saints of the world from time immemorial have been preaching to us about the absolute and universal truth of life, which they realised from a higher level of mental consciousness. They achieved it by hard practice, dedication, and introspection. They developed the desired level of energy by properly activating the sources of hidden treasures present within their bodies and minds. These sources are available in all human beings, but they need to be awakened by means of focused mental exercise. This has a striking similarity to the method of changing the electrical parameters of receivers and transmitters and thereby tuning to a desired energy band.

'The selfless, wise people, for the benefit of mankind, shared their knowledge and experiences through preaching, writing holy books, discourses, etc. in all ages and in all countries. If the contents of those are properly analysed, we will find that such teachings are the same and conform to the universal truths as governed by the laws of God.

'The law of gravity, the law of conservation of energy, properties of basic constituent of the Earth—like air, water, fire, earth, and ether—can never be changed. It is He who has created these for our planet, and it shall remain so as long as our planet exists.

'Science may discover some of the existing laws and may uncover the internal relationship of such laws but can never create any new element other than those that have already existed since the inception of our planet.'

Slowly the evening sun starts setting in the western horizon. The domestic animals and birds starts returning to their homes.

The four scientists has spend their entire day in the laboratory of God to understand His complex science. In fact, the research has not been done in a day, nor has it happened by design. It has happened because of prefixed destiny.

The priest suggests that they should take a short break. The sister goes back home and again brings some coffee with her. They have steaming hot coffee, which stimulated them. After finishing the coffee, they start getting ready for the next session.

The elder brother agrees that the principle of radio and telecommunication and the process of transmigration leading to reincarnation are similar. But the arbitrator brother questions, 'How do we know whether reincarnation is real or not?'

The priest replies, 'There are countless evidences throughout the world of people recalling the events of their previous lives. The veracity of the same had been established by several groups of people. Reincarnation is an established fact. Dr Ian Stevenson's work, which is an example for the Western world, is the proof of reincarnation. Dr Stevenson, a medical doctor and former head of the department of psychiatry at the University of Virginia, USA, has devoted forty years to the scientific documentation of past-life memories of children from all over the world. He had over three thousand cases in his files. Many people, even sceptics and scholars, agree that such cases offer the best evidence of reincarnation.

'In India, Swami Abhedananda, a direct disciple of Paramahamsa Ramakrishna and associate of Swami Vivekananda, in his book *The Life Beyond Death*, clearly explains the evidence regarding the veracity of reincarnation.

'The world's greatest philosophers, rishis, saints, and prophets have claimed the truthfulness of reincarnation through the ages. Therefore, this query shall not be valid any more for the subject. What remains unanswered is the process of reincarnation, which we have been trying to establish with the most acceptable logics for appreciation of the concerned certifying authorities. In fact, a complex process can be understood better if the same is broken down into several simple systems and then analysed separately. We have so far done the same from the beginning before we could reach the possible conclusion of the scientific mystery of rebirth.'

The umpire's next question is 'How can consciousness be related to electrical activities?'

This question is very quickly picked up by the younger brother. He says, 'Consciousness is one's awareness of existence, thoughts, sensations, feelings, internal knowledge, concerns, interests, etc. Therefore, the consciousness remains in the state of subjective and subtle matter and is confined within the experience of one person. To understand this, we must know how the conscious mental state is related to our physical body? Is it merely an activity of the brain? What is the philosophy of the mind and its relationship with metaphysics?

'There are two traditional competing thoughts. One is materialism, and the other is dualism. While studying the gross body, we have stated that our minds are an outcome of neural activities that occur in the brain. The intellect or consciousness is non-physical and has been classified as a subtle body. However, some philosophers believe that consciousness is a neurophysiological matter. Therefore, a gap remains unfilled over the ages. The Vedas, Upanishads, Gita, Bible, Quran, etc. were composed at a time when there was no knowledge of various terminologies of modern science. Whatever was considered as non-physical in those days were later explained by scientists as physical matter. They established the relationship with other physical matter. To understand it more clearly, let me give an example.

'The believer of dualism is not able to explain how a non-physical substance can interact with the physical body. In terms of Indian philosophy, how prana binds or acts as glue between the physical body and the subtle body (atman) is the basic query of the general population of the Western world. Some of the Western philosophers, like G. W. Leibniz, Immanuel Kant, and even Sigmund Freud believed that consciousness needs to be viewed separately from physical matter. The definition of physical phenomenon over time has changed. We believe as facts those things which physics can explain in terms of physical phenomenon. The movements of God's particles are now within the ambit of physical domain. We still do not know about the existence of finer particles beyond boson. In several thousand years, the best of the scientists all together could explore only a very insignificant part of the universe. But the undisputed fact is that science still remains far behind in uncovering the major acts of God and His finest creations.

'Keep an infant in a closed black-and-white room for some years. Do not expose the baby to the outside world up to some years. Then one day, expose that baby and show it a red rose. It won't be able to recognise the matter as red rose. A red rose is named based on its colour. We learn it from our childhood and embed it in our memory. But from the infant stage, we have the ability to know it through neurophysical concepts or by actually undergoing the relevant experience of using our phenomenal concepts. The property of conceptualisation is inherent in the baby. Animals also have brains. We may understand their brain functions physiologically, but we are unable to fully comprehend how animals' brains undergo the developmental process. It is precisely here that the understanding of the concept of consciousness of a person arises.'

'Yes, my brother,' continues the sister, 'there is a gap between physiology and the understanding of subjective phenomenon of consciousness, which is inherently a first-person activity. Some knowledge about consciousness is limited to first-person knowledge. Even modern science cannot explain it. Our ancient saints, yogis, and rishis taught us that we can access consciousness through introspection, whereas science has taught us that our access to the brain is through spatial senses of our sense organs.'

She further explains, 'Two scientists, Francis Crick and Christ of Koch, in their works (1990–2004) claimed that our mental state becomes conscious when large numbers of neurons fire in synchrony and all of them have a frequency within the range of 35–75 hertz. But this correlation alone does not establish an acceptable theory for consciousness. This only gives information on the mental status.

The sister says, 'I would try to connect the two processes that we have discussed before. One is about DNA, and the other is about transformation of energy as explained by our beloved brother. If these two processes are combined together, we may get a possible explanation of consciousness.'

'The genome is the complete set of genetic information of human beings. This information is encoded as DNA sequences. DNA contains all the information that are available at a source, from where it receives its energy, when it acts as a receiver. In fact, human DNA is a biological Internet and is far superior to the one artificially made for our use. The sources of such energy automatically get selected by the parent according to their own DNA and associated with fractal antennas. This process is exactly similar to that of a radio receiver.

'It is estimated that the DNA information in a single sperm contains about 37 megabytes' worth of data. DNA can transmit electrical power. The sperm also has antenna, as explained before, and is capable of transferring and converting natural electromagnetic energy into electrical energy, which eventually can act as a driving force for the mind. It has been observed by researchers that DNA can be influenced and reprogrammed through specific voice commands and frequencies. The Russian biophysicist and molecular biologist Pjotr Garjajev explained the vibration behaviour of the DNA. He could modulate certain frequency patterns on to a laser ray and, with it, could influence the DNA frequency and thereby the genetic information itself. Since the basic structure of DNA alkaline pairs and language are of the same structure, no DNA decoding is necessary.

'One can simply use the words and sentences of a human language. This was experimentally proved. Living DNA substance in living tissue will always react to language-modulated radio waves if a proper frequency is used. We experience it in our daily lives, affirmations, mental trainings, hypnosis, etc. It can have strong effects on us, including our bodies.

'All thought processes are actually electrical waves of different qualities with respect to shape, magnitude, and frequency. Wave shapes are generally formed because of the combination of different harmonics generated from the magnitude and basic frequencies of the energy. The total area of such wave represents the total energy content within it. Our central nervous systems, CNS, have two types of cells—neurons and glia. These two cells give us our ability to act physically through our minds and sense organs. Neurons are the basic information-processing cells in our central nervous system. The function of neurons is to receive input information from other neurons, process them, and then finally send the output information to other neurons. This is similar to the baton, which passes the protocol of distributed digital control system in our modern technology. The connections between neurons, through which information flows, are known as synapses. All our motor information, sensory information, and cognitive information are processed by different types of neurons. To get a dimension of this amazing network, it may be remembered that about 10,000 types and approximately 200 billion neurons exist in brain alone. Each of those is connected to other neurons from 10,000 to 200,000. Glia cells support our neurons. Glia cells are forty to fifty times more in number than neurons.

'The incoming signals from other neurons are received through dendrites, some sort of information conduits which could be several thousand for each neuron, whereas the outgoing signal to other neurons flows through only a single axon. The cell body of a neuron is known as soma, which is a metabolic control centre for neurons.

'The fast long-distance communication of neurons is done through electrical signals, which are known as action potentials. The system is known as conduction. This is how a neuron communicates with its own terminal via axon. Communication between neurons is achieved at synapses by the process of neurotransmission.

'To start conduction, an action potential is generated near the axon. The action potential is an electrical signal with inherent qualities of frequency and magnitude, waveforms, etc. This occurs because of the movement of electrically charged particles (ions). The protein members of a neuron act as a barrier of ions.

'Normally, the membrane potential of a neuron is about 70 mille volts. Electrical signal is generated, which is then propagated along the axon until it reaches its terminal. This phenomenon is called conduction. Therefore, neurons send their outputs to axon terminals and to other neurons

---

or effectors (muscle cells). At electrical synapses, the output will be the electrical signal itself. At chemical synapses, the output will be the neurotransmitter.

'Neurotransmission or synaptic transmission is accomplished by the movement of electrical signals or chemical signals across synapses. Electrical signals carried by axons are action potentials. A momentary change (–70 millivolts to +30 millivolts) in electrical potential on the surface of a cell, specially of a nerve or muscle cell, occurs when it is stimulated, resulting in the transmission of an electrical impulse. At the synaptic knob or terminal, the action potential is converted into a chemical message, which in turn interacts with the recipient neuron. Presynaptic knob is the transmitting side, also known as synaptic knob, and postsynaptic knob is the receiving side (soma, dendrite, effectors). Synaptic knobs contain much membrane, which contains the neurotransmitter. The action potentials arriving at the synaptic knobs trigger the release of the neurotransmitter into the synaptic cleft.

'The time involved between these two actions is only about one to two milliseconds. Action potentials arriving at synaptic knobs open calcium channels in its membrane, which causes an inward movement of calcium ions. The calcium ions then trigger the release of the neurotransmitter from synaptic vesicles into the synaptic cleft. The synaptic vesicles fuse with the presynaptic membrane during this process. The membranes of old vesicles become part of the presynaptic membrane, and new vesicles pinch off from an adjacent area of the membrane. These new vesicles are subsequently refilled with newly synthesised or recycled neurotransmitters. Released neurotransmitters diffuse across the narrow synaptic cleft. At the postsynaptic membrane, neurotransmitter molecules bind to membrane-bound receptor molecules with recognition sites specific for that neurotransmitter. The binding of the neurotransmitter to the receptor triggers a postsynaptic response specific for that receptor.

'These responses can be either excitatory or inhibitory, depending upon the properties of the receptor. If receptor stimulation results in the postsynaptic membrane becoming more electrically positive, it is an excitatory postsynaptic potential. Excitation or inhibition depends on the properties of the receptor and not on the neurotransmitter. Receptors coupled with sodium or calcium channels are excitatory and produce a depolarisation of the postsynaptic membrane, whereas receptors coupled with chloride or potassium channels are inhibitory and produce a hyperpolarisation of postsynaptic membrane. Such receptors coupled with ion channels are known as ionotropic receptors. Synapses are junction complexes between the presynaptic neuron and the postsynaptic neuron. These chemical synapses are part of a very adaptable and flexible communication system. These are dynamic structures that are capable of changing their molecular properties with changing circumstances.

'In electrical synapses, the presynaptic and postsynaptic members are partially fused. This allows the action potential to cross from the membrane of one neuron to the next without the help of neurotransmitters. Electrical synapses do not have much flexibility as chemical ones but act much faster.

'Summarising, the basic functioning of the human brain is dependent on the neurons or brain cells. A neuron is an electrically excitable cell which processes and transmits information by electrochemical signalling. The neurons, unlike other cells, do not die or do not divide but remain intact during their entire lifespan, if not lost. Our memory is the strength of synaptic connections between the brain cells. This strength can be altered by our lifestyle and eventually by our minds.

'We, with our preliminary knowledge, have tried to understand the elementary functions of the brain, communication protocols of our electrical signals, formation of memories, and commanding processes to various organs.

'Still a question remains unanswered. Who triggers the voltage-gated ion channels to cause the action potential, and who drives it?

'There is no doubt that the mind is superior to any other organs, including the sensory ones. We should always remember that it is the mind which stimulates our brains to act. All good or bad intentions first arise in the mind, which is then discriminated with intellect, senses, and old memories. Thereafter, the action potential is stimulated by the mind.

'Therefore, the next important function is the mind. The human mind can be classified in three states—the conscious mind, the subconscious mind, and the unconscious mind. The conscious mind keeps a person aware of the status of every moment. The subconscious mind consists of accessible information if we focus on the same. However, the degree of desired focus varies with the status and location of subconscious memories. The unconscious mind consists of primitive, instinctual wishes and the information that we cannot access. During birth and in our childhood, we unknowingly acquire huge amounts of memories and experiences that remain buried in the unconscious mind and some in the subconscious mind. These unconscious and subconscious forces drive our behaviours.

'The human mind, along with the brain, deals with memories and the ability to act, read, command, build logics, etc. for the physiological body. The brain alone can potentially be understood as an information-processing and control system. To a large extent, this statement is correct for other animals as well. Internal parameters of the body—like temperature, salt content, water content, blood glucose level, etc.—are also controlled by the act of the brain, which is known as homeostasis. Homeostasis gets significantly influenced by the mind. The system acts on the engineering principle of negative feedback.

'Again a question arises. Who manages this super computer?

'Genes, as we understand, determines the general formation of the brain and also determines how the brain reacts to experience. Scientists around the world are still searching for the physiological basis of human intelligence. The only consensus is that intelligence depends not just on the efficiency or power of various brain regions but also on the strength of the connections that link those.

'Richard J. Haier, a professor in the School of Medicine at the University of California–Irvine, uses brain imaging to study higher cognitive processes. He opines, 'These early attempts to find the physiological basis of intelligence were limited by a lack of modern technology. With the advent of modern medical imaging, it becomes possible to look for more subtle differences than you might find with gross anatomy.

'It is quite evident that science so far could not clearly explain the process of intellect. The brain has a natural tendency to ignore most of the information captured by the various sense organs while storing them in memory. Only the ones which are memorable or liked by the mind are stored for future reference. Therefore, a question arises. Who in the background prompts the mind to focus on certain selected information? It is believed that the human brain is a very powerful and sophisticated computer. However, the output of the same solely depends on the user. The mind is the controller, and the intellect is the ultimate user of this computer.

'Human intelligence is still a mystery to scientists. Nevertheless, scientists over the ages have been trying to know more about intelligence, with the ultimate aim of being able to improve the same so that it can be used for development of our society in a better way. The word *intellect* is viewed differently by scientists and philosophers. The scientists see it as a function of physiological and neurological act, whereas the philosophers visualise it as a link between the human soul and the mind. It is superior than the mind. The intellect can be classified in two parts—active and passive. The passive one is the potential of the individual's intellect, and the active one is the segment that the individual uses for commanding or controlling the mind.

'Hindu philosophers describe human intellect as a chariot for easy understanding of the relationship among the body, mind, and intellect. On a chariot, there are five horses, a driver, and a passenger. The horses are the sensual organs, the chariot is the body, the reins and bridles represent the mind, the driver is the intellect, and the passenger is the soul, who does not have any knowledge or control over the decisions the intellect makes. But because of the presence of the passenger, the driver is driving the chariot, and because of him only the final destination is known. The soul has a natural and continuous desire for divine unity; it is always in a state of divine bliss. But the intellect distorts the form of the soul in the same way a small amount of dye changes the colour of water even though its constituent remains same. It is the same principle involved in how the waveform of the carrier is changed by the signals to be transmitted by a broadcasting station. The subtle discontentment of the human gives commands to the driver of the chariot to go to a particular direction.

'Having understood to some extent the relationship among the body, mind, intellect, and soul, we may now look at the most elementary particles of the systems that drive all of us and the infinite universe. It is comprehended that the entire universe comprises of energy and matter. It is more unknown than is known. Scientists have estimated that about 68 per cent of the universe consists of dark energy and about 27 per cent consists of dark matters. All normal matters are what have been observed by our instruments so far and, when put together, are not more than 5 per cent. The estimated diameter of the observable universe is about 93 billion light years, which is practically infinity for us. The entire universe consists of three principles—space, time, forms of energy (including matter and momentum)—and the physical laws that relate them. Scientists could identify some of the physical laws and constants, like Plank's constant, gravitational constant, several conservation laws (conservation of energy, momentum, angular momentum, charge, etc.).

'The elementary particles of this universe are quarks, leptons, and those that interact via the Higgs boson. Science—in particular, quantum physics—suggests that everything in the universe is energy. The universal law states that everything in the universe moves and vibrates at some speed or the other. Everything we see is vibrating at one frequency or the other. Everything has its own vibration frequency (fundamental frequency). We did not believe these until science proved it to satisfy our very limited senses.

We initially disbelieved the opinion of Guglielmo Marconi, Nikola Tesla, and Dr J. C. Bose's work on the radio until it was demonstrated to our sense organs.

'Our ancient wise forefathers walking through very hard paths had perceived such universal laws and imprinted those in their works with their own and known manuscripts. They realised such truths through their extraordinary intellect and wisest consciousness. In India such realisations of the universal laws had been very well documented in the Vedas, Upanishads, epics, and other holy books. The matrix of causes and effects of such laws in human lives are very well versed in such holy books all around the world. Those laws and rules are universal and are the true dharma of mankind. Those had never changed and shall never change over time as long as our planet exists. The man-made dharma is only ways of living lives as per the convenience of societies and groups of people.

'It is only He who is the architect, creator, operator, manipulator, programmer, and manager of the universe, including the giant and supercomputer with infinite dimension.

The elder brother has a thoughtful question. 'The sun emits energy from its source every moment to Earth. How does the same return back or gets recycled? If a departing soul from a body returns in a new human body, then what is the source of population explosion in this world? That energy gets absorbed in various layers of the universe, in all objects of Earth. Some get reflected or refracted, and finally, on the decay of such objects or during transformations, it returns to its source. A perfect heat balance takes place in the universe.'

'These are good questions,' says the younger one, and then he started clarifying to the elder brother. 'How does one radio or television broadcasting station transmit a programme, and how is the same received by the ever-increasing receivers of the million listeners or viewers?

'The Earth's atmosphere has enormous space to capture energy of souls at its various infinitesimally small cells in accordance to the quality of the departed soul. It is stored in bandwidth as per its qualities. Therefore, in general, the precise individuality is lost due to homogenous mixing to our perception. On transmigration, the exact memory is lost, but the quality of the source energy is retained by way of the primary subconscious, which the philosophers termed as the karmic cycle.'

The elder one asked another valid question, 'Why are two children of the same parents sometimes different in nature?

The younger brother replies, 'It can happen because of the different states of mind of their parents at the time of conception. It is generally seen that twins are validly alike. As per the myths, it is easier to please Lord Shiva than to please the goddess Kali. How can it be explained? What happens after liberation?

'The energy resides in space in layers according to their inherent qualities (frequency and amplitude). While cleaning or filtering our own energy, we may strike the natural frequency of the layer of Lord Shiva before the goddess Kali. This early resonance with Shiva Shakti may be recognised as relatively easier to invoke Lord Shiva.

'Our rishis and ancient philosophers had visualised these energy layers in fourteen levels. The atman, originating from Satyaloka in the form of God, settles in seven higher and seven lower *lokas* (layers) depending on the impurities. The seven higher lokas are Bhurloka (Earth), Savarloka (heaven), Maharloka (saints), Janarloka (beings of light),

Taparloka (knowledge and wisdom), and finally, Satyaloka (absolute truth). The seven lower lokas are Atla, Vitala, Sutala, Rasatala, Talatala, Mahatala, and Patala.

'It is really amazing that the above bandwidths of energy were visualised by our ancient philosophers thousands of years before our modern science could discover them. Each of the seven upper layers has a corresponding chakra located along our spinal cord. The chakra corresponding to Bhurloka is Muladhara chakra, and other six are Svadhishthana, Manipura, Anahata, Vishuddhi, Agya, Sahasrara chakra. These chakras are the gateways to liberation. One has to open and pass through these gates one after another through the process of purification until the Sahasrara chakra is reached, which is the gate of liberation. On arrival at each station, one can sense the results as motivation to proceed further.

'The lower seven energy levels are generally associated mostly with animals and lower species. After arrival in Satyaloka, the goals of the noble souls of the world do not get fully achieved. There starts another voyage to the ultimate station of Brahmaloka through many cosmic stations located beyond the ionosphere and magnetosphere. The Brahma Shakti is the creative power that manifests the universe. The sound of *om* or the Big Bang produced two powers from consciousness or pure elementary energy—purusha (original consciousness) and prakriti (primordial nature). The waveform and associated magnitude and frequency of energy emerged. Vishnu Shakti, the preserving power that sustains the cosmos, and Shiva Shakti, the liberating power that brings about transformation and renewal, evolved. In a progressive sequence, gunas (properties) and tattvas (elementary principles) manifested all subtle and gross forms. The liberated saints of this Earth, having overcome the apparent shackles of earthly bondage of joy or misery, start their journey afresh in the quest for absolute consciousness that is the fundamental energy wave without any harmonics. The spiritualists believe that such liberated souls reside within the band of more purified energy and eventually go to the cosmic layers.'

'How can animals purify themselves without walking through the karmic cycle?' asks the sister.

The priest explains, 'Animals do not have the discriminatory ability. They follow the laws of nature. The animals get purified through the evolutionary law of nature over a very long period. It is through drifting of energy from one bandwidth to the adjoining upper layer due to infiltration.'

The umpire has one final question, 'What do you have to say about the three thousand case histories collected by Dr Stevenson, where people could remember the events of their past lives or could remember events during coma?'

The priest says, 'Such cases are extremely rare. It is theoretically possible. A song of a renowned singer is transmitted from a radio broadcasting station, and if we want to test how she is pronouncing a particular note and at what frequency that note is vibrating, it would be possible in our modern audio laboratory to analyse the same but not in our home radio receiver or even in the ears of ordinary listeners, who will only enjoy the overall song. We by now are aware that human receivers are inexplicably precision instruments. It may be a matter of chance that some human receivers can capture precisely a unique quality of subtle energy of departed souls which have maintained their own unique entity within the selective bandwidth that otherwise acts as a homogenous one.'

The umpire now asked the million-dollar question, 'How can we buy happiness? Where is it available? What is bliss?'

The priest, without any doubt, is the most competent person in the group because of his age, experience, and also for his chosen path; hence, he answers this question.

He says, 'People try to do everything in their lives to remain happy. There is universal good governance of God for the happiness of mankind. But we have always questioned the very existence of God instead of trying to research His laws in the quest for happiness. The consequences are now very much visible to us. We can today easily measure the unhappiness and miseries of the world, looking into the consumption of drugs, sleeping pills, medicines, bullets, arms and ammunitions, etc.

'Many common people at their old age become victim of psychosis because of the fear of losing external beauty, fear of ill health, and finally, fear of death. They are not aware of the inner beauty and the truth of the everlasting and glorious atman that resides within themselves. Even if some of them know, they do not believe it. The actual happiness along with the treasures of bliss is within us. Introspection is the key to the treasure hunt of life.'

The sole arbitrator suddenly intervenes, 'Are we not drifting from our subject?'

The priest acknowledges the same immediately and says, 'I understand that today's complete exercise has been a humble endeavour to explain reincarnation scientifically. We know only 5 per cent of the universe. This limited knowledge to fully understand the acts of God is similar to a small sugar candy trying to dive into an ocean to measure its depth. Today's valuable discussions reveal that reincarnation is a process similar to the working process of a radio broadcasting and receiver station.

'The jivatman or the individual soul is like the music or voice which we intend to broadcast to the receivers or paramatman or the universal soul. If the music or the frequency held by jivatman is good, the receiver receives it in a layer of good or positive energy known as heaven. This happens following the same principles of radio transmissions and receiving stations. Scientifically, these processes are known as modulation and demodulation theories. The physiologically inbuilt antennas and transmitters (as explained before) of each individual work in a way similar to a radio broadcasting station. On our death, the atman leaves the body, riding on the carrier waves of energy. While giving birth, the similar principle works. The energy received or tuned into by the foetus from the sperm and egg has a specific frequency band and amplitude depending upon the physiological receivers of the parents.

'If the quality of the receivers is good, the DNA of the foetus will in all probability be good. If the DNA of the baby carries positive information, the baby's unconscious and subconscious minds will also be very positive. If the environment and parenting are conducive to good development, the baby will grow with the desired quality of an ideal human being.

'The good news is, unlike any other animal, human beings can change their fate to either good or bad. The modulation wave formation is in our hands. The waveform of our jivatman is imprinted by the action of our minds and intellects. The liberation or moksha is the ideal waveform of human beings. If someone contemplates to achieve the same, the only way to do so is by acquiring peace of mind. It is very important to calm as well as sharpen the intellect.

One has to first win over his mind and gross body. With a trained and disciplined mind, the intellect can be tuned to arrive at the ideal musical waveform. The intellect then acts as a microphone of a radio station, which imprints the musical notes on the human soul. When the final moment arrives for the jivatman to leave the body, it is the wave shape, frequency, and amplitude of its inherent energy that determines the destination of its journey. The tuning in to a particular radio station or channel or frequency can be done only by a definite method, whereas that of the human mind and intellect can be done in many ways. Each of those ways showed by thousands of pious saints of this planet had proved to be the right paths to reach His kingdom.

'His kingdom is a splendid receiving station located within the universal soul. It can be reached by the quality of the departed human soul; the probability of its returning to the earth becomes very rare because of the unavailability of a human receiver to tune the enlightened energy from that source.

'Our wise people over the ages had been proclaiming this as liberation or moksha. They had always preached to us this message and also taught us the method of tuning our transmitters to attain liberation and unite with heaven, the pure bliss.'

In the late evening, the priest and his three disciples slowly enter the sacred glass room of the temple. They stand there with folded hands for a while and pray silently. The priest again tells them to remember that without His wishes, nothing can happen in this universe and therefore we should always surrender to him and introspect in order to purify our minds and intellects. We should make the best use of our birth as human beings.

He says, 'Look at the fly that is trying to go out of this room through the glass panels in front. It is under the illusion and thinking that outside of the illuminated temple is its happy destination. Every time it is trying to go out, it is hitting the glass and bleeding. But again and again, it is trying, whereas behind us towards the idols, the windows are open to the beautiful sky with complete liberation. It is now up to you which path you will choose.'

Before they disperse, the priest distributes some prasad (sweets) to his diligent students.

Just before their departure, the younger brother discloses a secret about their priest uncle which he has never shared before with anyone. He informs his siblings that their beloved priest uncle is an alumnus of his university; he graduated from the department of electrical engineering. He changed his lifestyle and reached this temple in search of peace.

'I started suspecting him from the moment he started participating in all kinds of discussions, including my core subject. So I did some research and confirmed my doubts.' He asks, 'Am I right, Uncle?'

The uncle smiles but does not reply. He thinks that it is his past which he has left behind long back, and he does not want to remember it while sitting in the temple of the Almighty. The temple, along with its deities, is the silent witness of this research work done by the brothers and sister along with the priest.

The temple's bell tomorrow morning may transmit the outcome of the subject research and, through its waves, to Him. His response through the hearts of the valued readers will be awaited eagerly by the brothers and their sister in the temple.

Our most basic common link is that we all inhabit this planet. We all breathe the same air. We all cherish our children's future. And, we are all mortals. (John F. Kennedy)

References

Holy Books

1. Bhagavad Gita: It is a 700-verse Hindu scripture that is a part of the Hindu epic Mahabharata, and it is a holy book in India (about 3137 BC).
2. Katha Upanishad: It is one of the main Upanishads, which are the concluding portions of the Vedas.
3. Atman Bodha: It is a treatise on the knowledge by Sri Adi Sankaracharya, a Hindu philosopher of India (AD 788–AD 820).
4. Bible: It is a collection of texts sacred in Judaism and Christianity (AD 95). It was penned by Apostle John around AD 95. The Hebrew Bible was written around 600 BC.
5. Quran: It is the central religious text of Islam, which Muslims believe to be the revelation from Allah to Prophet Muhammad (609 CE).
6. Guru Granth Sahibji: It is the central religious text of Sikhism (1469–1539).
7. Psalms: It is the third section of the Hebrew Bible.
8. Al-An'am: It is a chapter in the holy Quran.
9. Ecclesiastes: It is one of the twenty-four books of the Hebrew Bible.
10. Second Peter: It is a book in the New Testament of the Bible.

11. Kabbalah: It is an ancient wisdom of how the universe and life work.
12. Pistis Sophia: It preserves the teachings of Jesus.

Scholars, Scientists, and Eminent Persons in the World

1. Aldous Huxley (1894–1963): an English writer, philosopher
2. Arthur Schopenhauer (1788–1860): a German philosopher
3. Benjamin Franklin (1706–1790): a founding father of USA
4. Christ of Koch (1932–2013): an Austrian novelist
5. Chuang Tzu: a Chinese philosopher
6. Count Leo Tolstoy (1828–1910): a Russian one of the greatest novelists
7. Daniel Chiu: a professor in University of Washington
8. Dr Deepak Chopra (MD): an Indian born American doctor and author
9. Dr Eben Alexander (1953 born): an American neurosurgeon
10. Dr Francis S. Collins (MD, PhD) (1950): an American physician geneticist
11. Dr Hugo Largercrantz: a Swedish professor was president of the European society of paediatric research
12. Dr Ian Stevenson (1918–2007): a Canadian-born US psychiatrist
13. Dr J. C. Bose (1858–1937): an Indian scientist, primary inventor of radio and microwave optics communication
14. Dr Martin Blank: an American scientist from University of Cambridge and Columbia University

15. Dr Michael Newton (PhD): an American hypnotherapist
16. Dr Robert Lanza (MD) (born 1956): an American doctor and scientist
17. Dr Robert O. Becker (MD) (1923–2008): a US orthopaedic surgeon
18. Dr Stuart Hameroff (MD) (born 1947): an anaesthesiologist and a professor at the University of Arizona
19. Dr W. O. Schumann (1888–1974): a German physicist
20. Elisabeth Kubler Ross (1926–2004): a Swiss American psychiatrist
21. Francis Crick (1916–2004): a British molecular biologist, biophysicist, and neuroscientist
22. G. Marconi (1874–1937): an Italian inventor and electrical engineer known for pioneering work on radio transmission
23. G. W. Leibniz (1646–1716): a German polymath and philosopher
24. George Harrison (1943–2001): an English musician
25. Georges Lakhovsky (1869–1942): a Russian engineer, scientist, author, and inventor
26. Goethe (1749–1832): a German writer
27. Henry David Thoreau (1817–1862): an American author, poet, and philosopher
28. Henry Ford (1863–1947): an American industrialist
29. Immanuel Kant (1724–1804): a German philosopher who is widely considered to be the central figure of modern philosophy
30. Jean-Pierre Changeux (born 1936): a French neuroscientist
31. John McCannon: a writer and professor

32. Julius Caesar (100 BC–44 BC): a Roman statesman
33. Lutoslawsky (1913–1994): a Polish composer and musician
34. Mahatma Gandhi (1869–1948): India's father of the nation
35. Mark Twain (1835–1910): an American author and humorist
36. Nikola Tesla (1856–1943): a Serbian American inventor, engineer, and physicist
37. Origen (AD 254): a scholar and early Christian theologian born in Alexandria
38. Pjotr Garjajev: a Russian biophysicist
39. Pythagoras (571 BC–495 BC): a famous Greek philosopher and mathematician
40. Ralph Waldo Emerson (1803–1882): an American essayist and poet
41. Raoul Kopelman: an American scientist and a professor from Michigan
42. Richard A. Miller, Iona Miller, Burt Webb, and Dickson: scientists who researched and worked on DNA hologram successfully
43. Richard J. Haier: an American psychologist
44. Richard Philips Feynman (1918–1988): an American physicist and Nobel laureate for physics, 1965
45. Robert Monroe (1915–1995): an American radio broadcasting executive and founder of Monroe Institute
46. Roger Penrose (born 1931): an English mathematical physicist and philosopher
47. Searle (born 1932): an American philosopher
48. Sigmund Freud (1856–1939): an Austrian neurologist known as the father of psychoanalysis

49. Socrates (399 BC): a classical Greek philosopher, founder of Western philosophy
50. Soren Kierkegaard (1813–1855): a Danish philosopher, theologian
51. Stephen Hawking (born 1942): a British physicist, cosmologist
52. Swami Abhedananda (1866–1939): an Indian monk, direct disciple of nineteenth-century mystic Sri Ramakrishna Paramahamsa
53. Apostle Paul: the most important figure of the Apostolic Age
54. Trutz Hardo (born 1939): a German philosopher and regression therapist
55. William Jones (1746–1794): an Anglo-Welsh philologist
56. Rene Descartes (1596–1650): an eminent French academician, philosopher, mathematician, and scientist
57. Antoine Henri Becquerel (1852–1908): a French physicist
58. Marie Sklodowska Curie (1867–1934): a Polish French scientist who got the Nobel Prize twice
59. Pierre Curie (1859–1906): a French scientist who got the Nobel Prize in 1903

References of Quotations

1. Aristotle (385 BC–322 BC): a Greek philosopher and scientist
2. Carl B. Hoch Jr: a professor of the New Testament
3. Carl Sandburg (1878–1967): an American poet
4. Chanakya (371 BC–283 BC): an Indian philosopher, teacher, economist

5. Charleston Parker: a prominent self-taught theologian and scholar

6. David Starr Jordan (1851–1931): an American ichthyologist, educator

7. E. M. Foster (1879–1970): an English novelist

8. Elbert Einstein (1879–1955): a German-born physicist and philosopher who is known as the founder of modern science; a Nobel Prize winner in 1921

9. Fritjof Capra (born 1939): an Austrian-born American physicist

10. Gabriel Garcia Marquez (1927–2014): a Colombian novelist

11. Gautama Buddha (563 BCE–483 BCE): an Indian (greater) sage on whose teachings Buddhism was founded

12. Jean de la Bruyère (1645–1696): a French philosopher and moralist

13. Jeb Bush (born 1953): an American politician

14. John F. Kennedy (1917–1963): an American politician, served as thirty-fifth president of USA

15. John Lennon (1940–1980): an English singer and songwriter

16. John Muir (1838–1914): a Scottish American author, naturalist

17. Khalil Gibran (1883–1931): a Lebanese American artist, poet, writer

18. Kurt Cobain: an American musician and songwriter

19. Marcus Tullius Cicero (107 BC–44 BC): a Roman philosopher

20. Maria Montessori (1870–1952): an Italian physician and educator

21. Mark Twain (1835–1910): an American author and humorist

22. Maxim Gorky (1868–1936): Russian writer and political activist

23. Niels Bohr (1885–1962): a Danish physicist, recipient of Nobel Prize in physics

24. Owen Feltham (1602–1668): an English writer

25. Rabindranath Tagore (1861–1941): an Indian philosopher, poet, author of *Gitanjali*; he was the first non-European to win the Nobel Prize in literature in 1913

26. Rumi (1207–1273): a thirteenth-century Persian poet, jurist, Islamic scholar

27. Saint Augustine (AD 354–AD 430): Christian theologian and philosopher

28. Sri Ramakrishna Paramahamsa (1836–1886): a demigod from India

29. Swami Vivekananda (1863–1902): an Indian philosopher

30. Thomas Edison (1847–1931): an American inventor

31. Thomas Gray (1716–1771): an English poet and professor at University of Cambridge

32. Walter Russell (1871–1963): an American polymath, sculptor, and author

33. William Wordsworth (1770–1850): a major English romantic poet

Index

1.0   **Chapter-1: An ideal family:** - Birth of a child in a family-Question arise in mind of other grown up child- explanation by elders.

2.0   **Chapter-2: Concept of birth:-** Definition and physiological process.

3.0   **Chapter-3 : Social environment:-** Life style of a middle class family- Influence by a priest-Inquisitiveness of a boy- Alignment of thinking process.

4.0   **Chapter- 4: Mind, Body, and Intellect:-** Formation of mind- Controlling factors- Basic parts of physical body- Spiritual body- Relationship between the two- Subtle body- Manifestation of hallucination (Maya) and egoism (ahamkara)- Common golden rules for good governance of society- Mass education.

5.0   **Chapter-5 : Philosophy and maturity:-** What is liberation?- What are bad and good egos?- Need to train mind- Concept of soul (atman)- It's homogeneity- Effect of its contamination-Concept of purification.

6.0   **Chapter- 6 : Death in the family:-** Mourning-Rituals and their need- An eternal question " Where goes the soul?"- It's nature?

7.0 Chapter-7 : Science and Spirituality:- Quest to quench of thrust to understand the mystery of death.

8.0 Chapter-8: A Solemn Mission:- Self-imposed by-laws of the research work on mystery of birth and death.

9.0 Chapter-9: Transmigration:- Belief and proof of Re-incarnation- Existence of God and Soul- Universal divine energy- Formation of physical and subtle bodies- Revelations and preaching in holy books.

10. Chapter-10: Present proof of Re-incarnation:- Experiences of wise people- New era after discoveries of Radio activity and theory of Relativity- Transmigration is a subtle process- A spark for its understanding.

11. Chapter-11: Humble appeal to the valued reader:- To be in open mind.

12. Chapter-12: Beginning of the search:- The outline of the research.

13. Chapter-14: Physiological Body:- Brief description- Function of DNA- It's response to electromagnetic waves-Fractal Antenna- Body as power house.

14. Chapter-15: Spiritual Gross Body:- It's constituents- Pentamerous process for its formation.

15. Chapter-15: The Subtle Body:- Consist of Five organs of actions- Five organs of perception- Five Pranas- Five basic elements- Mind and Intellect- Nescience(avidya)- Ego- Nature of Atman.

16. Chapter-16: Science of the Subtle Body:- Consciousness a state of vibration- Influence of terrestrial and electrical environment on biological body. Electric field by nerve impulses.

17. **Chapter-17: Birth of a Human:** - Recapitulation of the process of birth.

18. **Chapter-18: Death of a Human:-** Recapitulation of the process of death.

19. **Chapter-19: Soul/Sprit/Atman/Ruh:** As explained in holy books and by wises- It's resemblance with electrical and electromagnetic energy.

20. **Chapte20: Cosmic energy, Ionosphere and other layers of Earth's Atmosphere:-** Formation of layers of cosmic and electrical energies in atmosphere- Propagation of electromagnetic waves- Electrical components in atmosphere- Seven layers in atmosphere.

21. **Chapter-21: God time and Man hour:-** Timeless Universe- Instant response of God.

22. **Chapter-22: As We Sow So We Reap:-** The Karmic cycle.

23. **Chapter-23: Purification process of the Soul:-** Route cause of un-happiness- Remedy explained scientifically.

24. **Chapter-24: Physiological Responses during Meditation:-** Use of internal feed-back system- stabilisation of mind- Aligning with Schumann's resonance.

25. **Chapter- 25: Migration of energy and it's accumulation:-** Soul is energy-Follows same principle- Its behaviour in electrical circuits- Resonant frequency- Impedance matching for transfer of maximum energy- Radio waves propagation.

26. **Chapter- 26: Radio/Tele Communications:-** Resemblance of human systems and components with microphone, antenna, transmitter, transformer, amplifier, receiver, filter of telecommunication system. A cross road of philosophy and science- A logical and scientific conclusion on the process of Transmigration/ Reincarnation and Liberation.

27. **Chapter-27: Humble Submission:-** Based on the postulate, scientific validation of some important preaching of the ancient wise men and spiritual leaders of the world.